THE BOMBSHELL EFFECT

A WASHINGTON WOLVES NOVEL

KARLA SORENSEN

DEDICATION

For my dad, who was the person who taught me to love football, and Peyton Manning, who will forever be my favorite player, which is why I still can't watch his retirement speech without crying.

CHAPTER 1
LUKE

WASHINGTON WOLVES

"I cannot believe you're the asshole who missed the team owner's funeral."

The sigh that came from my chest was deep and slow, a technique I'd mastered early in my career when I was trying to hold my tongue. My agent, Randall, was good at his job. Really good. In the twelve years that I'd been a quarterback for the Washington Wolves, he scored me enough endorsement deals that I barely needed to touch my salary. What Randall was not good at was being understanding when he thought I messed up.

Even though I hadn't messed up.

"Faith broke her arm, Randall." I rubbed at my forehead because of course, I felt like complete and utter shit for missing my boss's funeral. I didn't need him to remind me of the gravity of them burying Robert Sutton the Third in my absence.

He let out a short puff of air, his exasperation clear. "Someone else could've taken her to the emergency room."

Another thing Randall was not good at was understanding what it was like to be a father. A single father, at that. The extent of his fatherly instinct was to dump lukewarm water on the parched cactus that always sat on the window ledge in his office.

I nodded even though he couldn't see me. "Someone else *could* have."

When he started to speak, I cut him off.

"Except that's not how I do things. It's the first time she's ever broken a bone, and my mom is out of town. Don't push me on this. It's over, the media didn't care, and my endorsement deals won't suffer."

The vacuum of silence after I spoke told me two things.

1- I was crankier than necessary at his questioning my decision.

2- I was crankier than necessary because I was exhausted.

Those two things carried far more weight than they should have on my already weighed-down shoulders. To my right, Faith sat on the long gray couch and played quietly on her Kindle. One arm in a bright pink cast with only my signature on the fabric, the other deftly swiping across the screen for whatever game she was playing or book she was reading. The sun streaming in on her from the large sliding glass doors overlooking Lake Washington made her look far older than her six years.

I rubbed a spot on my chest, in the general area where her name was permanently inked into my skin because sometimes the thought of her growing into a young lady was enough to make me think I was having a heart attack.

Randall finally spoke, aware by my tone that I wasn't in the best of moods. "It's the off-season, Luke. The media will make a story of anything they think will get hits. Including you missing Robert's funeral."

"I'm not making a statement about it," I snapped. "The guys know I respected the hell out of Robert. The front office knows that. There's no reason I need to explain shit to anyone else. I shouldn't have to."

"Agreed." His tone was placating, which pissed me off even more. "You shouldn't have to. But you're in your mid-thirties, and you don't have Twitter, you don't have Instagram, your social media presence is worse than my eighty-year-old grandma's, which means your fans don't have the window into all your thoughts they feel entitled to."

There was a reason for that. When I got home after a long day of practice, I wanted to focus on Faith. I didn't want to take pictures and come up with hashtags or try to fit a clever thought into a hundred and forty characters. Or even worse, filter through the shit that used to come into my direct messages. The day Faith grabbed my phone and touched her thumb to the wrong place, opening up a message with a picture of a naked woman asking if I'd like to meet up, I deleted all my accounts.

I didn't want to see it, so I certainly didn't want Faith to see it. It had nothing to do with football. None of those things were necessary for me to win games.

"Boobies!" a two-year-old Faith had exclaimed. It was enough to drive a non-drinking man to drink.

Randall cleared his throat, and I forced myself back into the conversation.

"Randall"—I sighed—"I don't need those things to play football. Peyton Manning never did social media, and his career didn't suffer because of it."

"Are you comparing yourself to Peyton Manning?" he asked innocently. I wanted to punch him in the scrotum.

Faith winced when she shifted on the couch, so I pulled the phone away from my ear. "You okay, turbo?"

At her nickname, the one I'd given her when she was barely two, she flashed me a quick smile. "I'm okay, Daddy. Just hurt when I set it down too hard."

I nodded at her answer and let out a deep breath before I turned back toward the kitchen counter, bracing my fists on the gleaming white surface after wedging my phone between my face and shoulder.

"Listen," I told him, "unless a reporter shows up on my doorstep asking why I wasn't there, I'm not making a statement."

"Why not?"

The sound out of my mouth was pure skeptical amusement. He wanted a list?

Oh, media, how do I hate thee? Let me count the ways.

"Because it doesn't matter what I say, Randall. They'll make up their own version of the truth, twist my words, and make it fit their story with a neat little bow."

"Lord, you're cynical."

"Can you blame me?" I asked.

He was silent.

"I guess not." He cleared his throat. "But come on. One sentence."

"No."

The last conversation that I'd had with Robert before his sudden massive heart attack had been a good one. Substantial. He told me he was proud of all that we'd accomplished, but we had a long future ahead of us to keep achieving more. I told him he was a great owner, a good man, and he'd slapped me on the back.

I didn't need to share that story with anyone. It was my history with him, not to be used for a sound bite or fodder for public consumption.

Through the speaker, there was a sound of slight exasperation. "You're such a stubborn ass, Pierson. Haven't you ever heard of being proactive?"

I almost laughed. Almost. My lips curled slightly at the edges, because what flipped through my brain was dawn workouts, muscle work to combat the normal deterioration that professional football players fought against the second the season kicked off, and the hours of film I watched from the office perched in the northwest corner of the lower level of my house.

"Nope."

"Whoa," Faith said in a short burst of air. I turned around to see her off the couch, nose pressed to the sliding glass door. "She looks like Barbie."

"Who does?" I asked her.

"Who does what?" Randall said in my ear.

"I wasn't talking to you."

"The man signed your paychecks, Piers," Randall said, using the nickname that was common among my teammates. "You need to say *something* about the fact that he ended up with his forehead down on the dining room table. Did you know that? Right on his dinner plate."

"Holy shit, Randall," I muttered, pinching the bridge of my nose. Faith didn't notice my slip, or else I'd have to put a buck in the swear jar. "Have a little respect. He had a heart attack."

"At least he had the grace to do it before the season started. Maybe it won't upset the balance of anything too much. Do you know who's going to replace him?"

"After twelve years, I'm still not entirely convinced that you have an actual soul."

"Of course, I do."

Faith's jaw dropped open, and I peered through the doors but couldn't see anything. She was standing so close to the glass, I could see it fog up when she spoke. "Look at her bathing suit. I wish I could wear one like that."

Fatherly alarm bells clanged noisily in my head.

"Um, Randall, I have to go."

"You have to make a statement. Robert Sutton the Third was a class act owner, great leader, blah blah blah, something. Anything. Because I bet you a hundred bucks they'll make a big deal out of this."

"Daddy," she practically whined, "can we please go say hi? She's looking over here. I think she sees me!"

The hair lifted on the back of my neck because the house next to us had been empty for as long we'd lived here. It wasn't unheard of for fans to find out where players lived, but we'd managed to stay off the radar for the past eighteen months since we moved into the modest house on Lake Washington, just outside Seattle.

Well—I thought as I looked around the immaculate open space, the sprawling view from the back of the house, sun glinting off the water like a mirror had been draped over the surface—modest for an NFL quarterback.

But anyone with working knowledge of Google could dig deep enough if they wanted. Like the woman who showed up at the team hotel a couple of years back, found out which room I'd been staying in, and opened her trench coat for me when I thought she was from room service.

There'd been nothing underneath that trench coat.

If Faith hadn't been asleep in the room, I would have slammed the door shut in her face. Instead, she got an icy, "Thanks, but no thanks."

"Randall, I have to go."

"No," he said urgently, "you don't."

I pressed my thumb to the screen and tossed the phone onto the counter. Faith rose up on her tiptoes for a better look, and it made the brown braid I'd managed that morning swing across her back.

"Who you lookin' at, turbo?"

When she looked over her shoulder at me, her smile was as big as her eyes. "Maybe she's our new neighbor. She's so *pretty*, dad. You should go say hi. You should welcome her to the neighborhood. Maybe she's lonely."

If her rushed words, loaded with excitement and awe, hadn't touched on such a sore subject, I might have smiled. Might have laughed. Instead, I pinched my eyes shut because all I could hear between the letters, the words grouped together so innocently in her sweet voice, was a girl who missed a mother she never knew. Stuck with a dad who had a career so demanding that it probably seemed like nothing was ever really about her. Even though *everything* I did was about her.

When I stepped behind Faith, I kept my eyes down on her while I braced my hands on her tiny shoulders. So much about her fragile now after her broken arm. I'd had my share of bruises, a couple of concussions, tears in my muscles that had interfered with half a dozen games, and a sprained ankle two seasons ago that had cost us a chance at the playoffs. But nothing felt as terrifying as seeing Faith fall off the playground equipment, hearing her cry of pain, and seeing her fear when she was lying in that hospital bed.

Now, when my hands landed on her skin, all I could feel was the delicate length of bone, and all I could imagine was how far I'd go to make sure nothing ever happened to hurt her. It was illogical, completely irrational, but I could stop it about as easily as I could try to stop my heart by sheer willpower.

"Daddy." She sighed, tilting her head back to look at me.

"What, turbo?"

"You're not even looking at our new neighbor."

I lifted an eyebrow. "You don't know she's our new neighbor. Maybe she's lost."

Faith rolled her eyes and giggled.

Finally, I looked up. Definitely wished I hadn't.

Because if that was our new neighbor, then I was in hell.

Like our home, the one next door was three levels facing Lake Washington. The deck on the main floor, similar to mine, was large and stretched the entire length of the house, but it was normally empty. As long as we'd lived here, I had yet to see a single person anywhere on the property, save the regular landscaping crew that came during the non-winter months to keep it tidy.

It wasn't empty now. As close as Faith was in saying that she looked like Barbie, the first thing that came to my mind was why is there a playmate strolling across the deck next door?

In the few seconds that I spent, regrettably, cataloging what I was looking at, I felt like someone shoved a stick of dynamite under my firmly planted feet and lit a one-inch fuse. It was impossible to escape and inconceivable to ignore the effect it had on me.

Her legs were endless, tan, and toned; her stomach flat; her hair long and blond and full. The black bikini she wore barely covered her ample, clearly natural chest, and that was when I had to look away for my own sanity. My daughter was standing in front of me, and there was no good place that my thoughts could go when staring at a chest like the one currently on display at the house next door.

"Please, please, please can we go say hi?" Faith asked again, turning around and giving me her full arsenal. Eyes? Wide and pleading, the exact same shade of brown as mine. Her hands? Clasped together as best as her cast would allow and centered over her heart like I'd break it if I said no.

"We don't know who that is, sweetheart," I explained gently. "Maybe she's a new neighbor, or maybe she's just renting it for the weekend. What do I always tell you about strangers?"

Her shoulders slumped, and I felt like the Grinch. "She wouldn't be a stranger if we introduced ourselves."

"That's true," I conceded, "but we're still not going to say hi."

Looking down at her disappointed face, I saw traces of myself. But I saw a lot of her mother too, something Faith would only be able to recognize from the few pictures I had of Cassandra. Our fling had been brief, the effects now permanent, and she'd died in a car accident before Faith had turned six months old.

In those six months, I'd seen Cassandra's sweet and sexy nature slowly turn green with greed; her demands for child support increasing while the time she wanted to give me with Faith decreased at almost the same rate. Unless I paid up.

Her solution to my firm denial to be her unending ATM was to sell some bullshit story to the gossip rags about our "romance." One I couldn't contest when she died a week later. At the risk of sounding like an asshole, I didn't want to brand her a liar when Faith would easily be able to use Google herself someday.

The fact that we'd already done a paternity test at Randall's insistence was the only reason my claim on her in the wake of Cassandra's death was uncontested.

The press had had a field day with that. The star quarterback was now a single father, and after the story she sold, my relationship with Cassandra had been romanticized to the point of being nauseating. It hadn't taken long for the frenzy over my story to die down, but it was enough to leave a sour taste in my mouth when it came to the media.

It was those aspects of the game that I hated. The groupies thinking that because I wasn't married, I'd climb in bed with anyone who spread her legs wide enough. The media prying into details of my life, piecing them together until they resembled a story they thought would sell magazines and up their ratings.

Faith pushed her bottom lip out in a pout when she realized I would not budge, but she didn't argue. Once she settled on the couch again with her Kindle, she gave me a sad look. "I'm just bored. There's no one for me to play with here, and I miss Grams."

Wearily, I made my way to the couch and sat next to her, slinging my arm around her shoulders until she was curled up into my side. "I know. She and Grandpa will be back in a few days, okay? You know she needs to take her vacations now because we need her help too much once I go back to work all the time."

"You're already working," she pointed out. The look on her face, sweet and a little sad, made my heart turn over. She wasn't wrong. I was at our team facilities every day to train, and we had team meetings every week. Not to mention practices taking up my days. It wasn't the rigorous, exhausting schedule of the regular season, but it was still work.

"When did you get so smart?"

She smiled and snuggled in deeper. "In first grade. I'll be even smarter in second."

The directness of her answer, so literal, made me smile and close my eyes. At moments like this, I could pretend I was a regular dad who made crappy peanut butter and jelly sandwiches, who did lopsided braids because my fingers were too big to be nimble when faced with all her hair. I could pretend I didn't worry about whether the media would sensationalize my absence at Robert's funeral, or if the bombshell on the deck was a random groupie trying to get a closer look.

My phone buzzed on the counter where I'd left it, and I dropped a kiss on Faith's head before I went to grab it.

. . .

Randall: Turn on ESPN, you asshole. You owe me $100. Let me know when you want to make your statement.

Instantly, it was like someone dropped a steel beam over my shoulder blades. I could feel the weight of it so clearly that it made my back ache. Aiming the remote at the TV mounted on the wall opposite the couch, I flipped to ESPN. The familiar desk and studio background of *SportsCenter* came into view. When I saw my picture in the graphic on the upper left of the screen, I scowled.

"Yesterday, friends, family, and members gathered to honor the life of Robert Sutton the Third, longtime owner of the Washington Wolves, who passed away suddenly last week from a massive heart attack. Noticeably absent, however, was the team's longtime quarterback, Luke Pierson. A source close to the Wolves organization told ESPN that there was tension between Sutton and Pierson over the past year, stemming from Pierson's inability to make it to the Super Bowl for the second time in his career. His time with the Wolves has been plagued by injury and disappointed hopes from one post-season to the next."

Her co-anchor glanced to the side with a sly smile. "Would you miss your boss's funeral?"

She took on a shocked face, and I wanted to punch someone again. Preferably Randall. "Of course not. I love my bosses."

Off-screen, you could hear the muted laughter of the camera crew.

Her co-anchor lifted his hands in a *what are you gonna do?* gesture. "Maybe it's nothing, but when the leader on the field can't show up to pay his respects to the guy leading off the field, I think there's something wrong with that."

She nodded. "Agreed. There's definitely a story here, and it can't bode well for the Wolves heading into the regular season."

Her smile was bright and practiced as she faced another camera. "We'll be right back, so stay tuned."

I punched the off button on the remote harder than necessary and braced my hands on my hips. "Son of a bitch."

"Daddy." Faith giggled.

After scratching the back of my neck, I fished a dollar bill out of my wallet and dropped it on her lap as I walked past. "Sorry, turbo." Frustration made my skin feel hot, my hands restless and tingly. "I'm going to go downstairs and work out for a little bit, okay? Yell if you need anything."

On the way down to my home gym, I grabbed my black boxing gloves and hand tape. And I kept my eyes off the slider when I saw movement on the deck again.

There was absolutely nothing there that I needed to see.

CHAPTER 2
ALLIE

WASHINGTON WOLVES

Honestly, I'm not sure what I was thinking. Baking was not my thing. In fact, as I stared down at the mess in front of me, I couldn't think of a time that I'd ever attempted to make cupcakes before. But something about the current season of my life was making me want to try new things. Try things I used to think I couldn't do.

A blob of bright pink frosting slid off the cupcake and onto the granite counters. Like putting frosting on homemade cupcakes, apparently. I knew the cake itself didn't taste bad, but when you bought a box with only like, four instructions, it was hard to mess that up. Even for me.

As the frosting slowly melted off each cupcake, I picked up my phone and pressed the home button.

"Siri, why is the frosting melting off my cupcakes?"

Oh, saying it out loud somehow made it worse. What twenty-six-year-old didn't know how to frost cupcakes?

After scrolling through a few links, I winced at the realization that you're supposed to let the cupcakes cool first before adding the frosting. Very carefully, I scraped the pink blobs off each cake and then set them in the empty fridge to cool off a bit.

Once they were in there, I turned and looked around the house, which was just as empty as the fridge. It had been years since anyone in my family had been to this place.

That made me blink for a second, the stifling weight of repressed grief making my lungs into cement until I could breathe through it.

My family. My family was just me now.

Okay, nope. I hadn't cried yet, and I was not going to start now. Not going to travel that path when I had cupcakes to worry about.

In the healthiest possible way, I would actively deny that I'd buried my father the day before, whom I hadn't seen in three years, and that I was standing in the house left to me when my mother died more than twenty years earlier and had been sitting empty for the past five.

Since I'd last been here, some things had been updated, maybe because my father held some tenuous hope that I'd come back from Milan and live here. New kitchen counters and appliances. Flooring in the bathroom that I'd never seen before. But still, there was barely any furniture. A single chair facing out toward Lake Washington. A bed with a massive gray headboard in the master suite covered with a plush light pink quilt. Some stools pushed up against the kitchen island.

It was a blank canvas on which to start a new life.

Blank was just a nice word for empty, wasn't it? The silence around me was deafening, and instead of diving into it like I maybe should have, I turned and found my Bluetooth speaker, cranked up some Kesha, and started a new batch of frosting. It was certainly preferable to wading into my emotions.

Just as I had that mentally healthy thought, my phone started ringing, and I used the side of my pinky, the only part of my fingers not covered with frosting, to answer the call.

"'Lo?" I said, breathless from dancing around the kitchen.

"Miss Sutton? It's Miles Kuyper from the offices of DeHaan, Kuyper, and Marston."

I sighed. My dad's attorneys. I'd already met one of the suits when he sat across a sterile desk and told me I was the sole beneficiary of my father's estate, outside of the charities he mentioned, which would receive healthy checks. "Hi, what can I do for you?"

He cleared his throat. "Is it possible for you to come into the offices again this afternoon? We have a slight addendum to your father's will that we need to inform you of."

My brows bent in as I swirled some frosting over the next cupcake. "Umm, sure. Is everything okay?"

"Oh, it's fine. Everything is fine. Just an additional bequest that we weren't aware of last week."

I glanced at the clock on the wall. "Sure. I can be downtown in about an hour if that works for you."

"Excellent. See you soon."

He hung up first, so I left my phone on the counter and got back to frosting.

Twenty minutes later, I stepped back and nodded in satisfaction.

They weren't beautiful, but at least they wouldn't appear in a Buzzfeed article of epic Pinterest fails like my earlier disaster. But now I had two dozen pink-frosted cupcakes and no one to share them with.

My mouth twisted in a frown as I stared out at the sun-soaked lake.

To my right, I saw a flash of movement. The blue house next door to mine had a massive sliding door overlooking the lake and framed in it was a little girl staring at me with her hands pressed against the glass. When she noticed me looking, her face spread into a huge smile, and she waved frantically.

Unbidden, my lips tugged up on the sides in a grin. I waved my fingers in her direction, and impossibly, her smile grew like I'd just thrown her a glitter-covered pony.

Like the house I was standing in, hers was large and immaculately kept. I couldn't see much past her, but she had her nose against the window like I was her only entertainment. She moved to the right, and I saw a flash of pink, the exact color of the cupcakes on the counter. A cast covered her arm, and the fabric was so bright, I almost pulled out my sunglasses.

The idea sprang into my head like a flash, and I decided not to consider the complete foreignness of what I was about to do.

People brought baked goods to new neighbors, right? Wasn't that what normal people did?

As I set a few on a paper plate—a perfect circle of imperfectly frosted cupcakes—I had a moment when I wondered if they'd recognize me. Would her mom answer the door and know that I was Alexandra Sutton, daughter of a rich man, famous only because of his money and my ability to pose well in nice clothes and post shit to Instagram?

Okay fine, I'd done a few spreads in lesser-known magazines, but it was enough that I'd earned money on my own.

But maybe she wouldn't recognize me. Maybe she'd be friendly and open the door with a smile and invite me in for coffee, or even better, a glass of wine.

I felt better about that. Maybe we could be friends.

Before I walked out the door to find the small stretch of road that connected our houses, both on the end of the street, I slipped my flip-flops on my feet and shrugged a white cover-up on over my bikini. In the mirror hanging on the wall next to me, I gave myself a quick once-over. My hair was insane from sitting out on the deck, but my face held enough color from the sun that I didn't need any makeup. For a second, the fresh-faced woman looking back at me looked so much like my mother that I paused and stared.

Everything about me, from the heart-shaped face to my full pink lips, was directly from her. Well, not my eyes. I got my ocean blue eyes from my dad. Getting good genes was like winning the lottery because I'd learned in twenty-six years that even if you were born with money, some people had no trouble being assholes to you. But smile prettily at them, and it was a sad fact of life that if they liked what they saw, they'd be more willing to give you a chance.

So with my cupcakes clutched carefully in both hands, I walked over to my neighbor's with a smile on my face.

The garage doors were closed, and the covered front door was shadowed since it was angled away from the sun. If I hadn't seen the girl in the slider, I would've thought the house was empty. Because of the way the street curved around with large trees and hedges, our houses were fairly protected from the traffic of the road. Making friends with them would be good.

Not that I struggled with being alone.

Nope. Definitely not.

My smile wavered a little bit as I came up the concrete steps to the large front porch. Two tall potted plants flanked the glossy white door, and the windows stretched up along either side of it were frosted for privacy. I was about to knock when my hand froze. Balancing the cupcakes carefully in one hand, I finger combed my hair with the other.

"Allie," I whispered, "she won't care if your hair is perfect. Just be yourself."

With my smile stretched wide, I took a fortifying breath and knocked firmly on the door, stepping back slightly so I wasn't creepy close to her when she opened it.

There was no answer, so I swallowed down the feeling that I was making a mistake and knocked again, a little bit louder this time. In the frosted window, I saw a flash of pink and then it was gone.

"Hang on a second," a small voice yelled through the door, and then I heard the unmistakable sounds of her feet running in the opposite direction.

I blew out a hard puff of air and shifted on my feet. "Don't chicken out, don't chicken out, don't chicken out," I chanted. Meeting strangers was the worst. Because you had that moment where their reaction to meeting you was completely unfiltered. It was usually in their eyes and the set of their mouth.

While I breathed through the nerves and anticipation, I could hear her little voice again, coupled with heavier footsteps. My smile spread again, as genuine as it was practiced. The door swept open, and my heart dropped into my stomach.

Maybe it was because he was so tall, easily four inches past six feet, with broad shoulders and strong arms covered in ink. Maybe it was because his dark eyes were devoid of any sign of welcome, and his hard mouth was set in a straight line, framed by a jaw that would make Annie Leibovitz weep if given the chance to capture it on film. Definitely, definitely not the smiling mom I expected, the one who'd invite me in for wine and conversation overlooking the lake.

"Can I help you?" he asked evenly, but there was zero warmth in the low tone.

I swallowed and kept my smile wide and friendly.

"I, umm, I came to bring you these." I held out the plate of cupcakes, and he stared at them for a weighty second. If it were possible, his eyes got even flintier. His chest was heaving, and the white T-shirt he wore was soaked in sweat as if he'd been working out. His hands were wrapped in boxing tape, and it made my stomach curl, but not in the good way that you want your stomach to curl when standing in front of a gorgeous, sweaty man. "I just wanted to introduce myself."

"Why?"

My smile dropped a fraction. "Why did I bring cupcakes?"

His eyes met mine, and one dark brow lifted slowly. The cold, icy flush of embarrassment slipped down my spine, which I straightened stubbornly.

"Why did you want to introduce yourself?"

"Because I thought it would be a nice thing to do," I told him, pushing brightness into my voice and refusing to drop my smile further. *Asshole.* That was the unspoken addition to the end of my sentence.

"I don't eat sugar." He folded his arms over his chest.

"Okay, fine." I pulled the plate closer to me like it was my very sugary, cupcakey shield. Rational, I know. "Sorry I was trying to be neighborly."

"Neighborly?" he repeated, and his mouth twisted like he had just sucked on a lemon.

I lifted my chin and smiled again, determined to salvage this. "Yes. *Neighborly.* Your ... daughter waved at me, and I thought I'd be nice and come say hi."

If I thought he looked cold before, it was nothing compared to the way his face transformed at the mention of the little girl.

His eyes narrowed and pinned me with enough ice that I actually stepped back. "So you're as smart as you are original? That's good to know."

My mouth dropped open. "Excuse me?"

"I have a list of reasons used by women prettier than you, blondie, and that's on the flimsy side when it comes to reasons you show up on my doorstep."

The absolute freaking nerve of him made my jaw pop open. "Who the hell do you think you are?"

One side of his lips curved up, but it was cold. "Uh-huh. Can we be done now?"

"Are you kidding me right now?" I gasped. It was amazing how the body could switch from cold to hot without changing the shape of your skin and bones because now I was on fire.

"Do I look like I'm kidding?" He flicked his eyes up and down my body, and my sugary shield was no match from the derision I saw on his face. "You can go back next door now. We're set on baked goods for the foreseeable future."

You know, there were moments when I prided myself on my even temper. My ability to stuff my immediate reaction and keep a pleasant expression on my face, honed by years of practice of being marginally well-known and judged for every single piece of my life—from my face to my body to my upbringing and my parents' money.

This wasn't one of them.

Everything I'd been shoving down for the past week since I got the call about my dad's heart attack, all the silence that I'd ignored because it was hiding too much, the empty house, my empty family tree, the shitty cupcakes, and the fact that it was difficult enough for me to lift my hand to knock on the door in the first place, oh, it all came roaring through my body in an ugly, messy rush of anger.

That was the only reason I had to explain why I shoved the plate of cupcakes at his chest.

The pink frosting stuck to his shirt for one horrifying, sluggish moment while he gaped at me, and I gaped at the plate like it hadn't come from my hands.

But I closed my mouth and took a calm step backward. The plate fell, and so did the cupcakes when he swept his hand down his chest. The sloppy pile at his feet made me gulp with a whole different set of nerves.

But I lifted my chin and give him a smile as sweet as fresh lemonade, the kind that usually garnered me a few hundred thousand likes.

"Enjoy the cupcakes, asshole."

I turned on my heel and walked back to my empty house with my head high, my face hot, and my hands shaking. Behind me, a door slammed, but I didn't hesitate. Not until I was back in the safety of my empty house, slumped against the firmly closed front door.

If this was my fresh start, it was off to a fabulous start, I thought miserably. Then I caught the time on the clock and groaned. I had less than thirty minutes to freshen up and get downtown to meet with the lawyers.

Whatever it was that my father had left me, in addition to oh, millions and millions of dollars, had better be good because all I wanted to do was curl up on the couch with a giant bottle of chardonnay.

———

"I'm sorry," I whispered. "Can you please repeat that?"

Underneath my hands, the surface of the desk was ice cold. Or maybe that was my hands. Miles Kuyper had enough grace to look embarrassed, and he cleared his throat before pushing a pile of papers toward me over the glossy surface of his desk.

"Which part?"

"All of it," I ground out irritably. I didn't spare the papers a second glance but kept my eyes trained on his rat-like face.

"Yesterday, we found this addendum to your father's last will and testament. It, uh, wasn't filed immediately, which is why we missed it when we initially met with you to discuss your inheritance upon your father's untimely death. I assure we've had a firm discussion with the clerk who made the clerical error."

I blinked rapidly, fleetingly wondering if maybe I was stroking out. Or that LSD laced the cupcakes I'd shoved in my mouth on my way out the door.

"I don't care about the clerical error," I said in a warning voice. "You're seriously telling me what I think you're telling me?"

He sucked in a quick breath and nodded carefully. "Yes. Two weeks before his heart attack, your father updated his will, transferring his ownership of the team into an irrevocable trust, so that you would become sole owner of the Washington Wolves organization in the event of his death."

My stomach slid down and landed somewhere in the vicinity of my Pigalle Plato Louboutins. The red patent leather shone brightly underneath the garish lights in the ceiling of the office. I almost started laughing when I realized that it was almost the exact red of the team's colors.

That stupid effing football team. The great love of my father's life. He'd definitely loved it more than me. After my mother's death, he threw himself into it with a fervor that I could only now recognize as distraction. But his distraction had turned to obsession, the thing he lived and breathed for.

"May I call you Miles?" I asked quietly, still staring at my shoes.

"Of course, Miss Sutton." His answer was deferential. That was something I was used to with people like him. He knew I held the money and, apparently, a good deal of power now that my father was gone.

I folded my hands in my lap so that he couldn't see how badly they were shaking and tried to meet his concerned gaze as evenly as possible. In reality, I was just trying to keep my shit together. Every inch of me felt like it was vibrating, shivering uncontrollably with the immense feeling of being out of control of my own life.

"What in the absolute hell am I supposed to do with a football team, Miles?"

He looked confused. "Is that a rhetorical question?"

My head dropped, and I started laughing. I rubbed at my temples. "I don't even know."

"May I call you Alexandra?" he asked carefully.

I lifted my chin and nodded. I was so tired. Maybe Miles wouldn't care if I slumped down on the floor and took a nap. Maybe Miles had a Xanax he could share with me. Maybe Miles had vodka in his desk that I could chase that Xanax with. "Allie is fine."

"I'd suggest that you call your father's assistant, Joy, tomorrow morning. I have her phone number, and maybe she'll be able to explain some of this." He smiled sympathetically. "Unfortunately, your father didn't leave a letter or note with this addendum. I wish I could give you more clarity, but he didn't explain his actions to us, and it wasn't our job to ask."

I counted to ten, breathing deeply the whole time. "So ... this, this inheriting a team thing, does it happen often?"

He thought carefully before answering. "While your father is the only team owner we've represented, I do know that as of 2015, this was voted in as something that could be legally done. The taxes on the purchase of a team are incredibly high. Him putting the team into a family trust was a prudent choice, which was the purpose of the Irrevocable Trust Law in the first place, allowing current owners to ensure that the team stayed within the family without causing a financial burden to the person taking over."

"Oh, good," I said faintly. My heart felt like a rusted tin bucket behind my chest, clunky and useless. The last business venture I'd attempted had failed within the first year—a jewelry line that I'd invested a substantial amount of money in—and the conversation I'd had with my father afterward had consisted of him bemoaning the fact that I couldn't find something that I excelled at, something that was worthwhile and made a difference.

And now I owned a group of men who threw around a leather ball for millions and millions of dollars.

I started laughing. My head tipped back from the force of it, the sound springing from the pit of my belly, loud and full. I wiped at my eyes when the laughter started leaking down my face.

Poor Miles, he stared in horror as the laughter turned to deep, body-wracking sobs. I'd made it through the phone call about my father, the flight home, and the funeral without shedding a single tear.

Now, I couldn't stop them. When I pressed my hands to my face and leaned forward to try to stem the way my shoulders shook and how my cheeks inevitably turned bright red from the flush of emotions, he cleared his throat. I peeked through my fingers and saw him leaning forward to hand me a handkerchief.

With a pitiful sniffle, I reached out and took it from him, wiping under my eyes and trying to calm my breathing.

Everything inside me rattled around in a confusing mess. Anger, confusion, and grief. Other than pictures, I hadn't seen my dad's face in years, and now I couldn't remember if his skin wrinkled around his eyes when he smiled. Panic swept like a messy wave.

What was he thinking? I couldn't own a football team.

"Are you okay?"

I blew out a long breath, but didn't feel like I could speak without another wild swing of emotions, so I nodded. When I tried to give back the small scrap of white fabric with blue stitching around the edges, he shook his head. "Please, keep it. I insist."

In my still shaking hands, I balled up the fabric and gripped it tightly. "Thank you."

"Do you need anything else?"

Another bubble of laughter popped out of my mouth, but I coughed over it. "Just that phone number you told me about. I ... I think I'm going to need it."

CHAPTER 3
LUKE

WASHINGTON WOLVES

"That was shit. Do it again. Keep your elbow tucked in and snap those hips around."

My chest heaved as I glared at my throwing coach, Billy. In his mouth was the ever-present toothpick, the wooden end bouncing around his gray-whiskered mouth as he chewed frantically.

"I did snap my hips around." My hands were braced on said hips. My elbow throbbed, and I knew I'd need a hell of a massage after practice.

He lifted an eyebrow when Jack Coleman, one of our wide receivers, smothered a laugh. Jake wore light pads, like me, and we were doing reps on the turf practice field in the training facilities outside of Bellevue. Normally, music pumped through the speakers while we threw the ball over and over and over, making rep after rep until both Jack and I were soaked in sweat and ready to murder each other over each missed catch or wobbly throw. Today, it was just the sounds of the team working.

"Snap them faster," Billy said, sounding completely bored. That's when I knew I needed to keep my mouth shut because when he sounded bored, it meant I probably had a shit ton more work to do to make him happy.

I nodded to Jack, who took off on a post route. With light feet, I jogged back a few steps and pulled my arm back, fingers gripping between the white laces. When Jack pivoted to the right, I snapped my arm forward, snapping my hips straight, keeping my other elbow tight into my ribs. The ball was a perfect spiral as it arced toward Jack, landing deftly into his waiting hands.

He whooped as he ran into the unguarded end zone, and I blew out a breath. Billy harrumphed behind me.

"Better."

It was better. Which meant I'd need to do it a thousand more times for it to feel like second nature. "I still don't like how my elbow feels when I tuck it in like that."

"Because you want to stick it out in the air like a damn chicken," he grumbled. "How the hell do you think you injured it in the first place?"

Couldn't argue with that. Things that I could get away with in college, along with a hundred other things, didn't cut it anymore at almost thirty-six. I had to work harder, longer, study more, and pay attention to every single muscle that I trained until it was rote —far more than my younger teammates.

They still partied each week while I was at home braiding my daughter's hair and watching film during the off-season while she slept. I was up at four to work out at home while they were still passed out, so when they finally got to the training facilities, we could focus on passing routes, doing reps to change the way I threw the ball so it got where it needed to faster and more easily, with less strain on my elbow.

Jack jogged up to us and tossed me the ball, a stupid ass grin on his face. "Better, old man. I didn't even have to reach for that one." He held his hands out, arguably the only other hands on the team as valuable as my own. "Dropped right in like a perfect little leather baby."

I shook my head. "The thought of you with a child is terrifying."

Billy clapped me on the shoulder and walked away. Jack

laughed and ran backward, holding his hands for the ball. I lobbed it easily, and he still missed it. Idiot.

"Faith loves me. Don't you, turbo?" he called out.

From the side of the practice field where she was sitting up against the wall reading a book, she giggled. All the guys called her by the nickname that I'd given her as soon as she learned how to run, faster than any child had a right to be.

"Faith is a terrible judge of character," I said dryly.

He winked at my daughter. Faith did love him. He was often over for dinner when my mom cooked or on holidays when he couldn't make it back home to Michigan. He was a second-year player out of Michigan State, and since I graduated from Michigan, we'd bonded pretty quickly. That, and he was a helluva receiver, which we'd been missing for a couple of years. Going into this season, we were already projected to do better than we'd done in years, simply because of his presence on our team.

He finished toweling off his face while we walked in Faith's direction. "Why's she here again?"

"My parents are visiting my sister. Normally, they wait until right after the season ends or a bye week, but Kaylie just had another baby. Once school starts back up for Faith, it's not such a big deal for my mom to be gone."

"Why don't you just like, hire a nanny or something?"

"Because this is cheaper," I said with a raised eyebrow.

Shortly after Cassandra died, my parents just up and moved to Seattle. Without a second thought, they sold the modest ranch in Brighton that they'd lived in my entire life and graciously allowed me to buy them something equally as modest near Faith and me.

It wasn't something I asked them, but they knew I'd need the help. Nobody wanted a stranger to raise my daughter, not in our family.

Jack rolled his eyes. "You make twenty-two million dollars a year, Piers."

"And most of that is sitting in nice investment accounts,

making me even more without me needing to lift a finger. You should take notes."

He stretched his arms over his head. "You sound like Robert."

We both fell quiet at his mention of our late owner. Jack was right; Robert had been financially brilliant, and the best advice I'd gotten since starting for the Wolves hadn't been from paid financial advisers but from Robert.

"Yeah," I said quietly. "I guess I do."

"What do you think will happen?" Jack asked, looking as young as his twenty-two years suggested. Sometimes I forgot that he was still a damn kid, barely old enough to legally drink. Not that that stopped him. "They haven't made any announcements from the front office."

I shrugged. The whole situation gave me a sick feeling in the pit of my stomach because the team being sold to a new owner could have untold and unpredictable results. Teams had moved cities for less—not to mention how it could affect coaching positions, how the money was spent, and who ran the front offices.

"Robert was smart," I told him. "He spent twenty years building a machine that ran seamlessly without much interference, so maybe Cameron will take over."

Cameron Mikaelson was our president and CEO and had been for the past ten years. He'd do a good job, and we'd continue exactly as we were now.

"Maybe," Jack said doubtfully. "Wouldn't we know that by now, though?"

Around us, teammates continued to do drills on the bright green turf lined with white. Some were jumping, some tackling, some running. Laughter and cursing and deep voices yelling at each other to do better, be faster, be stronger echoed around us. The red and black logo on the metal walls of the practice field looked freshly painted underneath the bright lights.

I loved that logo—the wolf with his head thrown back in a triumphant howl. It represented twelve years of sweat and blood and dedication that I'd redo in a heartbeat. Every injury, every snap, and every win and loss had brought us right here.

And I was their leader. Maybe I wasn't the coach or the suit in the front office, but on the field, I was the guy who screamed in their faces when they needed it, slapped their helmets when they made an uncatchable catch, stretched for an impossible tackle, got sacked from staying in the pocket too long, and then stood and took the next snap in order to get them the ball.

I was the guy who'd held a shining silver trophy only once before in his career and desperately wanted to do it again. And if I didn't step up at moments like this, then I wasn't deserving of the position of team captain.

I laid a heavy hand on Jack's shoulder. On the field, he was all about running his mouth and crazy touchdown dances that pissed off the safeties who were defending him. But then looking at me, all Midwest country boy, he looked every bit as young as his twenty-two years.

"What matters is what we're doing right here. We practice and get better, and in three weeks, we'll start another season and win, no matter who's in that corner office. It doesn't affect the work we do or the hours we spend making ourselves better, okay? They can't make us win or lose. That's on us."

Jack nodded and elbowed me in the stomach. "Yeah, you're right."

"I'm always right," I told him. Faith was watching us with a tiny smile on her face. She loved being at the facilities. Loved hanging out with the team, loved hanging out with their kids and wives and girlfriends. It was a trait she'd undoubtedly gotten from Cassandra because I didn't have much extrovert in me. But Faith, she loved being around people. "Aren't I, turbo?"

She giggled. "Not always."

Jack crouched down and leaned in to her conspiratorially. "Okay, sweetie, you'll have to give me a list of when he's been wrong, so I can use it against him."

Faith twisted up her lips and glanced at me. Just like it did every single day, my heart turned over painfully. Maybe I didn't get out and party, but she was worth every second of it. Then she opened her mouth.

"Well, he wasn't very nice to our new neighbor."

Damn it, damn it, damn it. I'd used every single shred of control not to replay that strange interaction on a loop since she'd chucked the entire plate of cupcakes at me and waltzed away like a queen.

Jack pretended to take notes on his phone. "Tell me more."

"Faith, we need to go."

"No, you don't," Jack said. "Proceed, fair lady."

Faith leaned in. "She looks like Barbie, and she brought cupcakes over after I waved at her. And Daddy wouldn't let me come to the door with him, and then he was mean, and he dropped the cupcakes everywhere."

"Is that so?" Jack drawled. I glared at him, kicking at his shoe, which he swatted away easily. "Barbie?"

My daughter nodded. "But prettier."

Jack's stupid face got very serious. "Prettier, you say?"

Faith's eyes widened dramatically. "Way prettier."

"What was she wearing?"

"Okay," I interrupted, leaning down to pick up Faith's bag. "That's enough."

Jack pouted about as much as my six-year-old when she stood next to me. "But her story was just getting good, old man."

Faith scampered off, and I punched him in the chest.

"Ouch, asshole." He rubbed at the spot where I'd hit him. "Seriously, though, what happened?"

I shrugged a shoulder. "Chick showed up at the door wearing a bathing suit and holding a plate of cupcakes, which she threw at me when I told her she wasn't very original."

His face froze, then he shook his head in disgust. "You are such a waste of a professional football player. Do you know how many guys wish for that shit to happen?"

I clapped him on the shoulder. "Just wait. It will happen to you too. The second you decide you don't want to sleep with random football groupies, they can smell it like a newly opened bottle of free champagne and will start showing up everywhere. Usually with very little clothing on."

"Promise?" he asked dryly.

"It's only fun the first few times." I cut him a look. "Trust me. Once you realize they'd screw anyone in a jersey, it gets a lot less exciting."

"I just, I just don't think that's the case."

"What, that it gets old?"

"Come on," he practically whined. "You're telling me she was at your front door and *nothing* happened?"

I narrowed my eyes at him with a look filled with so much annoyance that he actually backed off. Which was amazing because Jack had the self-control of a puppy whenever he wasn't on the field. It's why he slept with any woman with a pulse (slight exaggeration). Since he regularly hassled me about my lack of sex life, this was exactly what he didn't need to hear.

He didn't need to hear that Playboy Barbie had, indeed, showed up at our front door, even more stunning up close than she'd been from a dozen yards away on her deck. Standing there in the shade of my porch, I could see the blue-green of her eyes and the small beauty mark above her perfect, pink lips. It didn't matter that she'd covered her black bikini. The loose fabric covering that body didn't hide the fact that she was a ten. Maybe even an eleven.

"Nothing happened."

Although it was written all over his face that he didn't believe me, he wouldn't push me either. He knew better. And for that, I was glad because the last thing I wanted to do was discuss the kind of woman who was now living next door to Faith and me.

There'd been a moment, a fleeting, insane moment, where I wondered if I'd pegged her wrong when she shoved the cupcakes at my chest. Her eyes flashed furiously, but not from rejection. I'd seen that look often over the years since Faith came along.

Rejection had a distinct coldness to it, a disbelief that made features hard and unflinching. That was not what I saw from Playboy Barbie.

But my problem wasn't what flashed in her eyes because if I was lucky, I'd never have to talk to her again.

CHAPTER 4
ALLIE

WASHINGTON WOLVES

There was a beat of silence. Then laughter. All the laughter. Actually, if I'd been sitting across the small kitchen table back in our apartment in Milan, I think Paige would've spit all over my face.

"Okay," I said, settling into the couch delivered earlier that morning. It faced the lake, which usually helped to lower my blood pressure instantly, but my best friend's laughter in my ear upon hearing the news that I was now the sort-of-not-really proud owner of a professional football team was having the opposite effect. "I get it. Haha, so funny."

She made this weird sucking sound and I briefly wondered if she was choking, but I just rolled my eyes.

"I'm sorry, Allie," she wheezed. "It's just ... you ... a football team." And the hysterics began anew.

Spread out in front of me were binders upon binders. Stacks of paperwork requiring my signature. Ridiculous articles I'd googled about "how to own a professional football team" and "what do team owners do in the national football league."

Surprisingly, they weren't very helpful in my current predicament. My brain was overloaded with facts and figures, team structures from around the league and why they were or weren't successful, bios on the people who apparently now worked for me.

Incredibly successful men who now worked for the woman known for the pictures she took and the jewelry line that was now defunct, which left my savings account less full than it had been two years earlier. Though, once all my dad's money was transferred over to me, paperwork signed and completed, that would change. Holy bananas, was that going to change. I'd always had a steady stream of money because of what I'd inherited from my mom, but this ... this was on a completely different level.

My dad had been rich AF.

When I didn't respond immediately with, *Oh I know, isn't this so funny!*, Paige cleared her throat and took a deep breath. "Talk to me."

The back of my head found the couch, and I stared up at the bright white ceiling. "I don't even know what to say, Paige."

"Are you going to keep it? I mean, you could, like, sell it, right? Make a shit ton of money?"

"Believe me when I tell you that I do not say this to sound pompous, but as of last week, I already have a shit ton of money."

Most people wouldn't have sounded so glum when they said something like that. Oh hey, I inherited mega, mega millions, and here I sit on a relatively affordable couch in a relatively modest home (comparatively, of course) feeling like someone just tossed me into the middle of the Pacific with nothing to hold on to.

"So you don't need to sell for the coin," Paige answered. "But no offense, sweet cheeks, what exactly do you know about running a football team?"

Now that answer was easy.

"Nothing. I know nothing about running a football team." I lifted my head and leaned forward to snatch the binder off the top of the pile. A courier had dropped off a large box sent over by my father's assistant, Joy. She'd cooed and clucked over the phone, telling me that I didn't have a single thing to worry about. That everyone would help me. That everything would be fine. Told me to take a day and read over all the paperwork, call her with any questions, and take the time to wrap my head around what this might mean.

Joy was my new best friend. Not that I'd tell Paige that. Paige was my actual best friend and an actual fashion model, as opposed to me.

I knew my angles. I had six hundred thousand likes on my Instagram page, mostly by pervy men who liked the shots of me in designer bathing suits. Paige, on the other hand, had graced multiple magazine covers and walked in New York, Paris, and Milan fashion week more than once. She was one of the few people who felt real in an industry that was very, very fake.

"You're smart, though," she admonished. "Don't sell yourself short. You always told me what a good businessman your dad was even if he ignored your existence most of your life. Would he turn the team over to you without giving it any thought?"

"No," I admitted. It was an easy admission to make too because I'd turned that thought over in my head all night when sleep wouldn't find me. My dad was no fool. There were things about him that I couldn't stand, of course. That list was probably longer than the things about him that I loved. But I could never, ever call him stupid or impulsive.

Paige continued when I didn't say anything else. "There you go. You buckle down and do your homework. Maybe it won't be as bad as you think. It's not like you have to coach the team, right? Maybe you can just stand there and look hot and wear a power suit like a boss bitch. The media will eat it up."

I groaned. "They'll laugh at me."

"Maybe," she said in a quiet voice. "Just don't give them anything to laugh at. Show them you can do this. There's probably an entire building of people over there who will be willing to help you figure it out. Don't be afraid to ask for help, you know?"

Switching our call to speaker, I laid my phone on my chest and leaned back. "Yeah, you're probably right. I just wish I could figure out why he thought I'd want it."

When I talked to my dad—usually, no more than a couple of times a year—we stuck to safe topics and definitely nothing too deep. What I was doing, where I was living, veiled comments about me finding an actual job.

These were all things that Paige knew since I usually started pouring large amounts of wine before the calls were even over.

"Well," Paige said slowly, "maybe he thought you'd like it."

"Me? How many sporting events do I watch in a given year?"

"Zero," she said instantly.

"Exactly. There's no way he thought that." I shook my head and exhaled heavily. "My track record of not succeeding at life was well-documented by my father. Every failed business investment and every boyfriend who turned out to be another money-grub-bing douchebag were added to some list somewhere, I'm sure. This team was the thing he loved the most, and he knows that's a huge reason I never came back. Why he never pushed for me to come back. Because I could never be around him without being a constant reminder that I was his failure. The thing he ignored because it was easier."

Paige sighed heavily. "Lordy, this is heavy shit. And here I thought when I drove you to the airport that you were just going home to collect a massive check and you'd be back in a couple of weeks."

"So did I." Now, I didn't know what would happen or how long I'd be here. The empty home on the lake had been appealing because I wanted a bit of solitude while going through the process of burying my father. And now the quiet was almost making my ears bleed for what it was doing to my brain. Suddenly, I didn't want to discuss this anymore. I didn't want to think about this anymore. "Paige, it's so late there. Why don't you get some sleep, and we'll talk in a few days when I know more, okay?"

"Love you, boo."

"Love you, too," I said back. She disconnected the call, and I didn't move from my spot.

The sun was starting to set over Lake Washington, and from

my too-firm couch, it looked like the sky was bleeding a vivid pinkish orange, starting at the line of the horizon and working its way up in soft, blurry lines. I stared at the sun until my eyes hurt and I had to blink and look away.

From the balcony in our apartment overlooking the Fashion District in Milan, we'd been facing the wrong direction to watch the sunset. Every once in a while, we'd see the reflection of it in the yellow and brown and red buildings in the distance, and I wished desperately that I could see the colors as they changed.

All I'd had to do was walk a block over and stand on the opposite street corner to have a perfect view of it against the Italian skyline. A small effort on my part would have yielded a huge perception change.

It was enough to motivate me to get off the couch, which would hopefully relax over time. From the fridge, still pathetically empty, I grabbed a bottle of pinot grigio. The remaining cupcakes stared back at me, and I scoffed before slamming the door shut on them.

I hadn't seen the asshole next door or his pink cast-wearing daughter, but oh man, had I devoured a lot of those cupcakes. The amount of working out I did was so that I could eat shit like that, not so that I'd have to abstain. The cupboard next to the fridge held all the glasses, and I snagged a lowball with two careful fingers. With my Bose speaker tucked under my arm, I walked downstairs and made my way out into the long, narrow yard that ended at the lake.

A small patio table sat next to the hot tub that I'd yet to test out, and I sank into the chair that would afford me the best view. Carefully, I set down the wine and my glass, then connected my phone to the Bluetooth speaker.

While I sipped my cold wine, I felt the stress slip from my body. Finally, I settled on Imagine Dragons and let out another deep sigh when the music started, and I could sit and watch the colors bleed slowly into a deep blue.

As thoughts of the team filled my head, all the unanswered

questions looped and circled in an annoying beat that I couldn't stop. I turned the volume louder and closed my eyes, hoping that that would help, hoping it would drown out whatever was in my head. I needed to make a decision and stick with it. Own the choice for my future.

I could take the stack of papers on my coffee table and find someone else who would gladly take them off my hands. Or I could sign them, accept this strange gift my father had inexplicably given me, and try to make something from it.

Whichever choice I made, I'd own the hell out of it. I just needed a little more time. Some moments like this to sift through all the extra noise in my head.

Between the beats of the song and the pauses between notes, I heard other music. I looked out onto the lake and didn't see any boats nearby. No one was on my dock or the dock belonging to my next-door neighbor. Whoever was listening to the music turned it up louder, which did not help the cacophony in my brain, so I tried some breathing exercises to try to focus on my own music.

Then, like a string was hooked to my right, my head pinpointed where the sound was coming from. There was a row of tightly cut and neatly landscaped hedges between *his* house and mine. I leaned forward, and between the brief opening of the bright green, I saw someone sitting on the other side.

From the time I'd spent on my own upper-level deck, I knew that he had a patio as well, including a small lap pool, adjacent hot tub, and patio furniture surrounding a large fire pit that had given me an equally large twinge of envy. But now, I narrowed my eyes in a glare when I realized I could see ink covering the arm that I'd spied.

"Asshole," I muttered under my breath.

What pompous prick thought a random woman would show up on his doorstep with cupcakes as a thin excuse to have sex with him?

Fine, he was hot, and he probably got some blatant come-ons when he was out at a bar, but it's not like he was Chris

Hemsworth, newly single and carrying around a strip of condoms or anything.

I mean, fine. His eyes were like, dark and broody looking, and that jaw had the kind of edge that you could probably cut yourself on, but whatever. What arrogance.

I knew I wasn't hard on the eyes, but I certainly didn't walk around assuming that every man who spoke to me wanted in my pants. The ones that did usually made themselves known pretty quickly, and I'd done nothing, *nothing*, to make him lay that assumption over my shoulders.

Because the thought of how he'd so coldly dismissed me got my skin all prickly and hot, I grabbed my phone and hit the button to turn up the volume. And just to be spiteful, I went to my queue on Spotify and added a Britney Spears song.

Did I cackle under my breath when he, in turn, increased the volume of whatever classic rock song he was listening to, just in sheer anticipation of how he'd scowl when he heard my next song choice?

Maaaaaybe.

Did I turn the volume higher and then hold up my speaker while aiming it in his direction just as she started singing "Hit Me Baby (One More Time)"?

Hell yes, I did.

"Oh, come on," he bellowed from the other side of the hedge. "Are you serious right now?"

Instead of answering, I sank farther into my chair and enjoyed the feeling of pissing him off in a way that couldn't possibly come close to what he'd done to me the day before.

Suddenly, he was standing next to the hedge, glaring at me, only his chest and head visible over the vibrant green. I'd forgotten the color of his sandy dark blond hair and how it was a little longer on top than it should have been. From the bulge of his muscles, I knew his arms were crossed over his chest like it would somehow intimidate me.

I held his eyes and took a slow sip of my wine.

"Turn it down."

One of my eyebrows lifted slowly, and when I leaned forward, his shoulders relaxed slowly. Until he realized I was turning it louder.

Thunderclouds. It was the first thing that came to my mind when his face turned stormy. He looked like a thundercloud personified. But from my safe little distance, blocked by those flimsy hedges, I felt braver than I probably should have. Because he shouldered through the bushes and stormed in my direction, which churned up a bright flame of nerves that I wasn't expecting.

He towered over my seat, and I casually crossed my legs, allowing my foot to bounce to the ridiculous synthesized beat.

"Turn it down, please," he ground out.

"Oh, look at that," I said with a sickeningly sweet smile on my face. "He does have manners."

Even though his lips were pressed together, I could tell that he slicked his tongue over the front of his teeth.

"I'm trying to enjoy my evening, and this shit music is ruining it."

I nodded like I was interested in what he had to say. "I'm sorry to hear that. Did you get the frosting out of your shirt? It was very white, and the frosting was *so* very pink."

"No, I didn't."

When my smile stretched into something more genuine, he muttered a particularly dirty string of curse words under his breath. When I still didn't turn down the music, he reached out and snatched the speaker.

"Hey!" I yelled, jumping up to take it back.

He punched the power button with his stupid big thumb and set it back on the table with a loud thunk. "You're lucky I don't throw this in the lake."

Ooooh, this man was lucky I wasn't slapping the shit out of him. "*What* is your problem?"

Instead of an answer, he gave me his broad back as he headed in the direction of the bushes again.

Oh, no. I stomped after him as well as someone can stomp in flip-flops. "I was trying to be *neighborly*, you arrogant asshole. They were just *cupcakes*."

He spun around, and I froze at the fire in his face. "I don't want cupcakes. I don't want you to be neighborly. I want peace and quiet."

I held up my hands. "You've got it. I'll listen inside tonight. But the next time I'm out here first, put on some headphones and call it a night because I'm not budging."

The puff of air that left his mouth was so forceful that he sounded like a freaking racehorse. Without another word, he made a sharp pivot and pushed through the bushes again, then I heard his slider door close loudly.

"Men are so unbelievably stupid," I hissed. This is why God created vibrators.

After I sat back down at the table, I poured another glass of wine and sank back into the chair again. No muscled-up dickwad would ruin my night. I planned on steering well clear of him, and it didn't take a genius to guess that he'd do the same.

With any luck, I'd *never* have to deal with him again.

WASHINGTON WOLVES

O ne thing I learned early in my career was to trust my gut. If a defensive end twitched in a way I didn't like, I never questioned the zip along the back of my neck that told me a blitz was coming. If I started doing that, I'd hold the ball for a second too long, and a single second had the ability to change the outcome of a game.

Currently standing in the hallway of conference rooms at the Wolves front office, I couldn't erase the feeling of my gut screaming. Coach Klein pulled at the collar of his shirt, clearly as uncomfortable as I felt on the inside.

"Why are we doing this before the team meeting tomorrow?" I asked him quietly, just before we entered the room that held our GM William, our CEO Cameron, and the other two team captains besides myself. This morning when I'd woken with the sunrise, I had a text on my phone saying we were needed for a meeting regarding the new owner. Instead of the team as a whole, they only requested the small group of people who led the team. Meeting with the whole team would be during the regularly scheduled time about twenty-four hours later.

Coach Klein shifted again, and I gave him a strange look. "You okay, Coach?"

"It's the daughter."

It took me a second to place his strange comment, the sluggish gears in my head clicking into place with a loud, clumsy clack. "The new owner?" I hissed, eyes wide.

He nodded. "I shouldn't be telling you this, but I know you well enough that you can't filter your reaction for shit when something truly blindsides you." His finger pointed at me, and his gray eyes looked icy and hard under the lights. "And you need to be the one to set the example for the team."

"His daughter," I repeated slowly, choosing to ignore his entirely accurate statement that I didn't always react well in surprising situations at this level of importance. "His daughter is our new owner."

Coach scraped a hand over his haggard looking face. "Yeah. None of us have ever met her. I don't think she was around much the past few years."

"She wasn't around at *all*, Coach."

"You paying attention?" he asked grumpily.

My mouth flattened before I could answer. "No, but he and I talked about her a grand total of one time in the past twelve years. He wanted to know what my plans were for our bye week, which happened to be over Thanksgiving that year. I told him, then asked him the same thing. And you know what he told me? He'd had Thanksgiving at his assistant's house for the past decade because his daughter never came home."

Coach grimaced.

The thought of Faith ever abandoning me like that felt like someone was choking the air out of my lungs with tight fists. Yeah, the man was rich as hell, but his daughter was the only family he had. *Who does that?*

"She was living somewhere in Europe," I said when Coach didn't say anything. "Off playing dress up. Some business she'd tried to open failed horribly from what he told me. And now we're giving her the reins of *all* of this?" I gestured down the hallways.

Anger ripped through me, frustration like a hot wind coming

right on its heels. Because whoever she was, she hadn't done a damn thing to earn the right.

Coach rubbed his forehead and sighed heavily.

"Does she know *anything* about football?" I asked furiously.

"I don't know, Pierson, but you better not ask her that in this meeting."

I propped my hands on my hips and worked to breathe evenly. "I don't like this. I really, really don't like this."

"You don't need to like it," he reminded me with lifted eyebrows. "You need to play football and play it well. That is your job."

"Got it," I said through tight lips. A burst of laughter came from the conference room, and I put on my game face, hypothetically speaking. Coach saw the transformation and nodded in satisfaction. "She in there?"

"I don't think so. Cameron wanted to explain it to the captains first before she came in for introductions." He pointed at me again. "Now, no matter what you happen to think about this situation, remember that she lost her dad last week, and this situation can't be any easier for her than it is for us."

I barely held back my snort of disbelief. Yes, it must be terribly trying for the only child of Robert Sutton the Third. The woman probably became a billionaire the moment his heart stopped beating. Growing up with that kind of wealth at your fingertips was unfathomable to me.

The son of a school secretary and a mechanic meant that we never went hungry, always had a roof over our heads, and clothes that fit us, even if they were secondhand. But my roots were humble and as blue collar as the grease-stained uniform that my dad wore every single day of his life.

He'd drilled into my sister and me that wealth was fleeting, money wouldn't cure unhappiness, and if you were smart, you'd keep your head down, pay your bills, and live a life that didn't break your bank account, saving the rest so your family would have a good future.

Growing up in mansions and a world of private planes and boarding schools was as foreign to me as if someone had dropped me into a different country without speaking the language. The wealth I had now still felt fragile and flimsy, which was why I lived modestly. I never wanted Faith to think that her privileged life was anything she was entitled to. That it was normal. Because I damn well knew it wasn't.

"You coming?" Coach asked when I hadn't moved.

Following him in, I greeted the other two captains. Dayvon, our left tackle, was huge and hulking and terrifying when you didn't know him, and he was the only man I'd trust to protect my blind side, which he did amazingly well. He held his fist out when I passed, and I bumped mine against it.

"Hey, man, did you thank Monique for those cookies she gave Faith?" I asked him.

At the mention of his wife, he smiled widely, his teeth bright white against the dark skin of his face. "She wants to take that girl home with her every time you bring her in. Says that after having four boys, she needs to try one more time so she can get a little girl just like Faith."

I laughed, a small knot of tension unwinding in my chest as we spoke. I could do this. It would be fine.

Logan, our veteran safety and the captain representing the defense, lifted his chin in greeting. I did the same. No fist bumps for us or small talk since Logan was a quiet guy when you weren't part of his inner circle. Not something I would hold against him. He led the defense the same way I led the offense, by example and with thorough preparation.

Cameron, the team president and CEO, sat at the opposite end of the long rectangular table, flipping through some papers in front of him. When I reached the empty chairs on the other side of Dayvon, he held his hand out. His face looked more lined than usual, so maybe everyone was having some trouble adjusting to the change.

"Pierson," he said when I shook his hand. "Thanks for coming in."

"Of course." Like I had a choice was what I wanted to say.

Once I sat, Cameron took a deep breath and glanced around the table briefly. "I received a call from Robert's attorneys the day before last, informing me of a trust he'd created just a couple of weeks before his heart attack. Given that Robert and I enjoyed a forthright working relationship for many years, I have to assume he thought he'd have time to explain his actions to me, which, unfortunately, didn't happen. He and his late wife only had one child, and it was my understanding that her relationship with Robert was not a close one. I'm under the impression Miss Sutton has gotten as little clarification as we have to explain why he took these steps."

While that information settled into the tensely quiet room, I took a few moments to slow my racing thoughts. Perfect. Not only did she not earn this, but she also wasn't expecting it and had no preparation for what to do. It took everything in me not to bang my head against the table.

"The reason I'm explaining this to you now, before she and William join us," Cameron continued, referencing our general manager, "is so that we don't subject her to the awkward announcement that she had no warning she was about to own a professional football team. It's for this reason," his voice turned firm, and I knew that four of us were getting crystal clear instruction for how we were about to proceed with this meeting, and the team meeting the next day, "that we're making sure you—the leaders of this football team—are on board to extend her grace as she assumes this massive responsibility and ensure that the rest of the team does as well."

"Of course," Coach Klein said, his hands folded neatly in front of him. "Right, guys?"

Dayvon nodded. "Might be good to get some fresh blood in here."

Logan glanced at me briefly like he was checking my reaction before speaking. Or maybe it was because my hands were clenched into white-knuckled fists and my leg was bouncing furiously under the table. He looked away. "No argument from me."

I didn't answer right away because I felt like any words coming out of my mouth would be filled with the four-letter variety.

After another deep breath, I realized every eye at the table was aimed in my direction, and I lifted my hands up, knowing what they needed me to say even if it felt like chewed up glass coming up my throat. "She'll get every bit of the respect that we gave Robert."

Cameron let out a small sound of relief, his suit-clad shoulders dropping slightly. "Excellent. They should be here any second."

From down the hall, there was the indistinct murmur of William's low, gravelly voice along with an answering laugh. They were too far away for it to sound like anything other than generically female. I had nothing against a female owner, but still, my gut was screaming at me to run, that something was wrong, that shit was about to go very, very badly.

Despite my less-than-stellar interactions with my neighbor, I was no sexist. I wanted Faith to grow up to be any damn thing she wanted, which was why I'd worked my skin off my bones to ensure her those opportunities. So why was my spine crawling like I was situated in the crosshairs of a loaded gun?

Just before they entered the room, something snapped through my ears at the sound of her voice, but it was nothing I could place, nothing I could pin down with certainty. We all stood to greet her, and as soon as I got the first glimpse of her dress, everything around me slowed to a sluggish, weighted crawl.

It was almost as if my brain couldn't process what I was seeing, so the vision of her was reduced to blocks of color.

Tan shoes.

Tan legs.

Red dress.

Blond hair.

Red lips.

White teeth.

Blue-green eyes.

When it all snapped together, I lost my breath in a pained whoosh. This *could not* be happening.

As she smiled brightly at Dayvon, giving him her full attention, I realized she hadn't seen me yet. My next-door neighbor, the one who had called me an arrogant asshole less than twenty-four hours earlier, was the new owner of the Washington Wolves. And she hadn't seen me yet.

Suddenly, I understood the rampant tug of nerves and the unshakable feeling that something was about to go very, very wrong. I swiped my hand over my mouth and let out a slow breath, straightening my shoulders and holding my head up high. I could do this. I'd stared down three hundred-pound linebackers who wanted to rip the helmet off my head as they tackled my ass to the ground.

I could do this.

She turned in my direction, and I saw the moment it registered. The hitch in her step, the narrowing of her eyes, the slight purse in her scarlet red lips.

"*You*," she whispered.

Everything stopped. All eyes turned in my direction. The temperature in the room with that one hushed word from her went from cordial to downright glacial.

"Oh, shit," I muttered under my breath. She crossed her arms tightly over her chest. The chest I'd ogled while she shoved cupcakes at me.

There was absolutely no part of this that could end well.

"Well," Dayvon said, injecting obviously fake warmth into his voice. "Y'all know each other already?"

CHAPTER 6
ALLIE

I n all the mental prep work I'd done leading up to this meeting, I hadn't planned for this contingency. When I'd decided on my dress, heels, and hairstyle—not to look pretty, but to look kickass and mildly threatening—I didn't question whether I was ready to meet the men who led the team.

But the man in front of me, who'd lost all the color in his handsome face at my appearance, was something I could not have planned for.

And God bless my long buried acting skills and the little angels hovering around me at that moment because my voice was even and smooth when I spoke. "I'm sorry, I didn't catch your name."

Okay, maybe my acting skills were a touch rusty because the words sounded like ice picks coming out of my mouth all aimed in his direction.

His thick throat worked on a heavy swallow as he watched me extend my hand, nails tipped with my favorite OPI red, Vodka and Caviar, and my wrist tinkling with the slender gold chains I'd worn as my only accessory. There wasn't a single noise in the room as everyone watched us. The attention was heavy enough that I felt it raise the hairs on the back of my neck.

Like someone was trying to push his arm back down, he lifted it slowly, enveloping my hand in his own. His large fingers positively dwarfed mine, and the callouses on his skin were warm and dry, rough in a way that I was not accustomed to.

As the feeling of his hand on mine rippled down my arm, all the hairs there lifted, too, in a slow, rolling wave until they stopped at my shoulder. I wanted to rip my hand out of his, that wave was so strong. But there was no way in hell I would blink first.

"Luke," was all he said. There was a tightness in his voice that made my lips curl up deliciously.

William adopted a smile so fake it almost made me laugh as he stepped up next to Luke. No one was dumb in this room. It was clear we'd met before, and I could almost hear their questions as if they were shouting them.

How did you know each other?

What the hell did he do to her?

Did they sleep together?

"Miss Sutton, this is Luke Pierson, our quarterback. He's been with the Wolves for twelve years, so if there's anyone out on that field you can trust, it's him." William clapped Luke on the back, and he jumped, blinking away as his hand slid out of mine. My fingers curled into my palm as if they'd been zapped. "Luke, this is—"

"Alexandra Sutton," I interrupted, pinning Luke with as cool and even of a stare as I could manage even though my stomach was a tight, vibrating ball of unexpected nerves. "I guess I'm your new boss."

His jaw clenched, and his dark, dark eyes narrowed slightly on my face. There was a gleeful streak of energy that punched through my body when I smiled at him. Petty to the hundredth power, I could admit it. But as we stared at each other, I knew he was thinking about how he'd spoken to me when I showed up at his door and our exchange just the night before in my backyard.

Unlike the other times I'd seen him, he wasn't wearing a T-shirt and jeans. Today, his inked, muscled arms were covered in a simple blue dress shirt that fit him like it was custom made, which it probably was. It was a good look on him, intimidating just because of his sheer size but a good look nonetheless.

The coach cleared his throat, and I turned slightly to take his hand. He was a stern looking man in his fifties if I had to wager a guess. But his eyes were warm as he welcomed me to the Wolves, so I let out a quick breath.

The last person at the table that I hadn't met was a tall, lean man with a sternly handsome face and serious eyes.

"Logan Ward," he said with a firm handshake. He didn't smile, but there was still something about him that didn't come off as rude. Not exactly.

As we all took our seats, they waited until I'd taken mine first, and then all eyes were on me. Even Cameron—the polite, if a bit icy—CEO, was taking his cue from me for this small gathering, which had been called at his request.

The first man I'd met, Dayvon, gave Luke a quick, confused look, but he shook his head in a tiny, almost undetectable motion. His color was starting to return to his skin, but every inch of him looked tense and tightly leashed.

"Gentlemen, thank you for coming in," I started, making sure my fingers were knit together firmly before I set them in front of me on the table. When I'd walked into the building, an intimidating glass and steel thing trimmed in glossy black and red, I'd made a promise to myself that I would not show them an ounce of nerves. I promised myself that they would be able to find no fault in how I'd present myself as their team owner. The night before, as I got ready for bed, I knew what I wanted to do.

After washing my face, I dropped the towel on the counter and saw both of my parents staring back at me. In my nose and mouth, the color of my hair, and the heart shape of my face, I saw my mother. And in the set of my jaw and the aqua green of my eyes, I saw my father. Eyes that changed color depending on what I wore were one visible thing I'd gotten from him. Growing up, it had felt like his DNA was only a small shred of who I was as I couldn't identify anything innate as being Robert Sutton's daughter.

But looking into my eyes, I had to convince myself that he would not have given me this massive thing if he didn't believe I was capable of handling it. Forcing myself to believe that was the only way I was managing to stand, metaphorically, where I was standing.

The six men around the table watched me with a curious mix of wariness, curiosity, and anticipation, but they stayed silent until I spoke again.

"My father loved this team, and while it may have taken me by surprise to learn he was leaving it to me, I promise you that I will do everything in my power to continue the legacy of success he's built over the past twenty years." I smiled at each of them, my mouth only wavering in the slightest when I stopped at Luke.

He'd hunched over, pinching the bridge of his nose like he was in pain. Coach Klein elbowed him, and he sat up straight, looking anywhere but at me.

Cameron gave Luke a quick dirty look that surprised me, and William continued smiling like that alone would snap the tense cord between Luke and me.

Clearing his throat, Cameron gave me a tight smile. "Of course, everyone in this room is committed to that same legacy, and we'll do whatever we can to make this transition as easy as possible. Obviously, there are only a couple of weeks before the season starts, but if you're up for a crash course in football ownership, then we'll give you the best one possible based on what we've all learned from your father."

I was about to thank him when Luke's chair squeaked obnoxiously from the motion of him leaning backward. He froze when everyone looked in his direction. Coach Klein closed his eyes briefly, looking very much like someone was digging a knife into his ribs.

William just kept smiling.

"Thank you," I told Cameron. "Joy was kind enough to pass along the contact information for two other owners who she thought would be willing to speak to me. She thought that might be helpful as well."

William's smile broadened as he listened. "Yes, Joy is a remarkable asset for you. She worked with your father longer than anyone in this room did. Great idea. Good." He drummed his fingers on the table. "Excellent."

Luke scrubbed a hand over his face and made a sound deep in his chest that sounded like he was in pain. The reactions to that were varied. Cameron looked like he would strangle Luke with his bare hands. Coach was rubbing the back of his neck and staring at a fixed point on the wall. Dayvon was giving Luke an incredulous stare as if he'd sprouted a second head.

Me? I smiled. I thought about dragging this out just a bit longer when he was so clearly miserable. But it wouldn't help our current predicament to leave the rest of the room in the dark.

I cleared my throat in as ladylike a way as I could.

"Luke is my neighbor," I said. "In case you're wondering why he's acting like an insane person right now."

Cameron's mouth dropped open. William's smile fell, and Coach buried his head in his hands.

For the first time since we sat, Luke's eyes were directly on me, and I could clearly see the warm flecks of gold in the brown. He was just as confused as the rest of them, but still, he said nothing.

"As much as it pains me to say this—because my first impression of him was hardly a good one—don't be too hard on him right now. He had no clue who I was and vice versa." Casually, I rested my folded hands on my lap and held his stare.

He let out a slow breath and glanced over at Coach Klein. That told me everything I needed to know about Luke Pierson at that moment. He was a player, and the person he would defer to would be the man leading the team on the field, not from a luxury box or a corner office overlooking the Seattle skyline.

Finally, he spoke. "If you guys wouldn't mind, I'd like a few minutes alone with Miss Sutton." His eyes found me again. "To apologize for my previous ... behavior."

What I hated most was that I hadn't asked for privacy first. But second, I hated that his voice was low and commanding, without being overbearing. He carried his leadership as effortlessly as he wore that blue shirt. Like, I almost found myself getting up out of my seat and leaving the room, simply because he'd asked it.

Cameron gave me a look to question whether it was fine, and I nodded. After they'd filed out, William shut the door behind him with a quiet click.

And then we were alone. Faced off across a sterile conference table with the logo of a howling black and red wolf staring down at us from behind Luke's big, dumb, judgmental head.

He watched me. I watched him. And neither one of us spoke.

Finally, I gave a pointed look at the clock on the wall. "You're wasting prime apology time."

Oh look, the humorless man was not amused. He folded his hands on the table in front of him, taking up far more space in the chair than I did, his biceps looking very much like boulders straining under the fabric of the shirt. "Why not sell? You can't possibly want this team."

Oh, that observation rankled, but I refused to let him see it.

I tapped my chin. "Strange version of 'I'm sorry,' but I can work with it." One of my eyebrows lifted slowly. "If I thought for a second you were actually sorry for being a complete prick to me."

Luke slicked his tongue over his teeth and regarded me steadily. Other than those first few minutes when I'd taken him by surprise, I could now see the unflappable side of him emerging. The side of him that would manage a game with a steady, calm hand.

"I'm sorry that it was impossible for me to have any clue who you were when you showed up at my front door." He lifted a hand and gestured in my direction. "Similar to how you could have had no idea who I was when you shoved a plate of cupcakes at me."

My cheeks burned hot, and his lips finally bent in a satisfied smile.

"Still," I said with a sniff, "you weren't exactly giving me the benefit of the doubt, were you?"

"No," he conceded. "I've had years of experience behind me to back up the fact that when a woman who looks like you shows up at my house in a bathing suit, flaunting her ... baked goods, it usually only means one thing."

A woman who looks like you.

I nodded slowly, letting the slow burn of anger sweep through me.

He kept going, oblivious to what he'd just stoked inside my body and how high those flames could shoot. "So I apologize for being rude that day. And I apologize for turning off your terrible music in a way that might have been a bit heavy-handed."

"Your sincerity is blowing me away," I said dryly.

"You may not believe this, but this is incredibly sincere for me," he answered between gritted teeth. "I am sincere when I say that if I'd known who you were, I would have been polite. I would have taken the damn cupcakes from you and gone about my day. I would have ignored you last night. I would have shaken your hand without wanting to drop multiple curse words about twenty minutes ago." He leaned forward, and I found it hard to breathe evenly at the full force of his eyes, his personality, his everything at that moment. "And I am sincere when I say I hope that Robert knew what the hell he was doing because we don't need anything getting in the way of us winning another Super Bowl, which is the only thing I care about right now besides my daughter."

I knew his words weren't meant to make me feel small or cause me to fight the urge to curve my shoulders in protectively, but it's what I felt all the same. It took every ounce of moxie, every ounce of Sutton audacity to face him without flinching. When he finished his speech, I stood from my chair and looked down my nose at him. He leaned back, clearly surprised.

"I won't mess this up for you, Pierson. You don't need to worry your big, meaty head over that."

His eyes darkened ominously, but I held up my hand.

"You know nothing about me. You know nothing about the type of person I am. I'll treat you with the respect you deserve as the team quarterback, but you sure as hell better do me the same courtesy as the team owner. I may still be getting my footing, but I bet I could make all sorts of trouble for you if you ever felt the need to remind me what women *who look like me* usually do or say in your obnoxious, golden boy presence."

Luke's jaw was granite, his shoulders rippling with tension, but his mouth was shut, and that was all I cared about. More than likely, I'd want to pass out from sheer adrenaline once I wasn't in the same room as him, but I'd be damned if he saw that.

"After we leave this room," I warned him, "we start over. I won't hold what you said to me against you, the way you treated a perfect stranger who was trying to be kind, and *you* won't hold against me that I called you an arrogant, pretentious, narcissistic prick." I pulled in a deep breath and folded my arms around my waist. "Deal?"

From the chair, he unfolded his body to his full height, and the way he towered over me made me lift my chin stubbornly. I couldn't read a single thing in his eyes or in the set of his muscular body.

"Pretty sure you didn't call me all those things earlier," he said casually.

"No?" I shrugged. "Must have just been in my head. I think all sorts of interesting things when I'm not worried about when I'll get my next manicure."

Luke's nostrils flared, but he was smart enough to know he had zero grounds to keep pushing me.

My entire life, I'd used charm and a sweet smile to smooth over situations like the one I currently found myself in. This was the first time I tried on my badass bitch suit, and even if it didn't fit perfectly yet, at least I knew it was passable.

"Do we have a deal, Mr. Pierson?" I held out my hand again.

For one eternal second, he stared at it like it was made from poison, but then he took it. My arm zapped with energy, something quick and hot and annoying. The moment our hands separated, it stopped, and I felt the aftereffects strongly enough that I wanted to rub the skin of my palm.

"We have a deal, Miss Sutton," he said quietly and walked out of the room.

As soon as the door shut behind him, my knees gave out, and I sank into the chair.

"Awesome," I said into an empty room. "An excellent first day at work, I think."

CHAPTER 7
LUKE

WASHINGTON WOLVES

From the moment I woke up, I knew it would be a shit day. I'd forgotten to close my bedroom curtains, and as my room faced east, I opened my eyes to a painfully bright sun shining directly into my eyes. Like the day dawned with the intent to make my journey into wakefulness as harsh and jarring as possible.

I made my smoothie without a single glance toward her house. While I was actively not looking that direction, my blender broke. Four dollars made their way into Faith's swear jar. Faith's eggs ended up on the kitchen floor when she knocked her plate over on accident, and then she put her own dollar into the jar.

My mood was already so foul by that point, in anticipation of the team meeting, I couldn't even bring myself to punish her for her creative use of curse words.

I almost ran out of gas driving Faith to Monique and Dayvon's house.

During my workout, my elbow was sore and tight.

In the shower afterward, my shampoo bottle was empty.

Each successive thing reduced any remaining good humor I had into a snarling, snapping tangle of energy.

The team meeting was only about ten minutes from starting,

and by the time I found a padded seat in the main room, I felt very much like a leashed lion. If anyone dared get too close, I'd swipe with a heavy paw and pray to inflict damage.

What had Coach Klein said the day before? I didn't always react well when genuinely surprised.

While that was true, this was something different. This wasn't me. I wasn't the guy who remained steadily, purposely mute around my laughing, chatting teammates. Whatever they saw in the set of my mouth, my eyes, and my body language was enough for them to give me a wide berth. In front of me on the table was my binder for team meetings.

Scribbled notes in the margins, readable only to me. Diagrams with Xs and Os and lines and arrows, plays that unfolded in my head when I would sit and listen to Coach talk or our offensive coordinator discuss the defense we would be facing next. All the small things that I did on a daily basis that added up to wins during the regular season.

It was discipline—in every meeting, every workout, and every morning that I made my smoothie and chugged it down.

Sitting in that chair with my eyes shuttered and my jaw locked tight, I didn't feel very disciplined. I felt like screaming. The jumble in my head was messy, a tangle of past and present. My conversation with Robert about her business failures, her absence in his life, and how she was posting pictures as she worked her way through Europe while her father sat home by himself for every holiday. Her face at my door, cupcakes in hand. Her smile at the meeting yesterday.

It was a cacophonous, discordant mess in my brain; nothing I could make sense of even if I wanted to.

Of course, I wanted to. It was what I did every day on the field. To anyone else, a line of players shifting in motion looked like chaos. But I knew what it meant when someone went left, and another went right. When their eyes darted back to the edge of the field.

My fingers tingled with the need to scoop into my thoughts

and find the one thread that I could pull to make all this make sense. Any kind of sense. But I had the feeling that if I pulled the wrong thread, it would only tangle the knots further.

So I'd sit. And wait. And keep my mouth shut. Say a prayer to the football gods above that she didn't come in and fire everyone in the front office and replace them with Victoria's Secret models even if that would make Jack sublimely happy.

I let out a slow breath as the volume in the room increased with each new teammate appearing through the door. No Alexandra yet.

Just the thought of how they would react, how they'd see her, had me leaning forward and pinching the bridge of my nose. This was a disaster. It was everything I didn't want for us. Someone sat heavily in the empty seat to my right and nudged at my elbow.

Gomez, my center, laughed at the dark expression on my face.

"Who pissed in your Wheaties, Piers?"

All I did was sigh and lean back in my chair. "I just want this over with."

We'd played together for six years since New England traded him for two of our draft picks. He balanced me well, all smiles and jokes, amping up the O-line with his positive energy. His forehead wrinkled at my tone, but he knew me well enough not to push.

Then he leaned in. "I heard about her."

Of course, he did. I pinched my eyes shut and tilted my chin up.

"Heard she's hot. Like really hot."

Someone sat down to my left. "Dude, you've never seen her before?" It was Jack. Like I wasn't sitting between them, he leaned closer so that Gomez could hear him above the steadily rising noise in the room.

"No. I mean, I know she must have been at the funeral, but I wasn't exactly lookin', you know what I mean?"

Jack nodded. "Same. I looked at her Instagram last night."

"No shit?" Gomez asked.

I pushed my tongue against the inside of my cheek and glared at Jack, who was completely oblivious.

"She's got this one shot on a beach or some shit. Let me pull it up." He whistled under his breath. "No top. I'm tellin' you, dude."

Under my breath, I made a strange noise that almost sounded like a growl.

He ignored me as Gomez laughed. His thumbs flew across his phone screen, and I fisted my hands under the table to keep myself from choking him. Just as he whistled softly and turned to hand his phone to Gomez, someone stood in front of us and blocked the light.

Logan snatched Jack's phone out of his hand and tossed it back at his chest. Not gently either. "Knock it off, Coleman."

My eyebrows lifted slightly as Gomez sat back in his seat. Jack mumbled something that didn't sound very kind and shoved his phone back into his pocket.

"What's your problem?" Jack muttered.

"You have a sister?" Logan asked.

Jack looked away. That was a no.

"I have four. All younger."

My eyebrows went even higher.

Logan gave me a long look.

"Were you in that meeting yesterday or not?" he asked.

The undercurrent of his quiet voice was pure steel, and the implications, the fact another captain was chastising me, flanked by two members of my offense, made my face hot. "You know I was," I replied evenly.

Logan leaned in close enough so that no one outside the two of us would be able to hear him. "Then act like it," he bit out.

He sat in the row in front of us, oblivious to the fact that I was glaring daggers and knives and swords and all manner of weaponry at the back of his head. Later, when I didn't feel like I was one fraying thread away from punching someone, I'd have a talk with him about verbally reprimanding me.

Of course, when you're wading through the thick mud of a bad mood, you can't possibly entertain the notion that they're right in what they did. I shoved that train of thought down when Coach Klein and William entered the room. The volume around me flared quickly, briefly, until she walked in.

Then there was a hush, a vacuum of sound so intense, it was as if they all pulled in a breath at the same time. Inexplicably, it made me want to break something apart with my hands.

Her hair was pulled back this time, no waves or curls in that sunny, bright hair. No red lips. Skinny black pants, a loose white top, and a red tailored jacket covered her body. She looked sleek and bright and polished.

Rich. Powerful. Confident.

And I hated her at that moment because she was so beautiful that it hurt to look at her. Like waking up in the morning to find the sun aimed straight at me when I wasn't prepared for it.

The guys all shifted in their seats while William introduced her and gave them a similar brief overview of where we currently found ourselves as an organization. Tension rippled through the room in the sets of shoulders faced in her direction and in the eyes glued on her, unable to believe what they were seeing.

William gestured toward Alexandra, and she smiled at him gratefully. Jack actually had his hand covering his mouth, and I elbowed him until he dropped it. His eyes were wide and disbelieving, but he was smiling as if he'd just won the lottery.

She cleared her throat and folded her hands tightly in front of her, a tiny display of nerves that made me look away from her briefly. I didn't want to see her nerves. I didn't want to see her at all.

My eyes pinched shut tightly, and I saw Robert's small embarrassed smile as he told me he was eating Thanksgiving at Joy's house. Again.

Her voice knifed through my thoughts, and I pried my eyes open.

"Thank you all for being here. As William said, I'm Alexandra Sutton. Over the next few days, it's my goal to meet every one of you, and when I get that chance, I'd love for you to call me Allie. I know preseason starts in a couple of weeks, so while I can't promise you that I'll have the entire play card memorized, I do know what first and ten means, so I'd like to think I'm not completely hopeless." There was a small ripple of laughter through the room, and I vaguely heard one of my molars crack down the middle underneath the pressure of my jaw. Her body relaxed slightly, and I found myself winding even tighter.

Her smile straightened as the room quieted again. "I've spent the past few days immersed in facts and figures and charts and budgets. But those papers don't adequately convey the amount of love and respect my father had for the Wolves organization. It's humbling to know that he trusted me to try to fill his shoes." She glanced down at her spiked black heels and exhaled a laugh. "Metaphorically speaking, of course."

This was my nightmare. Staring at her, all I could see in my head was her on my front porch with that plate of pink cupcakes. Her sitting at her patio table and holding her speaker up in my direction. Her holding my gaze fearlessly the day before in our meeting while she laid out her terms of how this would go. And now we were joking about her shoes in the team meeting.

I'd keep my end of the bargain. When I shook her hand, slim and cool in my own, I meant it. I wouldn't do or say anything to disrespect her in front of anyone. But I also couldn't force myself to sit here and laugh and joke and think it was funny that the person who owned our team promised us that she knew what first and ten meant.

It wasn't funny to me. She posted topless pictures that my star receiver had already drooled over, and God knows what else was out there. I wanted to win another Lombardi trophy before I retired while she had bounced around Europe on her daddy's dime. I wanted to prove that I could make it to the top more than once in my career, that it wasn't a fluke.

Crafting a perfectly constructed social media presence was how she lived her life, and I would do anything to avoid that kind of bullshit veneer.

I wanted to play football. I wanted to win. And I wanted to do it without distractions and games and circuses surrounding the team. Let our performance do the speaking.

Allie's bright gaze briefly tangled with mine, and I refused to blink or look away. Her smile grew strained for just a moment, but then she visibly brightened. As if she refused to let me ruin this for her.

"When I was looking through some of my father's files, I found a scrap of paper with his handwriting on it." She held up her hand, and even from my spot a few rows back, I could see the frayed, torn edges. Allie stared at it for a second, and there wasn't a single sound in the room while we waited to hear what it said.

"*In times of difficulty, those brave enough to stay the course will be victors in the end,*" she read in a firm, clear voice. She glanced up. "Does anyone know who said that?"

I knew. *Of course,* I knew. Jack looked at me, clearly surprised I wasn't answering.

"Bo Schembechler," someone said from the front row, referencing the famous Michigan coach. A veritable institution for anyone like me who played at The Big House, who understood the weight of his name among the hallowed ranks of college football coaches.

Allie smiled at him. "That's right." Again, she looked down at the paper before carefully folding it up and curling it into the palm of her hand. "Before I found this paper, I wasn't sure whether I would accept this position, whether I would keep the team. And I'm not telling you this so you'll doubt my commitment; I'm telling you this so you can trust that I'll be honest with you when it's important." Her voice got louder, and her chin lifted as the energy in the room made a palpable shift. Something that rose in a sharp crescendo and split through the room like a charge. I could see it take shape in how they were nodding, listening intently to what she was saying.

She smiled, clearly seeing what I was. "I'm choosing to be brave enough to trust my father's decisions, to trust that all of us can work together to stay the course and be victors in the end. If you're brave enough to trust someone who has a lot to learn, who won't be afraid to ask for help, then I believe we can do incredible things."

"Hell yeah, we can," Dayvon said from behind me. Allie laughed along with everyone else. Except me. An irritating swell of something pushed through me. It wasn't admiration, not exactly. But in less than fifteen minutes, she had this entire room eating out of her hand. When I glanced around, my teammates were nodding their head, smiling, some even clapping.

No, admiration wasn't the right word. A grudging admission that I'd underestimated her was certainly part of it. A muted shock that I seemed to be the only one who felt uncomfortable in how this was playing out.

Maybe none of them had spoken to Robert about her. Maybe none of them would view that conversation with the same stomach-sinking gravity that I had as a single father myself. I wouldn't be the one to tell them, but I'd sure as hell keep my eye on her, for whatever good it might do.

While Allie exchanged a few smiles and a laugh with some of the linebackers in the front row, one of the women from the PR department went up to the front of the room.

"Okay, guys, just a few things and then we'll let Coach take over. We're going to wait another day or so before issuing a press release about the transfer in ownership because we'd like Allie to feel a bit more comfortable before the media gets hold of this story." She smiled, and it reminded me of a shark baring its jagged, knife-like teeth. "And believe me, this is a story that will be everywhere. We're working with Allie and Cameron to make sure this gets us as much positive attention as possible, so if any reporters reach out to you, catch you after practice, whatever, we're incredibly excited for the new direction that Allie brings to the Wolves while maintaining the strong working relationships that Robert forged over the past twenty years." She looked around. "Any questions?"

Oh, I had questions. But since most of them involved some variation of *are we done now*, I kept my mouth shut and waited for Allie, William, and the PR chick to leave. As soon as Allie cleared the door, I finally felt like I could pull a full breath into my lungs.

It should have been a warning that I couldn't breathe properly when she was around. But I ignored it. Focused on football. That was the only thing I needed to worry about. Everything else would blow over eventually.

CHAPTER 8
ALLIE

WASHINGTON WOLVES

Paige: TELL ME ALL THE THINGS! Did you survive? Are there hot players?

Paige: Of course, there are hot players. Not that you can do anything about it. You'll get sued for sexual harassment and abuse of owner power or something.

Paige: OH! And what did you wear? I hope the red suit. Your rack looks insane in that red suit.

Paige: I wish I had your boobs. I've never been so jealous of a DD in my life as I am of you.

Paige: WHY ARE YOU IGNORING ME?

. . .

Me: OH MY WORD. I was peeing. Calm down.

Paige: ...
    Paige: Don't you take your phone into the bathroom with you? What does peeing have to do with anything?

I rolled my eyes and settled into the striped chaise lounge, adjusting the top on my blue one piece before responding to her. Paige was ... for lack of a better term, in a serious relationship with technology. Her phone was her boyfriend. And a healthy relationship, it was not. I was surprised her thumbs hadn't fallen off by now.

Me: No, I wore the black cigarette pants, the white Michael Kors blouse, and the red jacket from that store we found right before I came back.

Paige: Hmm. Satisfactory. I still think you should've done the red suit.

Me: Probably not an appropriate choice, considering the amount of cleavage it shows. I WAS meeting the players for the first time.

Paige: I fail to see the problem. I would totally switch teams for you when you wear that.

My laugh felt foreign on my lips because it was genuine and unforced, and outside of whatever meetings I'd been attending, I'd been alone at home with all my football binders. No one, outside of Joy and the lawyers and Luke, knew that I was living in the lake house, and since the press release about me taking over the team went out, the sports world had exploded with the idea of a twenty-six-year-old woman owning a football team she inherited from her father.

It felt easier to hide out than try to come up with a succinct statement about how it was going, or how I felt about it. The truth was that I still didn't exactly know. Speaking to the team was the most comfortable I'd felt since this whole crazy thing started because I'd been met with smiles and welcome and warmth, and several of them went out of their way to introduce themselves once the meeting was over. Everyone I'd met had been polite and respectful, supportive.

Except, I thought with a slight glare at the blue house next door, *Luke effing Pierson*. During the whole meeting, he watched me like I was a ticking time bomb. Not once did he smile. Not once did he look at me with any hint of warmth on his chiseled face.

And what absolutely pissed me off was how quickly I'd searched him out in the room of large, imposing, handsome men. He certainly wasn't the only one with broad muscular shoulders. And he certainly wasn't the only tall, good-looking man in the room. There were many of them in there.

But his were the only eyes that I felt burning through the clothes covering my body.

"Get him out of your head *right* now," I said out loud. I blew out a breath and adjusted my sunglasses. It was a beautiful day with cloudless sapphire skies and enough breeze in the air so lying out in the sun wasn't stifling. It came off the lake and crossed my yard, bringing with it the sounds of boats, laughter, and some music coming from somewhere far in the distance.

What I needed was a distraction.

Stacked on the ground next to my chair were more binders that Joy had given me. I'd read them the day before until my eyes started crossing, but it was all helpful. Overwhelming, but helpful.

Thankfully, I wouldn't have to concern myself with most of the details.

There was a CFO who worried about the money. A manager who worried about the talent. A president who worried about ... everything else. The truth was that my father had spent the past twenty years hiring people who knew their shit.

He was the figurehead, but they ran the team and ran it well. My main concern was making sure that the Wolves didn't suffer because of my surprise presence. I knew as well as anyone that the media could spin many tales, as long as they got people to tune in, and I wanted to keep the players from resenting me.

I leaned over and grabbed the binder that held the team roster. Joy had each player, each coach, and each coordinator sectioned off with brightly colored tabs for easy reference. I flipped page by page, looking at their picture and saying their name and position out loud. Some of the faces I recognized from the meeting, but most I didn't. Of course, they'd all been at the funeral, but most of that day was a blur of handshakes and air kisses, condolences and black suits and the numb realization that I had no living parents.

I finished looking at the page for Jack Coleman, a smiling guy who I recognized as the one sitting next to Luke at the meeting. The wide receiver from Michigan State had been with the team for two years. His numbers could've been impressive, or they could have been shit; I really had no idea. His smile was wide and care-free in his picture, and I found myself smiling back.

Idly, I flipped to the next page and froze. Luke's image smiled up at me.

Smiled.

That smile did weird tummy-flipping things to me.

It was a small smile, no teeth showing, but it was so foreign that I stared open-mouthed. Honestly, it did such spectacular things to his face that it wasn't freaking fair. The man could've been a model. But like one of those rugged, non-pretty boy models.

Feigning the same casual interest that I'd read the other files with, I skated my finger down the line. Luke Michael Pierson from the University of Michigan. Third-round draft pick twelve years earlier. He was the backup quarterback his first year with the team. During the second game of his second season, the starting quarterback ruptured his Achilles' tendon, and Luke took over with the ease of a veteran QB.

They won the Super Bowl that year and hadn't been back since.

A noise from the hedges made me snap the binder shut because I would be damned if he caught me staring at his picture like a heart-eyed teenager. When I looked over, though, it wasn't Luke who I saw; it was a flash of bright pink and a purple T-shirt among the leaves.

The little girl didn't move again until I looked away, then I heard another rustle of leaves. This time, I could see her face, big brown eyes and long brown braids hanging on either side of her face.

Tapping my thumb against the binder in my lap, I thought about my options. Luke told me to stay away from his daughter, but that was when he thought I was a football groupie or something, coming to offer myself up as a bodily sacrifice.

Snort. Give me a break.

Now, we were co-workers, for better or for worse.

I slid my sunglasses to the top of my head and squinted over at her. "Hey. You doin' a little landscaping in there?"

She giggled and pushed her way into my yard, face flushed and smile wide. "No, I'm not allowed to help with the yard yet. My daddy mows the lawn."

I looked down my nose in her direction. "Your dad does? Wouldn't you guys, like, pay someone to do that?"

Her face turned serious. "He said as long as he has working legs and two hands, there's no reason to pay someone for something he can do himself."

Huh. That was ... not what I was used to.

"Oh, okay. Well ... good for him." I smiled at her, at the way she watched me like I was a unicorn that had just pranced in front of her. Kids were like a strange little alien species to me. None of my friends had kids, and I had no nieces or nephews to hang out with. So I figured I might as well treat her the way I wanted to be treated when I was her age. As if I mattered. "What's your name, sweetie?"

"Faith Pierson." She puffed out her chest. "I'm six and a half." I nodded sagely. "That's a good age."

"What's your name?"

"I'm Allie." When I held my hand out for her to shake it, I thought she might burst open from the force of her smile. "It's a pleasure to meet you."

"You too, Miss Allie."

"How'd you break your arm?"

She let out a heavy sigh and walked closer to my chair. "I fell off the monkey bars."

"Ouch." I gestured for her to show me her cast, and she held it out. When I saw Luke's signature and a couple of other players' too, I smiled. Gripped in the skinny fingers of her other hand, I spied a small black marker. She saw me looking at it and opened her mouth, but she didn't ask. "Can I sign it?"

I smothered my smile when Faith nodded excitedly and shoved the marker into my waiting hands. Very gently, I held her cast in one hand and found an empty spot up by her wrist to scrawl my signature.

"Wow," she breathed. "That's the prettiest writing I've ever seen."

"You know," I started, very aware that Luke would be furious for me digging. Digging. Asking. Whatever. He could suck it. "I saw you wave at me through the slider. I wanted to come over and say hi. Maybe meet your daddy and mommy."

I held my breath when she looked up at me. Okay, fine, it was *shameless* digging. But come on, what guy looked the way he did, made as much money as he did, had an adorable little girl, and wasn't attached? If he wasn't such an asshole, it would be practically a crime against nature.

"You met my daddy," she said, clearly confused.

"I did. I, umm, I actually work with your daddy too. We just didn't know it yet when I came over to say hi."

"Oh, cool! I can't wait to tell Grandma. She and Grandpa are visiting my aunt Kaylie and my new cousin, but they'll be back home to take care of me tomorrow because Daddy has to start playing games soon."

I squinted toward the sun. "Your grandma takes care of you?"

"When I'm not in school, but I'll be in second grade this year."

Questions tickled the edge of my tongue, so I clamped that sucker between my teeth to keep from pressing this tiny, cute little child who had no clue why I was asking. Hell, *I* didn't know why I was asking.

Liar, liar, pants on fire, I sang in my head. I totally knew why I was asking. I hated how he wrote me off, how he treated me without knowing a single thing about me, and I hated that he was hot and that it bothered me so much.

Naturally, that meant I had to get as much information about him as possible.

"Well, I can't wait to meet your grandma when she comes back. Is she your daddy's mom?"

Faith nodded, trailing one finger over the spot I'd signed. "I don't know my mommy's mom. She died when I was a baby."

In my chair, I froze, not sure how to proceed. Good job with the questions, Allie. "I'm sorry to hear that. Your mommy's mom did?"

She shook her head. "My mommy. I don't remember her, but Daddy said I have her smile and her laugh."

And just like that, folks, my heart went kablooey in my chest. I was the biggest asshole in the entire world, thinking I would ask this cute kid a few innocent questions. Unsure of what to say next, I closed my eyes and tried to remember what I felt like when people had asked me about my mom when I was not much more than her age.

"I have my mom's smile, too," I told her gently. Were my eyes wet? I hadn't cried once about my father, but Faith's big brown eyes were absolutely gutting me.

"You do?" she asked. "Is your mommy in heaven like mine?"

I nodded slowly. "She is."

"Faith?" Luke boomed from the other side of the hedge, panic clear in his deep voice.

"Right here, Daddy! I'm talking to Miss Allie."

Well, shit. I slid my sunglasses back down like they'd shield me from the incoming wrath of Luke Pierson. Like he had the other night, he shouldered through the hedge with a furious look on his face. When his eyes moved from me to Faith, he visibly gentled.

Kablooey part two, ladies and gentlemen.

"You scared me, turbo. I didn't know where you were." He crouched down next to her and cupped her shoulder in one massive hand. "If you want to leave the yard, you have to come and ask."

"Okay, Daddy." She beamed at him. For a moment, I tried to remember if I'd ever smiled at my own father like that.

No, I hadn't because I didn't think I ever heard the kind of concern in his voice that Luke was showing Faith. In the bright sunshine, I could see the ink covering his arms more clearly. Dates and Roman numerals and a couple of names, all slightly faded like they'd been there for years. Nothing looked new in the way it was printed into his tan, smooth skin.

Stop looking at his skin!

"Can you go back home while I have a quick chat with Miss Allie?" he asked her in a deceptively kind voice.

My stomach sank like a rock, imagining him turning to me and asking what exactly I'd been talking about with his daughter. Slowly, I swung my legs over and sat sideways in a chair, using the striped towel on the ground to cover my shoulders. Before he stood, Luke's eyes flickered to my bare legs, and I very much wished I hadn't seen them do that because now I felt naked.

Faith waved at me as she ran back toward the hedge. "Bye, Miss Allie! Thanks for signing my cast."

"You're welcome, sweetie. It was nice to meet you."

Luke and I were silent as she slipped through the widening space in the hedge, apparently the unofficial spot that the Piersons walked through to get into my yard.

Once she was gone, and the sliding door into their house opened and closed, the silence between Luke and I bloomed into something big and uncomfortable, but holy shit, I was not going to speak first. Because what would I say?

Sorry, I was just pestering your daughter about your apparently dead wife? Girlfriend? Ugh, no matter how I phrased it in my head, I sounded like an asshole.

"So," he said slowly, all dangerous and low and quiet, and it raised goose bumps on my arms. "Care to tell me what the hell that little conversation was?"

CHAPTER 9
LUKE

WASHINGTON WOLVES

"Just being *neighborly*," Allie answered instantly. She followed it up with a sweet smile that set my teeth on edge. Aviator sunglasses sat on her face, and I didn't like that I couldn't fully see her, as they blocked her eyes from view. But I didn't have to see them to know that they were the same color as the lake today.

Now, if I was a less stubborn man, someone less determined once I'd chosen a course of action, I might have been worried about why I was thinking about the fact that Allie's eyes matched the lake when the sun hit it just right.

But I wasn't worried. It was a natural reaction when you'd been celibate as long as I had to notice things like that.

It was natural, damn it.

"What did you talk to her about?"

Allie tapped her chin and leaned forward, but I kept my eyes trained on my own reflection in her sunglasses, not on the deep v of her simple navy bathing suit. It shouldn't have looked as sexy as it did. But I'd wager a guess that on her, anything would look sexy.

"Well, first I asked her if she knows what your type is." She paused, cocking her head to the side while I rolled my eyes. "Oh wait, no I didn't. That's not right because my world doesn't actually revolve around you."

When I braced my hands on my hips, she stood from the chair and mimicked my pose. Except on her, it just looked like something you'd see in a fashion magazine. With her mussed-up blond hair, the high cut of her suit on those impossibly long, toned legs, and the curve of her hips into her waist and back out at her breasts, Allie Sutton was a fucking stunner.

I hated it.

And because I hated it, I found myself snappish and surly just from being in her presence with no buffer, no one waiting in a hallway for us to be done.

"My daughter is off-limits." I hardened my face, making myself bigger in the space between us. Except she did the same.

"Your daughter came over here, thank you very much. Do you want me to ignore her? Make her feel like she's a nuisance?" Allie scoffed, shaking her head at me in ... disgust? Disappointment? "Get over yourself, Pierson."

"Of course, I don't want you to make her feel like a nuisance," I ground out.

"Good. Because I know how that feels, and if she talks to me, I'm going to talk back."

My brain hiccupped over that, and I tried not to give her a narrow-eyed look of suspicion. What was that supposed to mean?

Something about standing in front of her made me feel like a fraud. The thought came from the part of my brain that had the flimsiest of filters. She'd been raised with every opportunity presented to her. She could've done anything with her life, choices laid out in front of her like a smooth arc of cards from a dealer's hands, probably on a silver platter.

Just by being born to the right people, she now wielded an immense amount of power. She could fire anyone in the front office if she wanted, any of the men and women who made the Wolves run smoothly day in and day out.

Which was why I wasn't stupid enough to snap back at her

even though the words were ready to spring from my mouth with ease.

"Don't worry, I'll tell Faith to leave you alone," I said before turning and going back home. I heard that sound again, the annoyed huff that scraped my skin like a cat's tongue, rough and uncomfortable.

When I let myself back in my house, I took the stairs two at a time and found Faith sitting on the couch, my phone in her hand, and she was smiling at the screen.

"I'm talking to Grandma, Daddy." Faith turned the phone, and my mom's face greeted me.

I gave Faith a mock angry look. "Who taught you how to FaceTime?"

"You." She giggled.

With one hand, I ruffled her hair. "What a terrible idea that was."

"Faith was just telling me about your new neighbor, Miss Allie," my mom said, voice heavy with meaning. "As in Allie *Sutton?*"

She'd heard the news then. I kept my face even since my mom had this horrible ability to see right through me. Especially when I didn't want her to.

"Hey, turbo," I said to Faith, "why don't you go play in your room for a little bit, okay? I want to talk to Grandma."

For a second, she opened her mouth like she was going to argue but nodded glumly instead. "I'll see you tomorrow, Grandma. Love you!"

My mom smiled. "Love you too, baby. I'll see you at the airport. I'll be the one with the suitcase."

Faith gave the screen a smacking kiss and ran down the hall to her bedroom.

"Your neighbor is Alexandra Sutton?" my mom asked immediately.

I rubbed my forehead and centered the screen so she could see me better. "Yes."

"Don't sound so excited about it." Her face was lined with concern.

"I'm not."

"What's wrong with her?"

She exists.

That was what I wanted to say. What was wrong with Allie was that she existed in the house next to me and at work, and I couldn't escape her.

"Luke," my mom said slowly when I didn't answer right away. "What did you do?"

I sighed heavily. "Can we just talk about this tomorrow?"

"No. I'm hiding from your sister."

"Baby made her crazy, huh? I bet it did."

She lifted an eyebrow. "Don't change the subject."

I shifted on the couch and briefly looked out the large glass slider toward the lake. I couldn't see Allie where she was sitting on her lawn, but I knew she was still down there. I'd seen the binders stamped with the Wolves logo stacked next to her chair.

Finally, I met my mom's knowing blue eyes. "I wasn't exactly *kind* the first time I met her."

"And the second time you met her?"

In lieu of an answer, I scratched the side of my face.

"Oh, Luke."

"I didn't know who she was," I snapped.

"And that's a good excuse? Your father and I raised you better than that."

That was the problem. Even my own reasons for still being an ass to Allie were rooted in my own issues. My own past. Things that, if I was honest, had absolutely nothing to do with her, despite what Robert had told me.

The insidious claws of my own prejudice toward the type of women who wanted to sleep with me merely because of the size of my paycheck, because I put on pads and a helmet for a living. They didn't care about any other part of me. In fact, I was interchangeable. If I'd swapped out with any of my teammates, they wouldn't care.

Cassandra had been that type of woman. And she wasn't the first like that who I'd slept with, but because the consequences of my fling with her had been far-reaching and so life-altering, it left sand and dust in my mouth anytime I thought about venturing down that road again.

It was the cheapest part of this rich life I now led. And Allie had looked like the prototype of that nightmare. That wasn't her fault, and I knew it. I just didn't want to say it out loud.

I didn't want to voice that she represented all the things I actively sought to keep out of my life, out of Faith's life. That I'd had a prejudice against her even before I'd ever met her, which also wasn't her fault.

"I know you raised me better than that," I told my mom. "But you also didn't raise me to be an idiot. It's for Faith's benefit that I am just a little suspicious."

"But you don't have the reason now." She shook her head and looked away from the screen, her disappointment like a shard of glass wedged under my skin. "Think about what that poor woman has been through. She lost the last parent she had in this world."

"She didn't exactly see Robert as it was."

She clucked her tongue. "So judgey. Who does she have now? *No* one."

"She's got an entire football team," I said dryly.

Like only a mom can, she ignored my wonderful attempt at sarcasm. "Have you apologized to her?"

I slicked my tongue over my teeth. In only the most technical sense. But had I meant it at that moment?

With embarrassment, I had to admit to myself that no, I hadn't. She'd stood by that table, secure in the knowledge of the position she now held, whereas my own felt flimsy and fragile. Shift too far in one direction, and it felt like I'd tumble off my perch with the team. So, I'd said the words, but that was it.

"Kind of," I told my mom.

Even from a thousand or so miles away, when my mom narrowed her eyes at me, I wanted to shrink away. "Luke Michael Pierson, you go over there right now and try again. Bring Faith the phone, and I'll keep her occupied. You apologize to that nice woman."

"How do you know she's nice?" I muttered grumpily.

"If she didn't fire your ass, then she's probably nice."

I had to lift an eyebrow in concession. "Good point. I mean, there's that pesky little thing called a contract, but ..."

"Go."

"I'm going." I stood from the couch and brought Faith the phone. She snatched it and started showing my mom all her dolls that she'd set up in a tea party. Alone in her room with blank-eyed toys for company. No wonder she went to talk to Allie. "I'll be right back, turbo. You stay here and talk to Grandma."

"'Kay, Daddy."

I kissed the top of her head and slowly walked back downstairs as if a rusty-edged guillotine waited for me and not Alexandra Sutton.

As I opened the slider, I knew why. Because they could both inflict massive damage if used properly.

Careful to close the door quietly, I made my way across my own emerald green lawn with slow and steady steps, making sure my head and gut were in line.

She was just a person.

A person who'd been subjected to the ungracious side of me that I wasn't always proud of, but still used like armor. A person who'd only risen to the bait when I'd practically forced her to. A person who'd extended me more grace than I'd extended her. And she'd made my daughter smile with enough force to light the entire state of Washington.

As much as it pained me to do so because it felt like I was betraying his memory, I had to set aside what Robert had told me as if it was proof of some crime she'd committed.

Maybe her manners were superior because that was how she

was raised. Maybe it was because she was a nicer person than I was. Either way, I was a big enough man to admit that I could do better when it came to how I treated Allie.

From the other side of the hedge, now visibly battered in one spot from the newly introduced traffic between our yards, I heard a deep sigh.

I pinched the bridge of my nose and felt a deep welling of shame.

As soon as I walked through the hedge, her head lifted on a sharp snap of surprise.

"Is it okay if I interrupt for a couple of minutes?" I asked.

Allie licked her lips and then nodded, those sunglasses still covering her eyes. Instead of towering over her while she laid on the chair, I gestured to the patio set. "May I?"

"Of course."

Pulling one of the chairs out from the table, I angled it toward her and sat, rubbing my hands along the tops of my thighs. Her fingers, long and graceful, tapped on the surface of the binder in her lap when I didn't immediately speak.

"My apology the other day," I started, closing my eyes briefly before I spoke again. "It sucked."

Allie let out a surprised laugh. The hand on the binder lifted so that she could push the sunglasses into her hair. Her face was free of makeup but still held no less impact than when she was fully made-up. With it or without it, I knew that I was looking at one of the most beautiful women I'd ever seen.

The thought made me swallow hard. Because how she looked didn't matter. How I treated her did.

"We all have our reasons for why we do what we do," I told her; a vague explanation, but it was all I wanted to give. "But my reasons don't matter in this instance. They don't really have anything to do with you, so they shouldn't affect how I treat you. So I apologize for how I've spoken to you, and I hope we can start over."

For a moment, her eyes narrowed as if she doubted my sincerity, so I refused to look away. It wasn't easy because those thick-lashed eyes, bright and vivid in her flawless face, were surprisingly astute.

"Apology accepted," she replied quietly. "And in turn, I'll apologize for calling you a pretentious prick after the meeting."

My lips hooked up on one side in a begrudging smile. "Well, not an unfair label, given the circumstances."

"True."

I pointed at the binder. "What are you working on?"

"The roster," she said, flipping open to a page. "I want to know everyone by name by the time preseason starts."

The page she was on was Logan's, and I grimaced thinking about how he'd done what I should have been doing at that team meeting. "Ward is okay."

"Yeah?"

I shrugged. "For an Ohio State grad."

Allie smiled politely, but I could tell she didn't get the reference.

"Our colleges are rivals," I explained.

"Ahh." She squinted out at the lake. "Does that stuff really matter once you're in the pros?"

I shook my head. "No, it doesn't. We all want the same thing now. All working toward the same goal. It makes it easy to forget all the things that seemed so big when you were playing college ball."

Her thumb tapped lightly, and I could tell she was thinking, especially when her eyes darted over to me briefly. "I'm sorry if I crossed a line by talking to Faith."

I held up my hands. "No, you didn't. I have a tendency to over-react when it comes to her."

She stared at the binder for a minute, not really focusing on the page. "I just remember watching my dad work and wishing he would ... I don't know, talk to me. Let me sit in there with him. Anything. She looked so curious, watching me from that hedge. I was looking at myself twenty years ago."

I shook my head because the shame I'd felt earlier made a hard right into embarrassment. My mom had called me judgey, and she was not wrong.

Twenty years ago.

That was when Robert bought the team, and she was just a little girl without a mother.

After a long sigh, I swiped a hand over my mouth. There were so many things she could relate to with Faith. A father who worked an ungodly number of hours in order to be successful. The void left behind from not having a mother around, and even though I tried very hard to live well below our means, having a life of wealth and ease, free of the everyday struggles most families had to deal with.

What kind of person would that shape Faith into? Would she travel the world, known simply as the daughter of a football player? It was a perspective that allowed me to watch Allie through the lens of curiosity instead of judgment. Like I'd finally given myself permission to view her more clearly and not through the foggy lens of my own bias.

"Can I ask you something?"

She smiled. "In the spirit of this football-related truce, sure."

I clasped my hands together, and they hung between my spread legs, elbows propped on my thighs. "The other day in the meeting, I asked you why you didn't sell, but you never really answered."

There was a spark of humor in her eyes as she watched me. It did something luminous to her as if someone lit a match behind a piece of wavy blue-green glass. You could see the glow, maybe even feel the warmth, even if you couldn't make out the source of where those things were coming from. "Maybe I didn't answer because you spit the words at me like they were weapons."

"Touché."

Allie sat up, bringing her knees up to her chest and wrapping her arms around the front of her legs. Staring out at the lake, she rested her chin on her knees and looked so much younger than she had the day before in front of the team. In comparison, I felt old and tired with battle-scarred skin and muscles where she was all lithe and firm with soft, full curves exactly where they should be.

"We all have our reasons for why we do what we do," she said, using my words from earlier. I dropped my chin to my chest and smiled. She turned her head to the side, cheek resting on her kneecap and her eyes aimed at me. Something new and uncomfortable tumbled through me with that look, and I absolutely refused to name it or unpack what it might mean. "Maybe someday I'll be ready to explain this one."

We sat in silence for a while with the sound of waves and rustling leaves, and boat engines rising and receding the only things breaking that up.

"I'm just ready to focus on football again," I told her, surprised by my honesty. "It's all the extra stuff that makes me cranky."

"You?" There was a smile in her voice. I didn't look at her mouth to see what it looked like.

It was a tenuous truce, only a few cautiously asked questions and vague answers serving as the foundation. But it was a start.

WASHINGTON WOLVES

"I hate this."

The PR lady (I was quite sure her name was Ava) gave me a steady look that told me everything I needed to know. Before she broached this topic with me, she damn well knew what my reaction would be. It was well known to the team that dealing with the media was my least favorite part of this job.

"It doesn't matter if you hate it or not. It's a huge opportunity." Her eyes were the same green as the practice turf, and I closed my eyes from the steely reserve I saw there. "When's the last time *Sports Illustrated* wanted to feature us on their season kickoff article?"

Never. But I swallowed that word down like I had a gun to my head.

Behind me, Jack was practically vibrating with excitement. "Come on, Piers, this is huge."

Slowly, I rolled my neck. "I don't want to do it. It will turn this team into a three-ring circus."

"Or," Ava said, "it will get our fans excited. The league is eating this up."

I gave her a dry look. "Of course, they are. If it can increase ticket prices or gain more sponsors, they love any sort of controversy."

"It's not controversy," Jack, the idiot, butted in. "She just happens to be hot. Hot people sell magazine covers. It's not rocket science, dude."

Ava pinched her eyes shut at his complete lack of tact. "Clumsy phrasing aside, he's not wrong."

From behind me came her voice. "Of course, he's not wrong."

It was my turn to shut my eyes, but against my arm, I felt the whisper of air when she stood next to me. Even though she didn't touch me at all, I felt her like a static charge. As if she had her own energy field that I had to plant my feet against or be pushed back by the force.

"Miss Sutton," Ava said warmly, giving Allie a respectful greeting even though they were the pretty much the same age.

"Allie, please." When I dared to glance at her, she was smiling at Jack. "And you're Jack Coleman, right?"

The kid puffed up like a peacock, extending his meaty paw as if he was bestowing a gift upon her. "That's right, ma'am. It's a pleasure to finally meet you." While they shook hands, his smile spread even further. "Or can I call you boss? I like that better."

The fact that he'd called her ma'am at all was ridiculous. Dressed in slim, dark jeans and a simple white T-shirt with some thin gold jewelry around her neck and wrists, she looked no older than he was. I'd long learned that the most dangerous of women were the ones who could wear something simple and look like they'd stepped from a magazine. No frills, no embellishments, just them. That was how you knew they were beautiful, and you knew they knew it too.

She cocked an eyebrow. "Allie is just fine." Briefly, she looked at me and sent a subdued—albeit polite—smile. "Luke."

I nodded my chin.

Allie turned back to Ava. "What are they asking for exactly?"

"They want to feature you, Luke, and Jack on the cover to kick off the NFL regular season. The article will be about you, as the new owner, and how you're stepping into a system that's been in place for years." Ava scrolled through something on her phone, and with every word out of her mouth, my skin crawled even further. They'd want me and Jack shirtless, no doubt, and Lord knows how Allie would be dressed, draped over both of us.

"Why just the three of us?" Jack asked.

Ava gave him a casual once-over. "Well, you're not hard on the eyes, and you two are easily the Wolves most recognizable players. Even casual football fans know the star offensive players at a glance."

"Who's the photographer?" Allie asked, and I gave her a quick look. Even in the team meeting, this was as business-like as I'd heard her.

Ava hummed and scrolled further down on her phone. While we waited, Jack spun the football in his hands and gave me a wide-eyed look of disbelief. I'd been on the cover of *SI* before, but it was a shot taken on the field of me hoisting the Lombardi trophy over my head. No photo shoots, props, makeup, bright lights, or reporters asking us questions for the sole purpose of digging for some juicy tidbit.

Hadn't I said this was my nightmare? Because this was my *nightmare*.

When she found what she was looking for, Ava said the name, and Allie lifted her eyebrows appreciatively.

"Is that good?" Jack asked.

"It is," Allie answered. "He does a lot of fashion photography too. My friend Paige has shot with him before. Said he's great to work with."

Against her denim-clad thigh, her perfectly manicured nails beat a furious rhythm. Ava noticed it, as did I.

"What are you thinking?" she asked Allie because I sure as hell would not.

Before she spoke, Allie glanced at me, then at Jack. There was a determined jut to her chin that I'd never seen before, even when she was chewing me out after that first meeting. Around us, the guys practicing gave her sideways looks as if she was an exotic animal let loose among our ranks. What made it even stranger—their watchful curiosity, the impression that they were all circling her warily—was that every single one of them were used to seeing beautiful women.

Beautiful women were a given, an expectation when you reached the level that we were at. Teammates were married to former Playboy bunnies, models, socialites, actresses. But she was more than that because of her position. Just take this small, private conversation as an example of how different Allie was when it came to what we were used to within the walls at work. The moment she showed up, the dynamic shifted.

The moment she showed up, we all deferred to her. It made me as wary as my teammates because it was usually a position that I held.

"Call them back and let them know that we'll agree." When I made a small sound of dissent, she lifted a hand, her eyes holding mine. "On the condition that they only photograph me. The guys can be there for a few questions, make sure I don't make a fool out of myself if too many football-specific questions come up, and we'll do a behind-the-scenes featurette for their website that includes the three of us. Something light, something funny. Something very shareable to drum up interest for the article."

Jack was staring at her in a way that could only be described as awestruck, and I wanted to smack the worshipful look off his face. Even if I felt a streak of appreciation for the way she'd read between the lines of what I wanted. Or didn't want.

"And if they push back?" Ava asked. Her fingers were flying over the screen of her phone.

Allie was confident when she answered. "They won't. Let's face it, this is the biggest story the league has right now, and last season, ratings were down by almost ten percent on every network that aired games. That's a huge hit for advertisers to the tune of millions of dollars, including outlets like *Sports Illustrated*. If people don't care about the stories, they're not buying magazines, and they're certainly not tuning into the games. If they're smart, they'll latch on to anything that will get fans excited to watch. And the fact that they reached out to us means they're very smart."

It was my turn for my jaw to pop open, and Jack snickered when it did. I snapped it shut, thankful that Allie didn't seem to notice. Seemed she was doing more studying than the team roster. Ava's hands froze over her phone, and she was studying Allie the same way everyone else was.

Who the hell was this woman?

When she snapped into motion, her movements were brisk and efficient, crackling with energy. "You're sure as hell right about that. I'll let you know what they say." She looked at all three of us, giving me only the slightest warning with her eyes. *Don't screw this up,* was what I read loud and clear.

On the field, they all relied on me with complete trust. It was off the field that I tended to cause a few ... participation issues. I hated post-game press conferences, especially when we lost. I'd answer a few questions, but I wasn't the guy to joke with reporters or go the extra mile to make them feel like they knew me.

If anyone would put a wrench in this agreement, Ava damn well knew it would be me.

When I didn't say anything right away, Allie turned slightly, giving me a patient look that seemed to non-verbally remind me of our tentative truce. Even though my very bones ached with the desire to just focus on football, focus on plays and games and offensive schemes and tape of my opponents, I promised that I would try. And I hated that that patient look was going just as far into me as anything else.

Then she lifted a slim brow like she was daring me to argue.

"Fine with me," I told Ava but kept my eyes on Allie. Her bare, pink lips curled slightly at the edges.

"Hell yeah," Jack said. "And umm, if they just want me on the cover with you, Allie, I'd be game even if the grumpy old man isn't."

She broke the connection when she turned toward Jack,

laughing as she did. "I'll keep that in mind. Maybe they'll let us take a few snaps just for fun."

"Are we finished here?" I interrupted, voice gruff and clearly annoyed. Ava gave me a surprised glance. Jack rolled his eyes, and Allie just studied me as if I was the wild animal, not her.

She wasn't completely wrong because I felt itchy under my skin, the anticipation of sitting behind some bright lights and watching her pose with Jack skittered like bugs I couldn't scratch away. Which was stupid. Completely, utterly stupid.

So why did it piss me off so much?

"We're done," Ava said. "Allie, if you could come with me, we want to get some stuff for the website and our social media."

The two women walked off, and I watched them until they left the practice field. As soon as the door snapped shut, the volume increased back to normal. As if the guys were tempering the level at which they spoke in her presence.

Nothing felt normal.

"Toss me the ball," I told Jack, and he did. "Slant route, about twenty-five yards."

Not needing any further explanation, he took off, and I dropped back. The ball between my fingers settled my skin, my brain clicking into the natural rhythm. I danced to the left and heaved the ball to where Jack was crossing the field.

It was just past his fingers, falling with an awkward bounce onto the turf. Like it never happened, he scooped it up and tucked it against his midsection, running toward the end zone where some defensive linemen were working out.

"Shit," I whispered.

After a few mediocre seasons, playoff disappointments when we did make it to the post-season, it had been a while since the Wolves were the center of the NFL media attention.

I didn't like it. Not like this.

I wanted us to be the focus because we were winning. Because Jack and I had developed an unstoppable offensive cadence because our defense hammered our opponents into submission.

Not because the most interesting thing about us was that we had a pretty face at the helm of the ship.

"I'm going to go hit the showers," I told Jack, suddenly exhausted. Coach watched me from the sidelines but didn't stop me as I walked out of the building. The hallway leading to the locker rooms was empty, but when I turned the corner, I heard the buzz of chatter.

A handful of reporters were standing off in their designated area, media badges around their neck and cameras in their hands if necessary.

"Pierson," one called. I kept walking like I didn't hear him, mainly because I couldn't stand the guy. He looked like a rat and always managed to ask questions that pissed me off. Most reporters weren't like him. Most were fair and respectful, but I think he had a history of paparazzi somewhere in him. The slime covered him like a coat he could never quite shed.

"Come on, Piers," he said in his nasally voice. "One question and I'll leave you alone."

With a sigh, I stopped. "What?"

His thin eyebrows raised slightly. "Aren't we friendly today?"

"If you have a question about football, just ask it. Otherwise, I'm not talking. We've got enough distractions around here to think about anything else, including my mood."

When he smiled, I should have been nervous because he held up his hands. "Nope. I'm good, thanks."

But I was too frustrated and too wrapped up in untangling the knots in my head into some semblance of normalcy, so I took the out when I was given it, going to the locker room for the coldest, quickest shower of my life so I could get the hell home.

If I'd known what would be waiting when I finally got there, I would have stayed in the shower all night.

CHAPTER 11
ALLIE

WASHINGTON WOLVES

For all of about ten minutes after I got home, I felt really damn good about my day. The *Sports Illustrated* cover, my interactions with Ava, Jack, and Luke, and the social media stuff we'd worked on afterward.

After letting myself into the house, I dumped my purse on the kitchen counter and made a beeline for my bedroom, where I stripped unceremoniously out of my jeans and top and changed into soft sleep shorts, a blue lace bralette, and a threadbare t-shirt that proclaimed my favorite color was pizza. The wine I poured in my stemless glass was plentiful, and the sigh that escaped when I sank onto the couch came from the depths of my very soul.

I was exhausted but exhilarated. It was a feeling I hadn't had in a really, really long time. It was like ... like when you pull a couture dress down your body and realize that it fits you perfectly. Like the silk was made to fit you precisely, and the seams were measured for all your curves and edges.

That was when my phone buzzed with a Google news alert.

Against Ava's suggestion, I'd set up a news alert with my name and the team's name. Now I understood why she thought it was a shit idea.

Wolves veteran QB sick of 'distraction' of the new owner, wants to focus on football.

The news outlet was legitimate enough that I couldn't dismiss it. But oh, how I wanted to.

I wasn't someone who got angry. Upset, yes. Annoyed, frequently. But anger was not an emotion that I could easily label when I felt a strange, hot thrumming through my blood. From the top of my head to the tips of my fingers, I felt a fuzzy, indistinct sensation crawl through me.

Maybe that was why I couldn't understand what compelled me to stomp down my steps into the lower level of my house, through the slider, across the patio in bare feet, and through that damn hedge into Luke's backyard. It'd been about three hours after I'd last seen him and well past the point when the sun had disappeared out of the sky.

So many thoughts went through my head; many combinations of four letter words that I'd never strung together in one sentence in all my twenty-six years. All because I had the sticky, messy sense that I'd been duped.

As a branch scratched my arm, I hissed under my breath. "Football truce, my ass."

The lower level was dark, so it was enough to make me hesitate before making my way up the steps to his deck. My anger, or whatever it was, ebbed with my indecision.

When I lifted my phone, the article was staring back at me, all ridiculous and infuriating. My eyes narrowed as my definitely unnamed emotion whipped back up like an icy wind. Just as I started across the patio toward the slider, a light turned on beyond the glass, and Luke came down the stairs with his own phone in hand and a frown over his chiseled face.

There was enough light on the porch that I slowed down, spread my legs, folded my arms across my chest, and waited for his traitorous ass to see me. He glanced up, then did an instant double take, but there wasn't a moment of surprise anywhere in his eyes or the set of his wide, unsmiling mouth. I saw his broad chest expand on a sigh, almost as if he'd been expecting me.

From across his backyard patio, through the double slider, to where he stood at the bottom of his stairs, we stared at each other. A weird, crackling stalemate that I could feel through all those barriers between us. Then he was moving, swift and silent until he pulled open the slider.

"I did not say that you were a distraction," he said hurriedly.

I lifted my phone as if it alone could prove him wrong, being all the damning evidence I could possibly need. The way he glanced warily at it did nothing to soothe my raised hackles. It was a look of guilt. "Well, you said *something*, Luke."

To my utter surprise, he growled and threw his arms out, muscles popping in his biceps as he did. "This is why I hate dealing with the media. They twist *everything*. This is why I don't want to do that stupid *Sports Illustrated* article."

"Stupid because they want to talk about me?" I snapped. "They're journalists. Journalists cover the big stories, and whether you like it or not, this is a big story."

His eyes darkened, and his jaw tightened, a pop of muscle where it took a sharp turn under his skin. "Oh, trust me, I'm aware."

That tone. The way his lips curled around the words like they tasted bad, sour on his tongue, made everything inside me erupt, named or not.

"I didn't choose this," I yelled. He blinked in surprise, the heat in my tone knocking him back a step. "I didn't know that any of this would happen, okay? I came home to bury my father, and all of a sudden, I'm in this place where ... where people like you hate me instantly, and I have to worry whether my suit shows too much cleavage before I talk to the team because someone might think I'm a whore if I do, and all it takes is one thing like this, and I ..." My breath was coming faster, shallow little puffs of air that didn't inflate my lungs to the capacity that they should have, and it made my vision narrow dangerously with lines of black around the edges.

I placed a shaking hand over my mouth when hysterical laughter escaped past my unwilling lips, which were cold and disconnected from the rest of my body. Or that was what it felt like. All the pieces of me were separate, split apart from the panic pushing at my seams.

"Allie, stop," Luke commanded, grabbing my shoulders with hard, hot hands. My head snapped up in surprise, and all I could see were his eyes, a lighter brown than I thought they were from this close to him. "Take a deep breath."

Inexplicably, I complied. Just once.

He nodded. "Another."

Sweet, lake-scented air filled my lungs to capacity, and his face relaxed when I blew it out through my lips.

"Good." His hands loosened but stayed on my upper arms. "One more for me."

My eyes burned at the way his fingers curled over my skin. In the past two weeks, I'd shaken countless hands, but no one had hugged me since Paige, since the day I left Milan after receiving the news of my father's heart attack.

I was closer to Luke now, by a single step, and clutching my hands in tight fists between us, but the soft cotton of his shirt brushed against the skin of my knuckles. Through that flimsy layer, I could feel the heat of him, warmth projecting outward from his body as if he was his own furnace.

And he was tall. Luke was so much taller than I was when I wasn't wearing shoes. Tilting my chin up, I looked into his face while he watched me breathe again. Slowly, my limbs snapped back into place, woven together by each deep pull of oxygen. Each block of sanity stacked back where it was supposed to go.

"It's okay to be pissed," he said in a low, soothing voice. "I'm pissed at him too. I hate that guy, and he twisted what I said into something I did not mean."

Looking away from him proved impossible, so I stood there in the dark, with his hands on my arms and his eyes trained on mine with unwavering intensity.

What in the fresh hell was happening right now?

He spoke again when I didn't. It was all I could do to keep breathing. "I'm sorry, Allie. All I said to him was that unless he asked me about football, I wasn't interested in any other distractions." He pinched his eyes shut. "Or something. I can't even remember. But it was more about him than you."

In the wake of his apology, which felt honest and direct with no wasted words or flowery excuses, I felt the frantic energy drain from me completely as if someone had siphoned it out.

"I can't have you making this any harder than it already is," I told him wearily. "And trust me when I say this is the hardest thing I've ever done in my life."

His entire frame moved closer, tiny fractions with each movement of his feet, but the space all but disappeared. Underneath his massive palms and long fingers, my skin was warm and dry. When his hands moved an inch up, down, that heat spread everywhere.

I wanted him to fold me up in his arms, which made no sense. But his steady instructions, the way he snipped off the wild edge of my panic with only a few words, and the smell of him all around me made me want to curl into him like a milk-sated kitten and sleep against the warmth of his skin.

"I wasn't thinking," he admitted, even closer yet. If I tilted my forehead down an inch or two, it would be resting against his chest. I'd feel his heartbeat. "Which is very unlike me, I can promise you that."

I shifted my shoulders, only the slightest wiggle, and his fingers were more fully on my back.

"Luke," I whispered, unsure of what I wanted, what I was asking, what I was even feeling. I lifted my eyes and met his, and he must have read the blur of my thoughts as it pinged back and forth between confusion and yearning, frustration and desire.

Because even in the dark, I could see all those things reflected in the way his eyes zeroed in on my lips. They opened slightly as if he'd used the tip of his finger to drag them open.

Instantly, he dropped his hands and stepped back. My shoulders were cold, despite the heat still clinging to the air around us. As if he was embarrassed, Luke rubbed the back of his neck.

"I know it doesn't help now, but even if I was furious with you, even if I thought it, I'd never say something like that about you to a reporter. About anyone who's part of the team."

Part of the team.

I blinked furiously against the uncomfortable lump of tears at the back of my eyes because it went a small way in warming where he'd held me. With the decision to stay, I was certainly part of something much bigger than myself. And I was just understanding the emotional ramifications of what that meant. What it could mean.

"It helps," I conceded quietly.

"I'll be more careful next time." His mouth curved into a wry smile. "Or I'll shut up entirely."

I nodded, appreciative of his attempt at humor even if I wasn't ready to smile back. "I know you're aware of the size of this story, but I'm aware of how many people would delight in seeing me fail, Luke."

He sobered. "I wouldn't."

"No?"

With a tightly clenched jaw, he looked over at the lake before he spoke again. "No. Because if you fail, it means we've done something wrong too. And that's not the kind of team we are. We support our own."

Gratitude was a soothing blanket around my shoulders, warming me to my very soul instead of just the surface of my skin.

I risked a small smile, just to see how it would feel on my face. "Even if that means you have to do the *Sports Illustrated* thing?"

The hand on his neck dropped, and he shrugged. A tiny movement made by huge, muscular shoulders made my smile grow.

"Owning the Wolves may be the hardest thing you've ever done, but an interview is that for me. I'll hate every minute of it."

"Hate is a strong word," I told him, studying and weighing the honesty of what he'd just said.

His mouth relaxed, but he didn't smile. "It's the right word. Unfortunately, I have a bit of a reputation when it comes to dealing with the media."

"Yeah?"

"Yeah. Because I don't." When I didn't say anything, he sighed. "Deal with the media. I just don't."

"How come?" I risked asking. The likelihood that Luke would answer me felt about as slim as me fitting into a size zero. But this man, so big and strong, sweet with his daughter and cold when he thought someone was infringing on his life with her, was one of the most fascinating people I'd ever met.

After a few moments, Luke gave me a guarded look. "I've been burned before, let's just say that. Whether I answered or not wouldn't have made a difference; it only would've made things worse."

I tilted my head. "You didn't want to defend yourself?"

"You reach a point in this industry," he answered carefully, "when you realize that hitting back at the people who say shit about you is a really easy way to waste your time. I'd rather use my time to be a better player. A better father. Everything else is just noise."

My heart turned over, the fascination growing in erratic pulses that stretched along my skin.

Of course, I kept that off my face when I spoke again, all cool and casual. "Even with all that, you're still willing to do the interview?"

His eyes traced my face. Just a quick glance, but it touched every part twice. It lingered longest on my mouth, and I struggled to breathe properly.

"Hopefully it doesn't kill me," he said quietly.

Stepping back but still facing him, I pursed my lips and

embraced the fragile sense of playfulness between us. As if I'd caught the edge of a butterfly with the tips of my fingers, and it was desperately trying to fly away. "Well, then you just leave it to me. I'll make it bearable."

Without waiting for his reaction, I spun toward the hedge, but not before I heard his muted reply.

"I guess we'll see about that."

WASHINGTON
WOLVES

Th>here were moments in a man's life when his pride must be swallowed down like a lumpy sock of coal. One of those moments was when his six-and-a-half-year-old daughter somehow manipulated him into a pool party with his boss/neighbor/star of the dream he had the night before but was actively trying to forget because it involved her in a bikini.

The day had started innocuously enough. The weather was beautiful and bright and hot. My mom didn't feel well, so I did my workouts from home, had a phone meeting with my offensive coordinator, and promised Faith we could go swimming.

Strictly following the house rule that she wasn't allowed in the pool if no adult was outside with her, she waited patiently on a patio chair while I ran inside to change into my board shorts and grab the sunscreen.

And that was when everything fell off the rails.

Because my evil genius daughter saw Allie sunbathing in her backyard, walked through the hedge, and must have begged her to come sit by our pool so that she could get in, thereby skirting around my absence and winning some quality time with the neighbor she clearly idolized.

That was the scene I walked outside to, folks. Allie sitting on the top step of my pool, wearing a slim cut red suit that looked nothing like the bikini she'd had on in my dream, and my daughter tossing a beach ball at her while they both laughed.

I had to pause and make sure I was awake because my dream had started in an almost identical way.

"Daddy!" Faith squealed from the water. "Miss Allie came swimming with me!"

"I see that," I said mildly.

Allie's hair was twisted up in a wet knot at the top of her head as she glanced between Faith and me. "I'm sorry, she asked if I could sit here because there's supposed to be an adult outside when she's swimming."

I narrowed my eyes at Faith, who beamed at Allie as if she'd just single-handedly given her the keys to Disneyland or something.

"She's right about that," I answered. "But I was just popping inside to change."

Allie wasn't wearing sunglasses, and her eyes tripped down my bare chest before quickly darting away.

She started to stand. "I can go."

"Noooo," Faith pleaded. Oh great, she pulled out the puppy dog eyes. They were practically a weapon of mass destruction when she unleashed them on someone who wasn't used to their power. "Can you stay for like, twenty minutes? Or maybe just an hour?"

Allie laughed at the clear misjudgment of time increments, and I rubbed the back of my neck. I wish I'd slipped on my sunglasses so that my eyes would have some sort of barrier, some way to block Allie from seeing where I was looking.

I didn't want to be looking at her. Truly.

But as much as I'd been able to ignore the foggy remnants of my dream all morning, it was all but impossible now.

In the dream, we hadn't touched. Not once. I woke up before it could happen, but it didn't lessen the impact. All I could remember now was how her slender fingers had worried the knot of her bikini where it tied behind her smooth, sleek back.

The way she looked over her shoulder at me and started pulling at the string.

"Twenty minutes," Allie told Faith, and my daughter smiled happily. "If that's okay with your dad," she said, glancing at me again.

As if I'd be able to kick her out and not have a mopey daughter to deal with for the rest of the day. But I was grateful Allie was asking my permission anyway.

I cleared my throat and set the tube of sunscreen down on the patio table. "Fine with me."

Faith dunked her head under water and doggy paddled over to the steps by Allie. Her waterproof pink cast looked wavy and distorted under the water but barely hampered her movements. Wouldn't it be nice if adults were so adaptable?

For instance, I should be able to adapt to Allie's presence, right?

By now, I knew she was beautiful, and I understood and accepted that she was in my life even though to what capacity was still a bit murky. So I should be able to just … deal with it.

"I'm going to be in second grade," Faith announced as soon as she swiped the water from her face.

Allie smiled at my daughter. "Yeah? You're gettin' pretty old, huh?"

"Did you like second grade?" Faith asked.

And thus the tone of this little impromptu pool party was set. Faith peppering Allie with question after question, each answered patiently and honestly, and not once did she look uncomfortable or annoyed.

No, that role was left for me.

I was more than uncomfortable because I was completely superfluous to everything that was going on. All I could do was sit at the edge of my pool, watching my daughter interview Allie with the skill of Barbara Walters, and try very much not to stare at the way Allie's bare legs swished back and forth under the water.

"What's your favorite flower?"

Allie tilted her head and pursed her lips. "Pink tulips."

"Really? Mine are daisies. Those are kinda like tulips."

I smothered my smile before Allie or Faith could see it because my daughter's clear insistence to form a connection with this woman was in every answer, no matter what Allie said.

Allie's favorite season was fall, and Faith's was spring, which both had leaves in it.

Allie's favorite color was blue, and Faith's was pink, and those were really, really close because they used them in *Sleeping Beauty* for Aurora's dress.

Allie's middle name was Leanne, and Faith's was Kathryn, which both had the letter 'n' in it.

Etcetera, etcetera, and we kept doing that for eighteen more minutes.

This was something I could adapt to. Surface level questions answered quickly and easily, and nothing about it shifted my perception of who Allie was as a person.

Then, with roughly two minutes left, Faith went in for her kill shot.

"Did you go to the same school I go to, Miss Allie?"

That long, tan leg stopped moving under the water, and Allie peered thoughtfully at my daughter.

It was the kind of question that should have been answered with the same ease as the others, but she took a deep breath, making her slim shoulders rise up and then down.

I forced my eyes away because I didn't want to be dissecting her body language.

"I didn't." She cleared her throat and tucked a non-existent hair behind her ear. "I actually went to a school where you sleep over."

Faith's eyes widened. "You *sleep* at the school?"

I leaned back and watched with unfolding interest, somewhere in my brain noting that this was a piece of the Allie puzzle that I might not want to know about.

Allie nodded. "I was a few years older than you, and my father thought it would be good for me to go to that kind of school. It's called a boarding school."

"Whoa," Faith breathed, no longer moving in the pool. "Can I go to a boarding school, Daddy?"

"No way," I said instantly, then gentled my tone when they both looked at me with surprise. "I'd miss you too much, turbo."

Allie swallowed and looked away, out at the lake, when it dawned on me how that might have sounded. I would miss Faith too much if I sent her away. Which might have felt like Robert didn't miss his own daughter because he did make that choice.

Shit, I thought in my head. This twenty minutes would completely upset the balance of whatever we'd figured out the night before.

The second I laid my hands on her, it started a new trajectory, something that I no longer controlled. Just like right now.

"I'd miss you too, Daddy," Faith said happily. "But sleeping over at school would be *so fun*."

She dunked her head under water again, which was why she probably didn't notice that Allie didn't agree with her.

But I noticed.

And I hated it.

Allie slid her hands along the tops of her sun-kissed thighs and gave me a tiny smile. "Well, I think my twenty minutes are up."

I nodded. "I'm sure she'll try to get another round out of you if you're still here when she comes up for air."

She laughed. "She's a great kid, Luke."

Faith came up and sputtered water from her lips, which made me smile.

"She's the best kid," I answered easily. It wasn't hard to say out loud, partially because I was biased, but if I took my own issues with Allie out of the equation, I was really damn proud that my daughter was being kind and curious and sweet with a new neighbor.

"Do you have to go, Miss Allie?" Faith asked.

Allie glanced at me and pinched her lips between her teeth to keep from laughing. She nodded. "I do, honey. But thank you for inviting me over. I had a lot of fun."

"Me too." She sighed.

When Allie stood, I could practically hear the soundtrack in my head to the slow unfolding of her swimsuit-clad body, which I'd see in only a few short hours at the photo shoot. What would she be wearing there?

She took a deep breath and looked at me for a long second. "I'll see you later."

Without waiting for a response, she winked at my daughter and went back into her own yard.

I didn't watch her walk away.

Refused to admit I wanted to.

The truth was that I still wasn't quite sure what to do with Allie Sutton.

WASHINGTON
WOLVES

"**I** hate preseason," Jack muttered. "Sitting on the bench makes me twitchy."

My smile came easily even though we'd lost our first game because I did too. We weren't supposed to say it out loud— telling our fans and the media that the practice was essential, that seeing the younger, more inexperienced players out on the field gave us a chance to watch how they performed.

But as the starting quarterback, I was forced to prowl the side- lines uselessly, feeding my backups play calls through a headset while watching them with a burning under my skin to be the one out on the field. It was clear enough why I couldn't be, the risk of injury in a game that didn't matter was too great, but that didn't stop the drive for me to sprint out there anyway.

Instead of inflating Jack's tirade, which had lasted our entire drive to the damned photoshoot and interview, I punched him in the shoulder. "Necessary evil, and you know it. They'll never get rid of it."

We'd decided to drive together since they really only needed us for the interview portion. Ava texted me earlier that we were combining the shoot and the interview because of Allie's idea for behind-the-scenes footage, which meant we'd have to look like we weren't complete slobs.

"I hate interviews," I told him. "Since we're in a sharing mood."

Jack snickered. "You say that like anyone *doesn't* know you hate interviews." He started ticking off his points on his fingers, which I was not allowed to break, unfortunately. "Everyone on the team knows you hate them. The front office definitely knows you hate them. And I don't know? Do you think the media knows you hate them? Yeah, let's count them twice."

I shifted uncomfortably in my seat. "You can't blame me."

Considering how much younger Jack was than me, he may not have been on the team when I was forced to deal with the fallout of Cassandra's story, followed by her accident and the glorification of "single dad QB," but he was old enough to remember it happening.

"No, I guess I can't." From the passenger seat, he glanced at me quickly. "Did you catch a lot of shit from PR about the article about Allie being a distraction?"

"A bit," I told him. That was all I planned on telling him, too.

By now, that whole thing had blown over, the happy byproduct of a media with a predictably short attention span. But the night I saw the article—receiving an ear-blistering phone call from Ava and stemming a panic attack from Allie in my backyard—was one I did not care to repeat. For numerous reasons.

Seeing her staring at me the way she had when she couldn't breathe, those big ocean blue eyes full of panic and fear and the sheer overwhelming size of what she was at the center of, I couldn't remember the last time I'd truly felt ashamed about something I'd done. Not just what I'd said to the idiot journalist, who'd twisted my words exactly the way I'd feared he would, but also everything leading up to that moment.

Allie had no reason to trust me. In fact, showing me that soft underbelly of what she was going through should have lit every warning bell in her head. If I was a lesser man, a weaker man, it would be so easy to use it against her. Manipulate her into quitting, selling, going back to the undoubtedly easy life she had before Robert died.

The shame was tangible enough that I was showing up early at the address Ava had texted me, ready to do what I needed to do for this whole song and dance with *SI*. It was the realization that leadership took on humbling forms from time to time. Doing things that I wasn't comfortable with, that I couldn't control, was just another opportunity to show my teammates that I warranted the respect they gave me every single week out on the field, during the week in practice.

"This it?" Jack asked, leaning forward to squint out the windshield at a nondescript gray building covered with gray brick. There were a few cars and a large white work van in the parking lot, and a small plant in a square black planter next to the door, which was painted bright red.

"I guess so."

Jack paused before he got out of my car. "Listen, I'm up for doing some shots with her for the cover because I think it would be bad as hell to have a *Sports Illustrated* cover under my belt, but I know they want us both."

I lifted an eyebrow. "Your point?"

"Just have an open mind about it. Maybe it won't be so bad."

Except it was worse.

It was much, much worse.

Which was saying something, considering after said panic attack, I'd had a dream about a scantily clad Allie and then had to live through the little pool set up by my darling daughter.

We were shown down a long, brightly lit hallway by a smiling assistant, ushered into a massive room filled with lights under white canopies, solid color backdrops draped strategically from the industrial style ceiling. The black backdrop was sitting empty ignored, but there was an ornate gold chair in the middle of it. Through the milling bodies of photographer's assistants, people with clipboards, Ava in the corner on her phone by a rack of clothes, and a hair and makeup setup that had me yanking on the collar of my shirt, there was Allie.

Jack and I froze when she came into view.

"Holy hell on earth," I said under my breath.

Pointed at her was a fan, making her teased, curled hair blow across her face. Sex hair. That was what it looked like. She never stopped moving, no matter how the camera clicked or the flashes burst in bright, fast succession. Some of the people in the room watched her, but most were going about their business, completely used to a beautiful woman moving the way Allie was moving for the camera.

But I wasn't used to it.

She was wearing black leather leggings, slicked tight to her long legs. On her feet were dangerously spiked red heels that matched the color of her lips. Moving slowly over her skin, pushing her hair out of her face and sliding against her bare stomach were her hands. Her hips pivoted back and forth in small, incremental movements. It registered somewhere in the back of my mind that there was music playing—something heavy with bass, a slow, pulsing beat with a guitar, and a rough, raw singing voice.

Allie hadn't seen us, so immersed in what she was doing, and I couldn't look away. Moving the way she was, eyes open and then shut, mouth curved in a smile and then set in a fierce line, she looked like a dancer. There was so much grace in every line of her raised arms—above her head, pushing her hair back—that I was completely entranced.

With tight fists, she gripped the sides of her black leather jacket, which was covering a white and red T-shirt that I recognized from some of the team's licensed merchandise, and pulled it open, her head tilted down to the side and her lips open in a visible inhale.

Yeah, I recognized the T-shirt all right. In block red letters across her chest spelled *Wolves*. But unlike the version in our shops and website, hers was cut in a ragged line just underneath her breasts as if it had been sawed off with rusty scissors. All it left beneath it was the tight, toned skin of her stomach and the perfect circle of her belly button. With the jacket pulled open like it was, she looked like every straight man's wet dream.

Who the hell thought that was a good idea?

Who dressed her? Shouldn't she be wearing a power suit? Maybe a turtleneck?

A muumuu. That would be best. Didn't we have a black and red muumuu, for the love of all things holy?

Jack snapped his fingers in front of my face, and I jumped.

The asshole was smirking at me, so I shoved his chest and walked over to Ava.

"Whatcha staring at, Piers?"

"Go screw yourself, rookie," I muttered. Great. Now I sounded like a petulant child who got caught with his hand in the proverbial cookie jar.

Yesterday, it had been Faith. Today, it was Jack. There were few things I liked less than being caught truly unaware, and it seemed to be happening more and more around Allie.

Moments when I didn't question who could see me because all I could see was her.

"Great, Allie," the photographer yelled from behind the constant click of his camera. A group of people huddled around a computer screen, commenting over whatever was popping up on the display. "Face front, spread your legs. Why don't you prop your hands on your hips to hold back the edges of the jacket. Yes, perfect. Perfect."

Click.

Click.

Click.

"A bit more of a smirk. Yes, exactly."

But I didn't look. Once he told her to spread her legs, my eyes stayed on the freaking concrete floor.

"Hey, guys," Ava said with a small smile, eyes never wavering from her phone. "If you want to have a seat over there, they'll fix your hair and make sure you don't look like shit for the behind-the-scenes stuff. We'll shoot that first, then answer some questions with the three of you. Allie already did most of her interview."

"How did it go?"

The words were out of my mouth before I could stop them. Jack coughed into his hand, a lame attempt at covering his laughter. Ava gave me a curious look before she answered. "Great. She had him eating out her hand in about five minutes. She should give you lessons on how to handle journalists."

"They didn't ..." I swallowed and tugged at the neck of my shirt. "They didn't ask about the crap with me?"

Ava's eyes softened slightly in understanding. "No. They want to highlight her, highlight the buzz around her, not knock her down a few pegs."

I nodded, still not convinced that this wasn't an elaborate trap. Especially with the way she was dressed and how sexy she looked. "Listen, I don't know how to ask this without sounding like a complete dick."

Jack hooted with laughter. "Since when has that worried you?"

Ava hid her smile like the professional she was. "Yes, Luke?"

I scratched the side of my face and gestured toward where she was still shooting, now without the leather jacket. *Sonofabitch* why was her jacket gone?

It must be eight million degrees in this room, but there was no reason for her jacket to be gone.

"Isn't this a bad idea? I thought ... I thought she'd be more ... umm ... covered."

Ava searched my face and glanced over at Allie, mulling over her words before she spoke. "We were pretty strategic in what we picked. What concerns you?"

Even though it felt like my face would betray me, betray how much this entire thing made me uncomfortable, I turned and watched Allie again. Now she was sitting on a black stool, one heel hooked over the bottom rung with her hands braced on her leather clad knees. The leather jacket was back on and zipped closed now, so only a few letters on her T-shirt were visible. For the first time since I walked in, she looked in our direction, locked eyes with me, and I felt it over every inch of my body.

I swallowed roughly, and she noticed. Her blood red lips curled.

Click. Flash.

"Hot! That was hot, Allie." Again, from the photographer, a grizzled, slightly older gentleman whose gray hair was tied back underneath a worn ball cap. "A few more here and we'll be done, I think. Spread your legs out a bit, like you're pushing on your knees with your hands. Yes."

"You don't think they're like ... objectifying her?" I heard myself ask.

Without a sound, Ava stood next to me, watching Allie move like a seasoned pro. After a few more clicks and a few more shifts of Allie's face, shoulders, legs, Ava finally spoke.

"You know The Body issue?"

Of course, I knew what it was. Athletes posed nude for *SI* every year; strategically placed hands and legs and arms and whatnot covered the necessary things that needed covering. Instead of answering, I kept watching Allie. After every few clicks, she'd seek me out.

As if she was checking in.

I kept my face impassive, but one particular tilt of her head reminded me of her sitting on the top step of my pool while she listened to Faith talk. Against the incongruous memories, I had to blink because they clashed in my head violently. Rarely did I ever have to struggle to figure something out, never to this extent.

Rich girl.

Determined.

Flighty.

Sexy.

Smart.

Thoughtless daughter.

Kind.

Centerfold.

Thoughtful.

I couldn't figure out if she was all those things or none of them, or which ones matched up with ease and which ones felt like contradictions. All I knew, standing where I was with dozens of strangers around me, was that I couldn't take my eyes off her.

"Do you think those athletes are being objectified?"

That gave me pause because no, I'd never thought that. The shots were tasteful, powerful even. "No," I said without looking at her. It was like once my eyes made the decision to latch onto Allie, I didn't have the power to look away. She was her own force of gravity.

"Allie is a beautiful woman. No matter what she wears, there's no hiding that. She has no desire to hide the fact that her beauty is, by society's standards, considered a sexy beauty. It's in her curves and her hair and her lips." As she spoke, my eyes tracked to each physical feature that Ava pointed out. "To try to ignore that would be foolish. So while we did do some shots wearing more sedate clothes, she's comfortable in this too."

Ava gauged my reaction before she kept talking. "And there's something powerful in the fact that she can own that side of her. It doesn't remove the power she holds in her position, and it doesn't take away the respect she's earned from those of us who have gotten to know her because she knows exactly what she's doing. And if she wanted to pose for the cover wearing baggy jeans and a jersey, we would've done that too." Ava shrugged. "But she didn't. This is her."

I'd never thought of it that way. But then again, I'd never been in the same position. I'd never had to think through how to present myself to the world like this. All I had to do was show up and throw the ball, not get sacked.

Maybe this was Allie, but I also remembered what she'd said to me when panic blew her filter to a million pieces. Remembered what she said to Faith about being sent away to school. Allie had been alone a lot, it seemed.

No matter what she did, she was alone in this position. Alone in thinking about how she presented herself to me, to the team, to the front office. And what I'd told her was that we supported our own. We supported our team.

The photographer had stepped aside to look at a computer screen, and Allie waited on the stool, her posture more relaxed now that he wasn't shooting. Her flawlessly made-up face was turned down, and her cheekbones caught the light in a way that made her look as if she couldn't possibly be real. As if she'd been carved by an artist or brought forth from the imagination of some master painter.

When she looked up, it was straight at me as if she knew I was still watching her. Because I wasn't embarrassed, I didn't look away. I didn't pretend I wasn't paying attention to every shift of muscle in her face. I didn't pretend I wasn't thinking about every word I'd said to her in my backyard while my hands curved over her shoulders. Had I meant those words or not?

Of course, I'd meant them.

However, I didn't mean to touch her like I did. It was an unconscious motion, my muscles acting on some instinct that I refused to name. Memorizing the way her skin had felt under my hands had been pure intuition. Moving closer when I should have backed away had felt like second nature. A reflex I didn't know I'd honed, after going so long without a woman to soothe, to comfort, to touch as I'd touched her.

Not with passion but with intimacy.

So yes, I'd meant what I told her.

There were a lot of things Allie had to do alone, making the decision she'd made, but this wasn't one of them. If she wanted the support, that was it.

Instead of asking Ava or the photographer, I tipped my chin and addressed Allie. "Do you still want some shots with us?"

The whole room went quiet.

The photographer shot his hand up. "I do."

Allie smiled at him, then stood from the stool. She walked over to Ava and me, and Jack, who was now hovering at my other shoulder.

"Why'd you change your mind?" she asked me.

I folded my arms over my chest, pretending I didn't see dozens of pairs of eyes trained right on us. "Just trying to mean the things I say."

Her lips didn't move, but I saw the smile in her eyes. She nodded. "Let's do it."

"Hell, yeah," Jack exclaimed, thumping me on the back. "Wait, I didn't bring anything else to wear."

Ava lifted a finger. "There are jerseys for both of you on the rack, or shirts to match hers if we want to go that angle." She looked at the photographer. "Any preference?"

He looked us over, fuzzy gray eyebrows low on his forehead. "T-shirts on them, have her wear a jersey over the leggings." Then he clapped his hands. "Come on, let's make it happen, people."

The room sprang to action. Jack got pulled one direction, me in another, and someone took Allie by the elbow and directed her behind a changing shade. It covered her just past her chin with the heels she was wearing, but she turned away and pulled the tattered t-shirt over her head, her blond mess of hair falling down her back.

Before it did, I saw two knots of bone at the top of her spine underneath her golden skin.

An assistant handed her two jerseys, one black and one red.

Ava walked up to Jack and me, tossing us plain white t shirts with Wolves stamped in red across the chest, a mirror image of what Allie had been wearing.

"Just had these laying around, huh?" I asked wryly.

"I don't suck at my job," she said with a tiny shrug. "But if I hadn't prepared for the contingency that you'd decide to do some shots, *then* I would suck at my job."

With one hand, I pulled my shirt off over my head, catching Allie's profile as she looked away quickly. I wasn't the most muscular guy on the team, my position demanding that I be tall and fairly lean. But if they'd asked us to pose without shirts on, I definitely wouldn't have embarrassed myself.

A flash of how Allie's eyes had trailed down my chest by the pool made me breathe deeply.

I slid the Wolves shirt on, not surprised when it was tight across my chest and biceps. Jack was grinning like a fool as a blushing woman in a headset brushed some powder over his fore-head and cheeks. She came at me with that same brush, her smile falling as she looked at the grim set of my face.

But I closed my eyes and let her sweep it over my skin.

"It just ... cuts the shine from the lights," she said as if she was apologizing for doing her job.

"It's fine," I told her gruffly. I opened my eyes when she was done, giving her a small nod. Those cheeks pinked up again. Leave it to me to be an asshole to a young kid whose only job was to powder noses. Ava was behind the privacy screen with Allie, using her hands to turn her around, then she looked over at Jack and me.

"The red, I think," she said quietly. Allie nodded, giving me a quick, searing glance before she peeled the black jersey over her head and tossed it away. Like she was checking to see if I was watching.

Did she *want* me to watch?

My stomach clenched at each flash of skin that I saw, each line of her neck or shoulders when she turned and allowed someone to pull the jersey down her body, covering the magnificence that I knew was underneath it.

I made my way to Jack, so I wasn't tempted to look anymore. Someone cranked up the music again as Jack and I stood in front of the white backdrop so they could test the lights.

The photographer gave us a brief handshake when he came to move the stool between us. Then he shook his head. "Can I get another stool? I think I want them sitting and her standing."

I took a deep breath. Maybe I'd had a brief psychotic break for suggesting this. It was the only plausible explanation.

My eyes caught Allie's as she came from behind the screen,

and I knew I'd lost my mind. When she told me she'd try to make it enjoyable, I was quite certain neither of us had anticipated *this*.

They'd clipped the red jersey behind her so that it was snug around her hips, showing off the curve of her waist. It was a dummy jersey, a bright white number one on the front. Maybe something they'd had specially made for her. Wherever they'd gotten it, it worked.

A makeup artist touched up her lips and swept more blush on her cheeks while someone ran a brush through her hair so that it looked sleeker than when we first arrived. With the deft twist of her hands, the stylist had Allie's hair curled over her shoulders, looking every inch the bombshell that she was.

When I first met her, I'd have bet a whole truckload of money that she preferred this. The lipstick, the face full of makeup, the team of primping people. But she looked so different to me now because every time I saw her at home, she was bare-faced and casual. Stunning in her simplicity because that was how deep her natural beauty ran.

It was as if someone took a jar of everything I'd thought to be true and threw it into a paint shaker until everything spun so fast that I couldn't remember what it looked like before. I'd crack the lid and see something completely different.

This was still the Allie who smashed the cupcakes against my shirt. But she wasn't.

Would she say the same thing about me?

The photographer eyed Jack and me. "You two need to loosen up. Shake your arms out, do some jumping jacks, something."

Jack actually did it while I just let out a deep breath and stood with my arms crossed over my chest. Allie walked between two assistants and stopped when she was facing me.

Her eyes traced the letters on my shirt, which were just below eye level for her. She mimicked my posture and smirked up at me.

Click. Flash.

I flinched, glaring out at the harsh lights. The photographer wasn't visible behind the lens of his black camera, but I could sense his instant excitement.

"Do that one more time," he commanded. "Allie, pop your hip out just a bit more. Yes."

With a small toss of her hair, she did as he asked, facing me again. This time, it was harder to feel like we were enemies because she was smiling. Her movements were small, not like before. Little turns of her head toward the light, angling her chin up at me, lips curved and then straight, gaze always locked on mine.

I stayed perfectly still as if I'd scare her away if I started trying to mirror what she was doing.

They'd done something to her eyes. Lined them with too much black. Made her lashes too long. It was too much because of how it made her face look. I felt as if I was trying to stare into the sun again, the jewel brightness of her face almost otherworldly, like a light bulb behind wavy blue glass.

"So, uhh, do you need me here or what?" Jack asked.

Allie laughed over her shoulder at him.

Click. Flash.

"Guys," the photographer said, "you sit in the stools. Cross your arms just like that, Luke. Same for you, Jack. Both look straight at the camera, no smiles. Good, good. Allie, you stand between them and just work your hands and arms a bit for whatever feels natural."

Jack and I did as directed, but the knot of tension twisted and turned under my skin when she stood between us. She started with her arms crossed like ours, then the music got louder, the bass heavier, and her body moved again. She never stopped her slow, smooth movements.

At the first touch of her hand on my shoulder, I managed not to jump out of my skin. On the back of my neck, I could feel the tips of her nails. Her hips canted in an angle, and the pressure of her fingers against my skin increased as if we were propping her up.

Click. Flash.

Those fingers slid across my shoulder, gentle and slow over the cotton of the shirt, and I kept my eyes forward, my face stern.

No smiles? Not a freaking problem.

What might be a problem was that if I stood, the entire room would see that our bombshell boss had just given me an inconvenient boner.

Breathe in, I told myself. *Breathe in and breathe out.*

Was she touching Jack this way?

I risked a quick glance to the side, and no, her wrist was resting casually over his shoulder, but staying firmly in place even as her fingers trailed over the line of my neck.

Breathe in. Breathe out.

My hands tingled, and my blood roared. This was unfettered, unencumbered attraction. And I'd forgotten how incredibly powerful it was.

"Great. This is great, guys." His finger snapped away. How many freaking pictures could you take of one stupid pose? "Now stand up slightly behind her. Someone grab a football, okay?"

Jack stood first. I recited my dead grandma's name in my head, over and over and over, until I felt like I could stand without embarrassing myself.

When I finally did, Allie was staring at me with a quirked eyebrow. I shook my head and went behind her. As I rolled my neck, it occurred to me that we'd exchanged two sentences since I walked in the door. That was it. And for some reason, I felt like she was the one in the room who knew exactly what I was feeling.

With that disconcerting thought, I waited patiently while they arranged for her to hold a football against her hip with one hand as she faced the camera. I propped my hands on my hips, as did Jack. When I inhaled too deeply, the front of my chest brushed against her back, and I saw Allie suck in a deep breath.

"Good. Jack, move to the left a bit." He looked around his camera and squinted. While he got situated, I cleared my throat. Allie glanced up at me over her shoulder, and I kept my face even, but inside, I burned.

Inside, where I could smell her, where I could feel her heat just in front of my chest, where I knew without checking that I could span her ribcage with one hand, I burned with a violent heat that I'd never felt in my entire life.

She blinked and looked back at the camera. So did I.

Click. Flash.

"And that," the photographer said in a satisfied tone, "is our cover shot."

CHAPTER 14
ALLIE

WASHINGTON WOLVES

There was music. And people cheering. Men stretching on the field in really tight pants. And I was frozen in the tunnel that led out to the field.

"You can do it, Allie."

I pinched my eyes shut and gripped Joy's hand. Her knuckles were large from some arthritis she said didn't bother her much. "Why does this feel so important?"

At her soft laugh, I finally opened my eyes. Would she think it was weird if I held her hand all the way out onto midfield? Probably.

This was freaking ridiculous. I knew it. When Joy and I talked about the regular season, she told me all about my father's rituals on game day. He walked the field while the team warmed up, speaking to each one. Once he'd done that, he retreated to his box, where he watched the entire game before heading home to eat some cherry chocolate chip ice cream, win or lose. Before his departure for frozen dairy, he'd visit the locker room to provide encouragement if they lost and join in the celebration if they won.

I'd made it through preseason, two losses and one win, but I'd stayed in my owner's box for each one, just trying to make it through each game without asking stupid questions.

But this ... everything was bigger and louder. There was a crackle in the air that lifted the hair on my arms, a churning, fast energy from the fans in the stands, already in their seats early just to catch a glimpse of the players as they warmed up.

"It feels important because it counts now, sweetie," she said, squeezing my fingers. "You go on out there and talk to your guys. You know all their names. I'd wager you know all their wive's and girlfriend's names, too."

I sure as hell did. That binder was worn from me studying it during the preseason.

I turned to her, taking her other small hand in mine. "How do I look?"

She smiled, then gave me a decisive nod. "Like a boss bitch."

My laugh was loud and decidedly unfeminine. "Thank you."

For as much as I'd love the looks we chose for the photo shoot, I went far more severe for the first game. It was away, so we'd flown out as a team a couple of days earlier, and I wanted to fade into the background as much as possible tonight.

Tonight, it was about the team. Everything was on their broad shoulders. My hair was slicked back in a low ponytail, my lips bare, my feet clad in flats. My jeans were dark and fitted, and the shirt I'd picked from the pro shop was bright white with a small Wolves logo on a tiny pocket over my right breast. It was simple, and I loved it.

My father maybe would've worn a suit, but this was me. I needed to figure out how I would do things. Which was why I let go of Joy's wrinkled hands and walked out onto the field with my chin lifted. Behind a few paces were two nondescript security guards with no necks and massive arms, a precaution that Cameron insisted on for our first regular season game, especially since we weren't at home.

So far, they'd shadowed me in a way where I didn't notice them. But out on the field, I was grateful for their presence. Phones lifted immediately as I started walking down the line of our defensive lineman stretching out their tree trunk legs. A couple of fans shouted my name, and I gave them a smile even though they were wearing the home team jerseys and not ours.

Dayvon, one of the captains I'd met on the first day, stood from a stretch and held out a meaty fist. I tapped it with my own. "How you doin' tonight, Miss Allie?"

I held my hand over my stomach. "Nervous. Is that normal?"

He laughed, and the sound was so warm that I found myself relaxing. "If you weren't a little nervous, I'd wonder about you."

With wide eyes, I stayed next to him and surveyed the massive field. Players ran drills, did stretches, laughed, and talked with opposing players and coaches. At midfield, standing tall on the bright green grass like a Greek god, was Luke. He dropped back and launched the ball down the field into the waiting arms of one of the tight ends. It was so effortless. So ... beautiful. He nodded and motioned for another go.

I hadn't seen him since the photo shoot. Watching him in this arena, the place he stepped up and became the leader, I had to fight the urge to lay my hand on my stomach again. He looked larger than life. Strong and fast. Sure in his actions. It was humbling to know how very out of place I was among them, but they were welcoming me anyway.

Maybe that was how Luke felt walking into the photo shoot. Oh, his face. Very little could have prepared me for the exact moment when we locked eyes from across that sprawling space. Whatever seed had been planted the night I freaked the hell out on his back porch had unfurled into something ... something that made me feel crazy when he was around me.

It was the tension snapping and vibrating between us, held aloft by the air, by his eyes on me.

With two strong hands, I shoved that out of my head, because this was not.the.place to be thinking about hot, tension-y things in regards to Luke Pierson.

After forcing a smile on my face, I made my way through the rows of players, all of whom seemed loose, happy, and relaxed despite the massive season they were about to undertake. Sixteen weeks of physically grueling work, even more mental prep, and possibly more if we made the playoffs. It was a small thing for me to make sure they saw my face each week and knew that I was paying attention to how hard they were working. Maybe that was why my father had done it. To remind them that he was paying attention.

It was enough to make me pause somewhere around the forty-yard line.

Had he done that with me? Had I even noticed?

Someone said my name again, and I looked into the stands to see three little girls holding up a sign, Wolves jerseys covering their bodies. The sign said *We're Team Sutton.*

With a hand over my heart, I made my way over to where they were leaning over the railing. The security guards maintained a respectful distance when the girls handed me a bright pink marker so I could sign their programs.

"Oh, thank you," one said in a shocked whisper.

"You're so pretty," said another.

"Enjoy the game, girls." I waved at them after I'd signed all their stuff, and the sweet giggles that followed me as I walked away were enough to make any bullshit I'd gone through worth it. The distraction was enough that I realized I'd missed the last handful of our team before they ran off to head back to the locker room, Luke included.

Maybe I was a chicken, but I let out a deep sigh of relief and made my way up to the owner's box.

————

When I walked into the locker room, the celebratory sounds were deafening.

Dayvon scooped me up in his arms, whooping and yelling. I could barely catch my breath from laughing, and my face hurt from smiling. Playing a division rival on their home turf had been a horrible game to watch. Horrible for me because it was so close.

Back and forth, the entire game, the two teams had stayed within one touchdown of each other.

With thirty-two seconds to go and down by three points, Luke had thrown a bomb down the field into the waiting hands of Jack, who evaded four defenders to run it in for a touchdown. My entire suite had erupted as well as the Wolves fans we had in the away stands, and watching the guys tackle each other on the field, I thought my face might split open from smiling.

During the entire walk down to the locker room, I felt very much like a bottle of champagne that had been violently shaken and only had one flimsy cork holding all the bubbles at bay. Joy was at my side, chattering happily about tackles and screens and play action, and all I could do was beam at every person we passed.

But that feeling was nothing compared to the explosion of the locker room.

It was addictive. Their happiness, the effervescent, powerful force was a high like I'd never known.

"Miss Sutton," Jack yelled from where he stood on a bench in our locker room. "We fuckin' did it!"

Dayvon set me down, slinging a heavy arm around my shoulder. It was then that I realized just how sweaty and smelly the locker room was. How sweaty and smelly every single guy in that room was. I gave him a smile and ducked out from under his arm just as Coach Klein stood in the middle of the locker room and motioned for silence. In his hands, he held a ball.

"All right," he yelled when a few players in the back were still whooping. "Great game, guys. You looked sharp, you looked fast, you looked hungry." More cheers and happy cursing, if there was such a thing. "But I'm most proud of how much you looked like a unit. A team. No one man more important the others, right?"

From my perch against a steel beam, I crossed my arms and watched the sweaty, smiling faces around me. *This was their church,* I thought. For them, this was a spiritual experience. Taking all the things they'd practiced and executing them so efficiently that they emerged the victor. It rolled through the space like a spirit, and I breathed it in, regardless of the smell that came with it.

Was it possible that I'd found my place among men such as this? One game probably wasn't enough to be able to tell, but a comfort seeped through me at that moment, something I'd never experienced before, and I wanted to grab it with both hands and hold tight with all my strength.

Coach lifted the ball, and everyone went quiet again. "The first game ball is an important one, isn't it?"

There were murmurs of agreement, everyone shifting in place as if they were too jacked up to stop moving. It was something I could understand as my fingers tapped along my arm of their own volition.

Klein held up a hand again, smiling now like I hadn't seen him smile once on the sidelines. "Pierson, get your ass up here."

Cheers went up as he made his way from the back. I tilted my head to watch him, my skin tightening at the mess of his hair, the tight white shirt pasted to his body with sweat, the grooves and curves of his muscles stark against the material.

He stopped next to Coach, hands propped on his hips, and a small smile on his handsome face. Underneath his eyes was that black stuff that I still didn't understand. He looked like he'd fought a battle—dirty and exhausted and happy. And ... hot. Okay, he looked hot. And sweaty. And hot.

With muscles. Sweaty, tattooed muscles

Damn it, Allie, I hissed in my head. Mental slap completed, I took a deep breath and focused on Coach again.

"This job never gets easier, but today, you made it look pretty damn easy."

Luke grinned, and my breath snapped to a stop in my throat.

Coach handed him the ball, and he held it up to the roar of cheers from his teammates. Then his eyes found mine. Desperately, I fought for the same happy smile that I'd given to Dayvon and to Jack. To the rest of the men in the room.

But I couldn't move my lips. It was all I could do to fight

against the blooming ache in my chest when he stared at me like that. It was the same way he'd stared at me during the photo shoot. Except now we were surrounded by dozens of people who would read that ... tension differently.

With more willpower than I thought I had at my disposal, I pulled my eyes away and talked briefly to Joy.

"We best be on our way, sweetie," she spoke loudly into my ear. "They're about to get naked, and I think my ticker would give out if I witnessed that."

I laughed, putting an arm around her shoulder.

Joy and I, followed by my nice security guys who'd waited outside the locker room, helped us navigate past some journalists who shouted questions. Because I wanted the focus to be the team, I waved and smiled but didn't answer anything. For now.

"So what happens after the game?" I asked Joy as we walked to where a driver was waiting to take us back to the hotel, which was about a ten-minute drive through downtown Houston.

"Some guys go out to dinner with their families, and some get their treatments, massage or chiro or acupuncture and relax until they can go to bed. But late afternoon games like this, usually you find some at the bar at the hotel if their families aren't here."

The leather seats of the car gave my fingers a new place to tap, and Joy noticed with a wry smile.

"Sorry," I said. "I'm not usually so fidgety."

She patted my hand and closed her eyes as she leaned her head back against the seat. "It's okay. It's exciting."

The car pulled up underneath the large overhang of the hotel, and the driver emerged to open the door for us with a deferential tap to his black hat. I smiled at him and waited for Joy before walking through the marble and glass lobby. No one looked twice at us, and before she exited the elevator on her floor, she gave me a soft pat on my cheek.

"Proud of you, sweetie. You did well today."

"Oh, I didn't do anything, but thank you."

Joy shook her head. "You'll see how wrong you are by the end of the season. I think it's going to be a good one."

On the quiet elevator ride up the next two floors, I thought about her words, rolling my neck against the constant hum of energy still thick in my veins.

The only sound in my room was the air conditioner, and as I sat on the edge of the king bed, white duvet cover neatly folded and white pillows perfectly placed, I knew I couldn't stay in my room all night.

Five minutes later, I found myself in the empty hotel gym, earbuds blasting G-Eazy and Halsey while I jogged on the treadmill. I made it a few miles before a stitch in my side forced me to slow, and my phone started acting wonky, leaving me without music. I used my towel to dab at my neck. In the wall of mirrors, I studied my reflection, wondering what people thought when they saw me now. The perception of me, with one title, had inevitably shifted.

Through nothing I'd done, I was now something more powerful than I'd been a month ago. It wasn't about the money either, because I'd had money before my father passed away. People treated you differently when you were wealthy, of course. But this was something else.

I looked the same. But I didn't feel the same.

Turning slightly, I studied my black leggings-covered legs that worked just as well as they had before. My white tank and pink sports bra were nondescript, my ponytail high on the top of my head. So why did I look different in my own eyes? Were the perceptions of others that powerful that they could change my perception of myself?

"You need a drink," I said out loud.

But since the gym was still blessedly empty, I laid on one of the mats and did some crunches and squats, and some light weight work for my arms. An hour and a half after I'd walked through the glass doors, I got back in the elevator and took a long draw from my water bottle.

I punched the button for the twentieth floor and sank against the wall. Just as the doors were about to shut, a hand shot out and stopped them.

The hand attached to Luke Pierson's tattooed arm.

His head snapped back when he saw me in the corner.

"Oh, hey."

I smiled. "Hey. Great game today."

His eyes started at my mouth and moved slowly as if he didn't care that I was two feet away from him and could clearly see all the places he was looking. And he looked. Luke Pierson was doing some intentional looking. Down the line of my neck, the V of my sports bra, over my simple black leggings and then back up. His dark eyebrows bent in confusion. Or pain.

I chose confusion.

"I felt like I'd go crazy if I didn't get some energy out," I explained.

"Yeah," he said, eyes locked in on my mouth. "I get that feeling after a game too."

Just as the doors almost closed, a young woman yelled out to hold the door. I leaned forward to hit the button, and Luke shifted backward as one, two, three, then four, five, and six teenage girls piled in.

They were giggling and laughing, chattering happily, and completely unaware that Luke Pierson was sharing an elevator with them.

He stood next to me, his arm brushing mine with every deep inhale that expanded his broad chest. I shifted next to him, raising a hand to dab at the sweat still gathered along my collarbone. His chin dropped to his chest, and I noticed him close his eyes.

Air left my nose in a hard puff, and he cut a look over to me.

One of the girls laughed so hard that she pitched sideways, causing Luke to jolt into me. To steady himself, he grabbed the railing along the back of the elevator. His fingers, tight to the metal, pressed against my lower back when I found my original spot.

Through my shirt, I could feel his knuckles, and I didn't move forward. He didn't move his hand. Except then he did. He pushed it over a few inches so that the length of his arm was across my back.

If I turned to the side, he'd have his arm around me.

At the fifteenth floor, they exited in a loud rush of giggles, some glancing back at us with flushed, excited cheeks.

Once they were out, Luke pulled his arm away, allowing a few inches between us.

I turned my head to the side to look at him, and his eyes were on my face.

Okay, if this went on much longer—this limited, full of subtext speaking, the small touches that clearly were not accidental, the bonfire hot eye contact—I would combust. My heart would ooze out of my chest because his stupid sexy laser eyes were turning my bones into gelatin.

"What floor?" I asked when he still hadn't moved.

Luke blinked, and I swear, my heart matched the quick movements. The air felt heavy and thick, and I licked my lips to see if I could taste it.

He was staring at the circular buttons, the number twenty lit up like an emergency beacon.

"You never hit a button," I explained when he still didn't answer.

"Same as you."

"Oh," I whispered. Why was I whispering? "Good."

The doors shut, locking us in together.

Good. Excellent.

CHAPTER 15
LUKE

'd never experienced silence like the one that filled that tiny elevator. Allie was within arm's reach, sweat making her chest shine under the harsh lights.

I wanted to lick it off.

My eyes pinched shut as the numbers dinged with each floor we passed. It was almost as if something had been suspended between us since the photo shoot, set into place when I laid my hands on her on my back porch. I didn't know what it looked like, this thing hanging in the air.

But, slowly, inexorably, it tugged me in her direction, making the space between us smaller and smaller even if I hadn't moved yet. Something inside me felt horribly off-balance, except for moments like this, when it didn't feel horrible at all.

It felt right.

Her mouth opened as if she was going to speak when her phone went off. The disappointment I felt was sticky and uncomfortable, and I wanted to wash it off me.

With a deep breath, she read something on her phone and gave me an inscrutable look.

"What is it?"

The elevator stopped.

On our floor.

With one hand, I held the doors open for her, but she didn't move.

"*Sports Illustrated* just emailed me a preview of the issue, in case I wanted to see the pictures before it hits newsstands."

I nodded slowly, pushing against the doors when they tried to close. "Okay. Are they good?"

Of course, they'd be good. I had eyes. They could've done the shoot with her looking exactly like she was right now. Scrubbed free of makeup, hair piled on top of her head, and sweat making her shine, she'd be fantasy fodder for every man with working eyes.

She certainly was for me.

"I can't get them to load." Her cell phone went dark in her hand. "Crappy signal in the elevator. I'll just use my laptop." She swallowed audibly and lifted her eyes to mine. "In my room."

The door tried to close, and I slammed my hand harder than necessary. She licked her lips and watched my face carefully as she walked out, her shoulder almost brushing my chest on her way out. I blew a long breath from my lips. That thing, the cord, the binding agent, the chemical pull between us tugged me further.

Off the elevator, there were two directions she could have gone. Given I had no clue where her room was, I watched carefully as she paused next to an ornate side table and gold framed mirror.

"Do you want to see them?" she asked, her eyes glowing wide in her face.

Remember when I said I felt off-balance?

That was a gross understatement.

With those words, the intent behind them, the hallway empty and hushed behind her, and tension vibrating between us like someone had struck a tuning fork with a sledgehammer, I knew that I was tiptoeing along a cliff's edge.

No harness. No safety net. If I slipped off the razor-thin line, we'd both tumble over into the unknown. But on Allie's face, given what she must be seeing on mine, she knew it as well as I did.

I swallowed, my eyes never leaving her mouth. It was a perfect mouth.

"No," I said, but it came out like a question, filled with uncertainty.

Her lips curved slightly. "Are you sure?"

"No." No uncertainty there.

The slight curve turned into a full-blown smile, her white teeth showing now, along with a flash of pink tongue. It would be soft and wet, her tongue.

"Well, that sounds like a personal problem, Luke."

Why did I like the sound of my name on her lips so much?

When I didn't speak, Allie turned and made a slow right; the same direction I needed to go to my room. What was I doing? This was complicated on an entirely different level than I was used to. My hands gripped the sides of my head, and I forced a hard breath through my nose.

But complicated or not, I wanted her.

That wasn't complicated. It was quite simple.

Allie wanted me, and I wanted her.

Normally, this was the moment when I remembered all the reasons I wouldn't indulge in a night of release, of spent energy and sweat-slippery skin. The consequences were never worth it to me.

This was different.

She was different.

In a few stretched-out seconds, I realized that Allie might be the only woman who would understand our precarious position. She didn't want me for my money or position; I didn't want her simply because she was willing and available. Despite the complications, she drew me in, yanking on whatever it was that had its hooks under my skin, under hers as well.

And I didn't want to fight the pull anymore.

I strode purposely, taking a right like she did, and she was standing in front of her opened door, the key just barely out of the lock, eyes on the exact spot where I turned around the corner.

"Change your mind?"

I didn't speak.

"Good," she said as if I had. Then she walked in her hotel room. Before I entered, I gripped the doorframe with both hands and let the breaths saw in and out of my chest. Maybe I wouldn't touch her. Maybe she'd show me the pictures, and then I'd be back in my dark, quiet hotel room with nothing but a sterile bed waiting for me.

Maybe.

Allie paused by the desk and glanced over her shoulder at me. Questioning, bright eyes, soft, smiling lips.

Or maybe not.

I pushed back and followed her, decision made. With the flick of my hand, the door slammed shut behind me. She was facing the desk again, and when I saw her brace a hand on the brilliantly clean surface, I saw the tremble in her fingers as she clicked a few buttons on her laptop screen.

"Whoa," she whispered when the page loaded.

I came up behind her, close enough that I could feel her heat but not touch her. The top of her head was just under my chin, so I could easily see over her shoulder at what she was staring at.

The cover was the exact shot predicted by the photographer. The last one he'd snapped, and even though I'd been there, even though I'd felt the explosive heat of that moment captured on film, it was like a punch to the gut to see it.

"The Wolves' New Alpha" read the title. Catchy. But what might have been cliché and silly wasn't. It only made the picture even more powerful.

Allie looked petite in front of Jack and me with that football balanced on her hip. Jack was smirking at the camera, his arms crossed like mine. Allie's red lips were open in a slight inhale, her eyes blazing blue in her flawless face. She looked fierce and strong and feminine.

But it was me standing behind her that was the most shocking. I looked savage. Territorial. My eyes burned into the camera with warning. With want. Her trembling finger came up and touched the screen just where I was staring.

"You look ..." she said quietly, her voice raw and soft, "like you'd rip someone's throat out."

"Yeah?" My head dipped so I could smell her hair. "That's not what I remember thinking about when they took that."

Her chin lifted, and my nose was in her ponytail. I took a greedy pull of air, and her phone clattered to the desk as she braced both hands on the surface.

"Wh-what were you thinking about?"

For a moment, I closed my eyes and simply breathed her in. The surging, overwhelming want made my hands curl into fists so that I kept from sliding them around her hips and under her shirt.

"You," I admitted in a rough voice. She emitted a soft mewling sound, and her back arched slightly, bringing her bottom snug against me. I dropped my forehead against the back of her neck and touched my lips to a delicate knot in her spine.

I'd been thinking about how she would smell, and now I knew. Something sweet and citrusy. I'd been thinking about how her bare skin would feel under my hands. Something I needed more experience with. What I'd felt so far wasn't enough.

So, so far from enough.

"Luke," she begged.

My fists uncurled, my fingers wrapping around her slim hips with ease. I pulled her flush against me, dragging my tongue up the gentle line of her neck until she angled her face toward me.

Slowly, Allie turned in the circle of my arms, her hands sliding up my stomach and chest, around my neck and into my hair.

With gentle pressure, she pulled my head down until my lips hovered over hers, neither of us willing to concede the last inch. My lips curled into an amused smile, and her eyes narrowed.

"Kiss me," I told her, my tongue darting out to lick my lips.

"You kiss me," she volleyed back. She wasn't averse to playing dirty because she arched her back again, pressing her breasts against my chest. I had to grit my teeth to keep from ripping her shirt in pieces with my bare hands, the desire to see and feel and taste so strong that she must have injected something into my bloodstream with that simple movement.

My hands curved down and gripped her bottom with rough fingers, and it made her forehead crease in agony.

"Why are you so stubborn?" she whimpered.

"Just me?"

Allie exhaled a soft laugh, and I sucked in the sound like it was the only way I could gorge on her. I'd take it. The thrumming of my heart was so violent, I knew I'd take anything she'd give me at that moment even if it was just this insane stalemate with no concession from either of us.

"Damn you," she groaned, surging up on her toes.

Her lips were soft and sweet, and I angled my head so I could go deeper, deeper, deeper. Her tongue curled around mine, and I licked the tip of it. Her fingernails dug into my scalp when I sucked her tongue into my mouth. My arms wrapped tightly around her waist, boosting her up onto the surface of the desk. Allie snaked her legs around me, trapping me against her, her hips writhing in a slow circle.

The kiss was demanding, but it was nothing compared to the drumbeat of vicious, biting desire that had my hands moving everywhere. Into her hair, along the smooth, feline curve of her back, under her shirt, where she was sleek and smooth.

She pulled away on a gasp, and I tracked biting kisses along her jaw while her hands scrambled to get underneath my shirt. Her fingertips dragged down the line of my abs, and I rocked into her, mindless from want and reckless in my drive to claim every part of her.

I wanted inside. Over. Behind. My hands filled with her skin, and my tongue slid over the parts of her that would be pale from being hidden from the sun.

I pulled back long enough to rip my shirt over my head, and Allie bit her lip as she watched.

"Look at you," she whispered, dragging a finger down the line that bisected my stomach, along the trail of hair that disappeared into my jeans. My muscles jumped when she did it again, with a light, torturous pressure.

I jerked my chin. "Your turn."

She tilted her head and leaned back on the desk. "Say please."

I propped my fisted hands on the desk and rocked into her slowly while my lips hovered over hers. With satisfaction, I watched Allie's eyes flutter shut when I hit just the right spot.

"You're such an asshole," she moaned.

Bending down, I dragged my nose from the base of her throat to the V of her sports bra and then gently bit down on the top curve of her breast. Allie arched up into me.

"I want to see you," I spoke into her skin.

"Yes," she hissed.

That was when my phone rang, a harsh, violent tone between our heavy, panting breaths.

It was Faith's ringtone. I dropped my head against her throat and worked to control my rapid heartbeat.

"Shit," I whispered and straightened. Allie slumped against the wall with a pained, frustrated expression on her face.

I dug the phone out and took one more slow inhale before I picked up the call.

"Hey, turbo. Can I call you back in five minutes when I'm in my room?"

"Sure, Daddy! You played so good!"

I pinched the bridge of my nose and backed up a step when Allie's legs unfolded from around me. "Thanks. I'll call you in a couple of minutes, okay?"

"Okay," she said brightly and hung up.

After I tucked the phone back in my pants, the sounds of someone walking down the hallway, laughing loudly, made Allie sigh heavily.

I understood the sentiment.

"That was Faith," I explained awkwardly.

She sat up and smoothed a hand over the top of her ponytail. "Yeah." Allie glanced at the door when more deep voices went past. "Probably for the best she called."

I swallowed that down like a bitter, chalky pill. She wasn't wrong. But as I pulled my shirt back over my head, I very much wished that she was.

We hadn't really thought this through. Who shared the room on the other side of that desk? If I could pinpoint voices in the hall, then someone would have been able to pinpoint ours.

Damn it.

My face must have betrayed my train of thought because she patted my chest in sympathy.

With a tiny, amused smile, Allie slid off the desk and gestured to the door. "I'll ... uhh, just make sure the hallway is empty."

It was, and I exited without fanfare, without so much as a goodbye, because I think we both knew exactly how bad it would look for us if I was seen exiting the owner's hotel room.

I sank heavily onto the bed once I was back in the privacy of my own and dropped my head into my hands.

Now I knew.

Knew what she smelled and tasted and felt like.

"You are such an idiot," I said out loud and flopped backward onto the bed.

Because now, there was no way I could forget any of it.

CHAPTER 16
ALLIE

WASHINGTON WOLVES

When I was doing my interview for *Sports Illustrated*, the reporter asked me a question that I wish I could answer differently. It wasn't that what I'd said was wrong or something not true. I just wanted to say something that was now more right. More true.

"What's the biggest thing you've learned through this whole process?" was what he'd asked.

"Besides what a salary cap means?" We both smiled, knowing this wasn't my real answer. Before I spoke again, I gave the question significant weight by pausing, thinking back on the last month. "I've learned that I'm capable of a hell of a lot more than I gave myself credit for."

I could tell my answer pleased him with the twist of his lips and the slow nod of his head. And I still felt that way. We'd won our second game, this time at home, the article absolutely blew up, was shared by millions on social media, and it was overwhelmingly positive. Two months earlier, if someone had told me that I'd be in that position, with this kind of reach, this kind of impact, I would've laughed my ass off. So my answer still held a firm grip on the truth.

But what was more true now was this: the gaining of knowledge was transformative and irreversible. I could never un-know the things that I'd learned in the past eight weeks. About myself, about the team, how incorrectly I'd viewed its impact in my father's life. About Luke.

Luke most of all.

Maybe it was silly that in the midst of all those things and the bearing they now held on my life, he was the thing I couldn't get out of my head.

Because I *knew* things now even if I couldn't really explain them.

For example, I knew that Luke was such a mothereffing good kisser, I'd almost let him screw me on my hotel desk.

I knew that his hands were huge and covered my ribcage with ease.

I knew that when he sucked on my tongue, it caused an involuntary clenching of my thighs.

I knew that when he rocked his hips against me, he was either hiding a steel pipe in his jeans or he was very, very blessed.

And I knew that I wanted to revisit all those things again. With regularity.

Maybe it was because I hadn't had sex in months. A really long string of successive months that should probably depress me if I thought about it, but that was mainly because most of the men who had balls enough to come talk to me and hit on me were usually egotistical assholes.

Hedge-fund managers and models who spent more time looking in the mirror than they did conversing with actual humans, or men old enough to be my father and somehow thought it was appropriate to proposition a twenty-six-year-old woman.

But Luke was different. I'd never met a man quite like him before. Okay, fine, I had to factor in that he loathed me on sight and wrote me off as a gold-digging, whore-y football groupie before I'd even opened my mouth, but even that was completely novel for me. It lent an element of refreshing honesty to our relationship, whatever that might be.

If Luke stripped off his shirt for me, if he licked my neck, bit the flesh over my spine, smelled my hair, and told me he wanted to see me naked, it was damn well the truth. It was in spite of what he'd thought of me when we first met. In spite of the fact that I owned the team he played for. In spite of every possible roadblock laid out in front of us.

Luke wanted me.

And, oh sweet baby wolves on the fifty-yard line, I wanted him too.

Knowledge. It rearranged your brain, allowing space, shifting your perception of reality and making sense of what the domino effect might be.

My mistake in this little bombshell was trying to explain it to Paige when we FaceTimed.

"I think," she said slowly, concern etched over her pretty face, "that you have lost your mind."

I laughed. "Oh, come on, you know what I'm saying. I know things now, Paige. I can't un-know them."

"Mm-hmm. You mentioned that. It's cute. You should make it a bumper sticker."

I lifted my hand so she could clearly see my middle finger on the screen.

It was her turn to laugh. Beyond where she was sitting on the sleek black couch, I could see our little patio set on the veranda, the uneven rows of tall, narrow buildings of Milan in the background.

"So … you know you want to bang your neighbor. It's not the end of the world."

"No," I agreed, "it's not. I've barely seen him since we got back from that game, though. The players' schedule during the regular season is insane. I don't know how he balances it, especially as a single father."

Paige propped her chin in her hand and grinned at the screen.

"It's so hot that he's a single dad. I Googled him last week when you sent me your post-kiss freak-out texts." She shook her head. "Allie, that man is en fuego. Like for real. He could be the long-lost Hemsworth brother, and I would not be shocked in the slightest. And he friggin' felt you up, girlfriend."

"I know," I groaned. "I can't stop thinking about it. About him. And I have a thousand other things that need to be more important in my head than one make-out session that might not get repeated anytime soon."

Through the screen, Paige smiled at me. "But you want to."

"I'm not even going to pretend like I don't, Paige." I tucked my knees up to my chest and stared out the slider. From where I was sitting, I could see his deck, which was empty. This time of day on a Wednesday, he'd be at practice or reviewing film somewhere with his offensive coordinator and the quarterback's coach. The level of his dedication—of all the players, the coaches, and the coordinators—was one of the most mind-boggling things I'd ever seen.

"What are you up to this week?" I asked her. "Any shoots?"

She shrugged, narrowing her gray eyes somewhere past the screen. "Nah, not this week."

"Paige."

"Allie."

"What's the body language I'm seeing here? It's weird. You're acting weird."

My friend did not fidget. She moved like a ballet dancer in shoots, could glide over a runway like her feet were made from clouds or something, but she made a weird twitchy move with her shoulders and started chewing on her lip.

"I don't know. I think I'm getting bored with Milan."

I clucked my tongue. "Well, duh, I left. Of course, you are."

We both smiled. Paige ran a hand through her dark red hair, one of her trademarks, and sighed. "Maybe that's it. I'm too much of an extrovert, and you left me all alone here, and I'm just ... ugh, I think I'm getting bored being a model. Point and click, pose, angle your shoulders, suck in your gut ..."

"You do not have a gut," I interjected harshly. "You're like a size one."

"I know that. But photographers are assholes."

"Not all of them," I pointed out. She rolled her eyes. "You know I'm right. But so what if you're getting bored with modeling. No one says you have to do it forever."

"Yeah, I guess. Maybe I'll come to Seattle and stay in your big mansion, and you can be my sugar momma."

Now it was my turn to roll my eyes. "I'm not in the mansion, and you know it."

"I know. Why aren't you, again?"

I looked around the family room, now fully furnished and feeling like me. The large couch, now with matching chairs, were soft and white. The hardwood floors had area rugs of dark blue and white covering it. Along the wall with the rock-covered fireplace, I'd found some tall white vases that I loved, each holding spiky green fronds. The bookshelves flanking either side were slowly being filled with pictures I'd found in boxes downstairs. Mom and I when I was little. She and my father on their wedding day.

The upper deck wasn't empty anymore. I had a long rectangular dining table in dark wood and chairs to match, which was where I ate most of my meals, looking over the lake. Someday, I'd have enough people over to fill the chairs, then I could light the candles lining the middle and not feel like I was wasting it on just me.

"It feels like my home," I said to Paige. It was the best answer I could give. "My dad's house is way too big for just me anyway. I really need to call a realtor and have them list it for me, furniture and all."

"There's nothing in there you want to keep?" she asked skeptically.

"Anything sentimental that was tied to my mom was brought

here. Anything from my childhood is in storage from when he renovated a few years ago, and anything else that I might find important is at his office." I shrugged. "That was just ... a house. And it's a house I don't need."

"Just add the sale money to your ever-growing pile of cash," she teased.

I stretched. "Don't you know? I told them to print it all off so I can swim in it. Every night, I lay it on my bed like a blanket."

She snorted. "I'd punch you if you were ever that obnoxious."

There was movement on Luke's deck, and I smiled at Faith skipping around the edge wearing a black and white Wolves' jersey over some sparkly leggings. Her dad was obscenely wealthy, just like mine was. Or like I was now. And she was happy to skip around a deck on a sunny day after school.

"It doesn't even feel real, Paige."

"What doesn't?"

"The money. Any of it. I could read financial statements until my eyes bleed, but my dad's wealth, my wealth, is this weird, abstract thing that I don't really have a firm grasp on in my head. I've been so focused on getting up to speed with the team, and it's like, I finally have to try to come to terms with exactly how much he left me with, and what I'm going to do with it."

Faith did a spin on the deck like a clumsy ballerina, and it made me smile. I hadn't noticed before, but she was wearing the number one on the jersey. The jersey I'd worn in the photo shoot. Ava had insisted that the pro shop start carrying them. And Luke's daughter had one.

My heart could hardly take it.

"Like invest in real estate or something?"

Another spin with her arms above her head and Faith had my brain whirring. I thought of the little girls at the first game, who wanted my autograph on their sign. Team Sutton, it had said.

"Like maybe a foundation." I tapped my finger against my mouth while my head spun with ideas. "You know how I told the reporter that I was surprised at how much I was capable of? It wasn't because anyone told me I *couldn't* do things when I was growing up. But I wasn't told that I could either."

Paige's expression sharpened like it did when she was interested. "So like leadership development?"

I felt a smile spread across my face. "Yeah, maybe. I know it would be a lot of work to get it up and running, but wouldn't that be amazing? Have a camp every year, go speak in schools, there are so many things you could do to help little girls recognize their potential."

"Well, holy shit, Alexandra Sutton. You're the boss for like three seconds, and all of a sudden, you're a mogul." She nodded. "I like it."

I liked it too. Just the seed of it in my head felt good. Felt important. Less like I'd been swept up in the tide of something and more like I was the one making the wave.

Paige and I said our goodbyes, and I walked over to the slider to watch Faith dance around.

Had I ever acted like that as a little girl? Probably. I just couldn't remember. So much of my younger years were hazy chunks that I couldn't recall; maybe because I spent more time with nannies and house staff than I ever did with my father. I had snippets of clear memories, but none of them were of me dancing around by myself in a home filled with love and support where decisions were made for my sole well-being.

Maybe that sounded terribly like I was a poor little rich girl, but the truth was that Faith was wealthy in something I'd never had. Luke loved her more than anything, and he didn't care who saw it.

Real men loved their kids like that. It was just another piece of the Luke Pierson puzzle that did absolutely nothing to stem the rise of desire inside me. And that probably meant I was screwed.

WASHINGTON
WOLVES

Three games. Three wins.

My offensive line had kept me from getting my ass knocked over all night, which was good because the Pittsburg D-line looked like they wanted me to be picking grass from between my teeth for the next week.

Normally, a win meant jubilation, a sense of relief, the knowledge that I'd fall into bed on Sunday night and sleep like the dead.

Instead, I found myself standing in my darkened kitchen, hands braced on the kitchen counter, body buzzing like someone had jammed a live wire under my skin. Without any lights on around me, I could see out into the dark night perfectly.

There were distant lights of the highway where it passed over the lake, boats floating out in the inky black water. And on the lower level of my next-door neighbor's house, I could see a long, delicate string of patio lights lit and hung in large swoops from the bottom of her deck, converging on a tall pole that was at the far corner of her hot tub.

It gave everything a warm, soft glow, and from my perch, I could see just the top of her head as she reclined in the tub.

Her shoulders were bare, her arms extended out along the edge of the tub.

It wasn't a live wire under my skin. It was Allie. And she generated a completely different kind of energy. It rolled off her like an uncontrollable, untamed force.

I wanted more.

I took a deep breath and rolled my neck on my shoulders, testing how my muscles felt. They were warm and loose after a vigorous treatment post-game by our staff masseuse.

Since our interlude at the hotel in Houston, I'd thought a lot about Allie. More than I should have been thinking about something that wasn't football related, but because it hadn't become a distraction yet, I allowed it. She was giving me space, treating me with polite respect when other people were around. Before the game, she always walked the field and wished the players a good game during our warm-up. When she reached me, I'd gotten no side-hug, no fist bump, no wide smiles or easy chatter.

But her eyes. They made my skin buzz recklessly because I saw the fire inside them that I felt burning through my bones.

And it was that polite respect that had me checking on Faith. She was snoring softly in her bed, face burrowed into her purple striped pillow. On her white nightstand, her star-shaped lamp cast her face in speckles of white and pink and purple. I sat on the edge of her bed and laid my hand on her tiny back just so I could feel the gentle rise and fall of her breathing.

It was something I used to do for months after Cassandra had died, when she was just a baby. Because she was a constant blur of motion during the day, the quiet moments when I could just watch her breathe felt like precious pockets of time that I wanted desperately to freeze.

It never woke her because unless she was sick, Faith slept like a rock. I leaned down to press a kiss to her temple and slipped from her room, leaving the door ajar. As I walked down the stairs, I checked the app on my phone that I used to monitor her when she slept. Normally, I only used it when I was downstairs working out, maybe doing laps in the pool after a game and I wanted the peace of mind that she was fine.

Now I was making sure it was working so I could go proposition my new boss.

The sheer absurdity made me snort softly. But did it stop me? Hell, no.

If anything, I congratulated myself on my genius because it was a perfect idea. The idea of Allie would likely become larger and larger in my mind until I'd wonder if I was making up the fierce heat that had combusted in that one perfect moment. Her ability to become a distraction expanded rapidly within the space of the unknown. Exploring this *thing* between us was the most logical way to control it.

As quietly as possible, I opened the slider onto my patio, leaving the lights off. The lights she'd hung over her own lower-level space gave me enough to navigate my yard. Thoughtful of her.

Once I reached the hedge separating our property, I took an admittedly creepy moment to look at her before she knew I was there. Her eyes were closed, her head still resting back on the edge of the hot tub as it had been earlier.

Slicked back and wet, her blond hair looked dark. Her face was bare of the makeup she'd been wearing earlier. And with the swirling water around her chest, no swimsuit visible, she looked naked.

Energy.

Electricity.

Whatever it was, Allie controlled it just by breathing. Maybe that should have had me turning back to my house, but I cleared my throat quietly and watched her sit up quickly in the water, eyes zeroing in on me instantly.

Not naked. Her strapless swimsuit was blue, the same color as her eyes.

Slowly, she sank back down in the water as I pushed through the hedge.

"Good game tonight," she said quietly, mirroring what she'd said in the elevator a week earlier. I smirked and folded my arms over my chest. Her jewel eyes lingered on my tattoos. I'd never met a woman who could load the silence with so much visceral, pulsing force.

"Thanks." I lifted my chin and waited for her to meet my gaze again. Not to be rushed, Allie took her damn time. "I had an idea just now."

"I hope you didn't hurt yourself in the process."

I licked my lips so I didn't laugh, smothering the smile instantly. That was why I was here. Exactly that. She wasn't afraid of me. Didn't elevate the idea of me to some god-like place that was so common for professional athletes. Most guys loved it, sought it out. It was why they did stupid shit like cheat on their wives in public places and not think about the consequences of getting caught. Because they thought they were above it all. That high was as addicting as any drug.

But I didn't want that. I never had.

Allie looked at me and saw Luke. Not Luke Pierson, professional quarterback.

And maybe that was a drug of its own for me because I was standing in front of her, willing to take this risk.

With a deep breath, I walked forward until I could prop my hip against the edge of her hot tub. "I have a proposition for you."

Her face didn't change, except for the slow lifting of a perfectly manicured eyebrow. "Yes?"

"I don't know about you, but what happened in that hotel room felt too good to ignore." I rubbed the back of my neck. "And believe me, I've tried."

"Me too."

"What if we make another truce?" I tilted my head to the side and thought. "Maybe truce isn't the right word. A suspension of our professional boundaries within a certain agreed upon amount of time."

Her lips twitched at my delivery. "And this suspension would get us, what, exactly?"

I turned so I could brace my hands on the edge, wet from the water surrounding her, the air thick and hot from the temperature of it. "Activities of the non-professional variety."

That did it. Heated her eyes to match whatever she was sitting in. It didn't seem possible that she wasn't increasing the temperature of the water just from whatever was running through her head.

"I'm listening," she said.

"My weeks are insane during the season, so I'm thinking one night a week. The only night when I can relax."

Her smile was instant.

"So Sunday nights then?" she asked, folding her arms under the water.

I pursed my lips. "Unless we have a Monday night game. Then you're on your own."

"I can manage that just fine," she purred.

Now I did laugh. "You are dangerous, Alexandra Sutton."

Her face went uncharacteristically serious. "Not to you."

To me most of all, I thought. But I kept it tucked safely in my head.

"Game nights," she repeated.

"Unless I'm concussed or have a broken limb," I amended.

Her lips curved. "I could be gentle."

I lifted my finger. "You just told me you weren't dangerous. Liar."

"And everything stays downstairs," she added an amendment of her own.

"Care to clarify?" I asked carefully, sure that she had a very good reason for asking.

"I like your daughter," she said quickly. "But I don't want her accidentally walking in on us in your room."

"Neither do I." I raised an eyebrow. "But she can walk downstairs too."

Allie licked her lips and stared intently at my face. "I don't want this to come out the wrong way, but I feel like bringing it upstairs, into the spaces that we live most of our lives, changes things. Makes them more serious."

I nodded. It wasn't coming out the wrong way to me. I understood exactly what she meant. My bedroom was my personal, private space that I didn't share with anyone.

I'd never considered sharing it with anyone. And the scariest part, the part I refused to unpack in my thoughts, was that I could picture her in my bed with stunning clarity.

In my silence, she nibbled on her lower lip briefly before she spoke again. "Maybe it's an arbitrary line. I don't know. It just feels … like an important boundary."

Maybe it was arbitrary. Maybe it wasn't. But I understood what she was saying. Hotel rooms and couches felt different than the beds where we slept each night. Which was why I agreed.

"You're quite a negotiator," I said in a quiet voice. I didn't want to spook her after something like that, but the fact she'd been thinking about my daughter spoke volumes as to what kind of woman she was.

Allie stood, water sluicing down her absolutely insane body. It was entirely possible I was drooling, so I clenched my teeth together to keep my jaw from popping open. The bottoms of her bikini were small, cut high on her long legs, and tied together by only a thin string on either side of her hips. The top could hardly contain her breasts, which, I knew from my limited encounter with them, would be a generous, overflowing handful, even for me. She was backlit by her strings of lights, giving her skin a flawless, golden glow.

At moments like this, it didn't seem possible that she was real. She must be a figment of my imagination, created by the part of my brain that wanted to stare at someone beautiful, someone sexy and confident. My hands shook from the need to reach out and touch her.

"Do we have a deal?"

I straightened and held out my hand. "We do."

She glanced at my hand and smirked. "I think we can do better than a handshake to seal the deal."

Allie exited the hot tub gracefully, picking up a fluffy white towel that was slung over the top of a patio chair. Standing there waiting for me, where I was frozen in place, she patiently toweled off her hair, then wiped it down her arms.

When she bent over to dry her legs, I almost swallowed my tongue. Allie stood and wrapped the towel around her, knotting it tightly before cocking her head. "Are we going in?"

I strode forward, not wanting a repeat of the hotel where I felt like I was chasing after her. Once I was standing in front of her, towering over her, I fisted my hand in the knot of the towel, so my fingers were underneath the edge of her swimsuit top. Her heart was hammering as I walked us backward, my hand refusing to let go of the material, the soft, wet skin under my own.

"I feel like a lamb being led to the slaughter," she teased as I reached behind me and shoved the slider open into her lower level.

"Good," I said once she'd cleared the door. I tugged her forward and placed my mouth next to her ear, licking the edge with the tip of my tongue before whispering, "because I am absolutely going to devour you, little lamb."

With both hands, I ripped the towel off and threw it somewhere. The slider door shut with an awkward clunk, and I backed her against it.

My mouth found hers hungry and hot, her tongue wet and cool, and I ate at her lips with a ferocious, lupine drive to take and take and take. The buzzing I'd felt earlier was nothing compared to this, to having her under my hands and mouth, to being able to sink my fingers into the luscious curves of her ass.

This was raw and unchecked, and I wanted to let my head fall back in a howl when she clutched at my back and dug her nails in. Short, hard puffs of air from my nose were the only reason I hadn't passed out, but the thought of taking my mouth away from hers made me feel like I'd incinerate from the inside out.

The sharp edge of Allie's teeth nipped at the tip of my tongue, and the bright, visceral tug of pain it gave me made me press into her so hard, I worried that I might hurt her. Step for step, though, she matched me.

Against the front of me, her hips moved restlessly, seeking the same thing that I was. Blinding pleasure, feral release, an unleashing of what we were both capable of.

The front of my T-shirt was wet from her suit, so I ripped at the back of it where it hooked together, unable to find a way to get it off her. Finally, I broke my mouth away and glared at it as if it had done me personal injury.

Which it had. Anything keeping me away from Allie Sutton's chest was officially out to ruin my life.

"How the hell do you get that thing off?"

Allie laughed. She bit her lip and looked up at me through her long, black lashes. "Come on, I've been told you're good with your hands. You can figure it out."

I growled, tucking my fingers in the front. Allie's chest heaved with labored, deep breaths, her eyes daring me. With one hard tug, I yanked it down, groaning when it was rucked around her waist, and she was finally bared to my eyes.

I bent down and kissed, licked, then when she gripped the sides of my head with both hands, I sucked. My fingers gripped her back as it arched sharply away from the glass.

"I love Sunday nights," she gasped, and I chuckled against her soft, warm flesh.

I leaned back and went to untie one string from the side of her suit over her hips when her doorbell chimed violently.

"No," she moaned. "No, no, no."

My forehead dropped into the curve of her neck while my breaths came out with the force of a runaway train. This could not be happening again. I wanted to howl all over again. The kind of desperate, grieving howl of a man who'd just tasted heaven and then had it ripped away with one stupid doorbell.

The bell went off again, and Allie whimpered. Or maybe that

was me. Even with the distraction, my hands didn't stop moving. The tips of my fingers dragged up the line of her spine and around her side to the warm, full weight of her breast, which I tested with my entire palm.

"You evil, evil man," she whispered.

Ding, dong!

I growled into her skin. "I hate whoever that is."

With gentle hands, Allie pushed at my chest, and I backed up slowly. Very, very slowly. With narrowed eyes, I watched her tug her swimsuit top back up into place.

"Let me just see who it is." She glanced up the stairs. "It's not like I get many visitors, especially on a Sunday night."

"I'll come with you," I said instantly.

She looked at me curiously. "Why?"

I found myself shrugging uncomfortably. "Just in case." Her slow, sweet smile made me roll my eyes. "It's not a big deal. I'll stay out of view."

Allie nodded and picked up the towel off the floor from where I'd flung it. Silently, I followed her up the stairs and waited just out of view while she carefully glanced out the window.

"Holy shit," she exclaimed, flinging the door open to reveal a tall, thin young woman with messy red hair piled on the top of her head and suitcases on either side of her. "Paige, what the hell are you doing here?"

"I told you to get my guest room ready," Paige said with a laugh, embracing Allie tightly.

Allie turned mid-embrace, giving me an apologetic look. I held up my hands and walked back down the stairs as quietly as possible.

"I missed you," I heard her friend say, just as I cleared the steps.

"You have the worst timing known to man, Paige," Allie said, and I smiled as I walked out the slider.

It was either that or weep.

And I had to be honest, weeping would probably come in about five minutes when I laid in bed.

Alone.

CHAPTER 18
ALLIE

WASHINGTON WOLVES

Something new about Paige since I moved away from Milan was her current obsession with *SportsCenter*. She said it was so that she could be as knowledgeable about football as I was, but I think she was just bored.

Over the next week, I came home to her curled in the corner of the couch, watching *SportsCenter* like it was reruns of *The O.C.*

Which was why I shouldn't have been surprised to walk in the door after our next game—a particularly grueling home loss—to find she already had a giant glass of merlot waiting for me.

"That was a tough one to watch," she said by way of greeting.

"Tell me about it." I toed off my heels and sank onto the couch.

We'd been beat on every level. Even though the TV was muted, the replay currently on a loop was Luke getting sacked.

Hard.

The ball had been stripped from his hand as he hurtled to the ground, and someone from New England had nimbly picked up the stray football and ran it in for an uncontested touchdown. Instead of watching the guy who scored, my eyes stayed on Luke, the way he twisted around to watch the player take what was his. I watched the way his helmet fell back onto the turf, and he punched the ground twice before standing up. Slowly.

He'd gotten hammered tonight. And not in the fun way, the way I'd been thinking about hammering and Luke all week.

"So," Paige drawled when she noticed what I was staring at. "Are you going to go over there? It is Sunday night. Your first Sunday night," she clarified as if I hadn't thought about it all damn week.

I chewed on my lip after another sip of wine. "I want to. But I don't know what the protocol is when he got his ass kicked, literally, on the field. He must be really freaking sore."

Paige's face brightened. "Sexy massage?"

I smiled. "Maybe."

She held up a finger. "I've got this oil I picked up in Venice. Take it with you. Rub all those muscles down and then ... you know, rub something else."

Her wink was obnoxious, but it made me laugh.

As much as I'd wanted to violently murder her for showing up when she showed up the previous week, it had been good having her in the house. She spent my money very well, helping me furnish the remaining rooms in just a few days' time. The last of it had been delivered the day before, including a new mattress and mahogany sleigh bed for the guest room that she'd claimed as hers.

Nothing about the house looked like it did when I moved in. It didn't smell musty with disuse. It was bright and clean and comfortable. Nothing stuffy or ornate. Probably not fitting for a team owner with more money than she'd spend in a lifetime, but I still loved it.

I liked to think that my mom was somewhere up in heaven, obnoxiously pleased that I was living in the home that had once been hers.

Weird how that house was what initially linked Luke and me. What would our relationship be if I'd even been three houses down? I'd never have met him before that first meeting. Never hated him. He never would've hated me.

The strength of our emotions was what made our current situation burn even hotter, in my mind. Without those initial exchanges, I couldn't help but wonder if Luke and I would've had the same polite, friendly interactions that I did with every other player, and that made me inexplicably sad.

"Am I crazy?"

Paige, very used to my random thoughts with zero explanation, just shrugged her slim shoulders. "I don't know. What do you think?"

I gave her a long look. "Not helpful."

She took a slow sip of her wine and stared out the slider. "I think there's a lot of potential for a messy fallout."

Paige wasn't wrong, but I hated hearing the words come out of her mouth. Even if I'd been circling around the same thing. "I know."

"You own the team he plays for," she said, lifting her fingers and checking off each item. "You're both public figures now; you in a way that's hugely magnified from before. His daughter idolizes you. And you live next door to each other."

"Okay," I interrupted. "You can stop now."

"You asked," she pointed out.

"I know," I moaned, dropping my head back on the couch. "So why am I ignoring all of those incredibly valid points and still thinking about how badly I want to go over there and see if he's waiting for me?"

Paige blew a raspberry with her lips. "Well, that is easy. He's not like any man you've ever been with. He's not a pansy or a neophyte or a narcissist or a creep. He's a *man*. And he's not intimated by you or trying to make you a pet."

I shook my head slowly. "And, Paige, the things he can do with his tongue, and I have not even been able to properly test drive that thing ..." I paused and laid on a hand on my chest. "It's a pretty novel experience for me."

She smiled. "Don't tell me stuff like that, or I'll weep into my wine with jealousy."

"I know that's part of it," I conceded. "The attraction is ... potent. But I just need to know it's enough to risk everything else."

Paige thought about that. "Risk what?"

I took another sip and let the wine roll around in my mouth. "What if the universe is trying to, I don't know, tell me something by the fact that we keep getting interrupted? That's not a coincidence. What if I'm doomed to fail at this owner thing, and getting mixed up with Luke will just make it so much worse if that happens?"

"Oh, my *gosh*," Paige said, reaching out to smack my arm. "That's easy enough, just don't fail. Luke is completely separate from that."

"Just don't fail, she says," I repeated on a laugh.

"I'm being serious! How many wealthy people, I'm talking obnoxiously wealthy people, own dozens of businesses and have absolutely no interaction with those companies? A lot. You're smart enough to trust the people to do their jobs, so you show up and make the fans and players happy and keep people interested and let them do their jobs. You won't fail. You *own* it; it's not like they can fire you." She rolled her eyes. "You're using this as an excuse because you think Luke and his magic tongue come with a lot of risk. No offense but you haven't had to take a ton of risk in your life."

Paige's face dared me to argue with her. Her stubborn little heart-shaped face dared me, complete with dewy skin and plump lips and wide, heavily lashed eyes that had made her career.

I glared at her, but I couldn't be mad. Something was inherently annoying about a friend who told the truth, even if it was a truth that might piss you off. It meant they were secure enough in your friendship and knew you well enough to take the leap into a tough conversation.

"I've taken risk," I muttered.

She laughed. "Not really. Yeah, you tried out some businesses, but you were never passionate about them. This whole thing is so much bigger, so much more important than any of that. It's okay that you care about it, but that's not why you're hesitating with Luke right now."

I felt the back of my neck bristle with the need to defend myself, so I took a deep breath. "I'm not hesitating with Luke." At her disbelieving look, I amended it. "Not exactly. I'm just making sure I'm not walking into something certifiably insane."

"Did it feel insane when he came over and asked you about it?"

My cheeks went hot at the memory, and I had remembered it a lot in the last week. "Not in the way I'm talking about, but yes, when I was in the hot tub, and he was standing there ..." I shivered. "I felt like I'd lose my mind if I didn't have his hands on me again. It was as if ... I was possessed, Paige."

"Then what's with the cold feet now?"

I wiggled my toes where they were propped on the coffee table. Nothing cold about them. They were just being lukewarm cautious. Something I wasn't used to when it came to my toes if I was being honest. "It's always different when he's not standing in front of me with his big hands and rippling muscles and sex eyes telling me he's going to devour me."

Paige slapped my arm, and I rubbed at it. "Oh, you bitch! I actually hate you now. Ugh. And a good dirty talker. I'll tell you why you're crazy. You're crazy for second-guessing this."

I found myself smiling. "You're probably right."

"Devour you, huh?" she said with a wide grin.

"Yup."

"Allie girl," she leaned forward and held up her wine glass, "I have condoms in my purse. Get your ass down there."

I took one last glug of wine and set it down on the table with a loud clack. When I stood, I glanced out the slider and saw the aqua glow of pool lights reflecting up at me. At the far end of his lap pool sat Luke, his arms spread on either side of him like a king lounging on his throne.

He wasn't looking up at me; his eyes were closed, and his head was resting back on the edge. Even with the distance between us, I could see the stacks of muscles in his chest through the wavy water, the black ink scrawled over it. Dates and names and pictures that probably all had some level of significance. As I stared, I thought about how those parts of him had felt under my fingertips and how they'd feel now that they were wet and cool from the water of his pool. He opened his eyes and turned his head, looking directly at me.

"Where were those condoms again?" I asked over my shoulder.

CHAPTER 19
LUKE

Watching Allie walk toward me, her features blurred in the darkness, her body covered by some white gauzy thing that floated around her like a cloud, I felt like I was in a dream. Some music video sequence where you found yourself holding your breath because of the carefully planned, drum-tight anticipation of what she'd do next.

I thought maybe she wouldn't come. Sitting in my pool, I wondered whether she would or not served as a surprisingly effective distraction from how miserably we'd played and how thoroughly we'd gotten beat.

That alone was enough to make me edgy because nothing distracted me during the season. Nothing.

"I'm not usually very good company after we lose," I told her when she came to the water's edge. The pool matched her eyes, which made her presence that much more potent, that much more powerful as if she was an extension of the water.

"Fine with me."

"I don't want to talk about what went wrong." My voice got harder at her softly spoken answer.

Her lips twitched. "Okay."

"I don't want a pep talk about how it'll get better and the season is sixteen games long."

"I wouldn't dream of it."

In the warm water of the pool, I held myself very still, my hands curling into fists on top of the concrete edge. The way Allie watched me was part fascination, part awe, and an amusement that curved the edges of her lips delectably.

"Since when are you so accommodating?" I all but growled.

"I'm always accommodating," she answered, her voice a low, hot lick of fire over my entire body. "You just didn't see it until now."

The puff of air that slipped from my mouth wasn't quite a laugh, but it was close enough that she zeroed in my lips with an intensity that rippled through me with all the subtlety of a tropical storm.

Hurricane Allie.

"So," she whispered, "what do you need to feel better, then?"

I tipped my chin up and stared at her for a beat. There were no sounds around us to cover our words, nothing that we could use as a distraction, as a reason not to hear every answer, see every response.

"You," I said.

In a loud rush of water, I turned and braced my hands on the concrete to lift myself out of the pool. It let me use more strength, exert more of what was humming under the surface of my skin than any sissy-ass steps did.

Allie backed up so she didn't get wet at my exit from the pool.

Her eyes tracked down my heaving chest, widening slightly when she saw exactly how much this conversation was affecting me. I couldn't really hide much under wet swim trunks.

Then they widened for a very non-sexy reason.

"Holy crap, Luke," she said, reaching out to slide her fingers along the early stages of a bruise on my side.

Annoyed by what that light brush of her fingers did to my

psyche, how much I wanted to feel it over every inch of me, I grabbed her hand and pulled it up to my mouth.

"It's nothing." I sucked the tip of one finger into my mouth, digging my teeth into the fleshy pad. Allie tucked her lips together between her teeth, and her eyelids fluttered closed. "But if you're concerned, there's no need."

When I sucked on another finger, she stepped closer, rubbing that finger along the edge of my tongue. "How about we take this inside? I think … holy *shit*, Luke." She broke off on a gasp. "It's just a stupid finger; how does that feel so good?"

I paused, and when she realized what she'd said, I smiled around said finger while she leaned into me and laughed. I slid my arm around her waist, gathering the gauzy material covering her body into my fist. It would rip easily.

"Yes," I said into her hair. "Let's take this inside."

When I turned for the entrance to the lower level of my house, I had to steady my breathing when Allie tucked her warm fingers into the waist of my swim trunks as if I'd somehow lose her on the way inside. As if she couldn't stop touching me.

Considering my profession, it had been a long time for me. No one I'd met had been worth the risk. To me, to Faith, and to the life I'd worked my ass off to build.

The slider opened without a single sound, and Allie followed me in just as quietly. The lights were off except for where my office was set up in the far corner. I pulled a white towel off the edge of my desk.

Allie's fingers gripped more tightly, and as I was drying off my face and chest, I felt her warm breath along my spine.

Her forehead dropped to my skin first, and I closed my eyes when her hands lightly drifted over my skin around my waist, meeting with sprawled fingertips spread over my abs.

With careful fingertips, she traced each neatly stacked set of muscles. Muscles I'd worked very hard to maintain at thirty-five years old.

She spoke against my back, her lips glancing my skin with each word. "When you pulled your shirt off at the photo shoot"—she paused, one hand moving up to skim over my chest, the other toying dangerously with the tie on my swim trunks—"the first thing I thought was that I wanted to bite you."

I let out a rough laugh, barely more than an exhale because I was trying very hard not to shove her down, tear her clothes off, and rut her like a wild animal who'd been left alone for too long. "Yeah? Where?"

She kissed my shoulder blade. "Right here." Then her fingers whispered along the V of muscle under my hip bone. "Definitely here."

Allie as the seducer was not how I'd envisioned this night playing out. My hands were shaking from my need, unsteady in how badly, how very, very badly I wanted to put them on her body in the same way as she was touching mine.

The whisper across my skin got louder, firmer when they skated over my biceps.

"Here," she said again. "I wanted to know just how strong you were. What you could do to me with all these places I thought about putting my mouth on."

If I was the wild animal being held at bay, she'd just ripped my rusty chains off with her words. I turned and gripped her face with both hands, sliding my tongue into her waiting, moaning mouth with a violent sort of drive to taste her.

Taste and taste and take and take.

She was sweet and wet, meeting each kiss with one of her own, deep, deep, deeper until we were wound around each other with too-tight arms and digging hands.

"I could ruin you," I told her between kisses. "I could do anything."

Allie pulled back, her eyes glowing unholy in her face. There was no part of her that wasn't stunning. "Promises, promises."

My hands weren't shaking anymore when I reached down and slowly pulled the hem of her dress up so that the hem was between my fingers. "Hope this isn't your favorite dress."

She lifted an eyebrow. "It might be."

Rip.

I wrenched it between my fingers, tearing it straight up the middle, teeth gritted and skin on fire. Underneath she wore simple white underwear, a white lace bra, and the skin that was the embodiment of every deathly siren come to life in one dangerous package. Golden, curved, endless inches that I fully planned to explore.

Tucked into her bra was a condom. I leaned down and licked across the top of the lace covering her, then pulled the foil wrapped package out with my teeth. When I leaned back, her cheeks were pink, her eyes bright, her breaths fast and uneven.

"I don't promise anything that I can't deliver, sweetheart," I told her after I'd tossed the condom onto the couch up against the wall.

I leaned down and gripped her underneath her bottom, hoisting her up in my arms. She wound her arms around my shoulders and moved sinuously against my stomach as I walked us to the couch. My teeth found the lace of her bra, and I bit. Hard.

Allie gasped my name as I tilted her onto her back but made sure she kept her legs locked around my waist as I knelt on the couch. It forced her lower body into an upward angle, and she arched her back more sharply, displaying herself like an offering. It was a feline movement, graceful curves and limber sensuality, someone who was totally comfortable in her own skin.

I spread my hand over her stomach, from pinky to thumb, and spanned her entire ribcage. My skin on top of hers was darker, rougher from misuse. Her skin under my calloused hands was pristine and unmarked, no bruises or breaks or violence to be seen anywhere on her body.

Not like mine.

Compared to her, with my inked skin, the bruises popping along my sides, and the scars from surgeries and injuries, I felt coarse and unrefined.

She looked up at me, her fingers slung over her head, knotted into the arm of the couch, impatient breathing and hips rolling against me when I didn't move. Her blond hair was mussed and tangled around her face. Her lips were flushed pink from the rough treatment my mouth had given hers. From the biting and sucking. *You are perfect*, I wanted to say. Instead, I dropped her legs so I could yank her underwear off. In a rare sign of shyness, she closed her knees while I stood and briskly untied my trunks. My hands were rough when I shoved them down my legs.

For two, maybe three heavy, pulsing seconds, we stared at each other.

"You're perfect," she whispered, and I had to blink for a moment at hearing the words I'd been thinking given back to me. It was disorienting in the sweet way she delivered them, which belied the sinful light in her eyes.

It hurt.

It hurt to look at her.

With those two words, I wasn't sure how to proceed. I wanted her over me so I could see her move. I wanted her under me so I could unleash everything burning hot inside me. I wanted ... I wanted ...

I just wanted her.

I held out my hand to her, helping her stand from the couch. She used her fingers and her palm to incite me further as I ripped the dress off her shoulders, then unhooked her bra and tore it off her shoulders.

Allie bit down on the skin over my heart as I walked us backward. Another bruise I'd have on my skin. My hands gripped her waist as I sat, and I lifted her easily to straddle my lap.

One of her hands clutched the back of the couch, and she moved over me. I slid my hands up the line of her back while she did, our lips tangling and sucking in kisses that never stopped, never slowed.

My hands got rougher, her movements more like a dance; my

teeth found her skin, her tongue found the edge of my neck, and her breathing got choppy and wild.

The moment I snapped my hips, we both stilled in a perfect suspension of breathing, of heartbeats, of time.

I'm so screwed, I thought. It was a realization that came far too late. Because I could never, ever forget that she felt like this. That like this, she was my perfect counterpart.

Allie pressed her cheek against mine as we both started to move, her breathing, her whispered words and pleas hot in my ear. For minutes, hours, I couldn't say, we moved against each other, her knees tight up against my hips, our chests sweat-slicked and sliding.

I felt the wave, felt it build up my legs, hot and silver and expanding like lightning in my blood, and only to crest into an explosion when Allie clutched my neck and then slumped against me.

One hand soothed up and down her back as we breathed heavily. Her hair was a tangled mess, and her clothes were in a torn heap on my floor.

And even with her still sweaty and sated in my arms, I knew I'd be counting down the hours until I could touch her again like this. How else I could see her and feel her, what new thing we could explore.

I always knew Sundays were my favorite day of the week, just not because it was now the day I got to screw my boss.

"Holy hell," I said out loud. If there was a moment of panic accompanied by that thought, Allie chased it away instantly when she leaned back and grinned at me.

"I love Sundays," she whispered.

"Yeah?" I asked with smug satisfaction at the sight of her. Rumpled and sweaty and pink-cheeked.

She smacked my chest, and I laughed.

I sighed and ran my hands up her back. Who had skin this perfect? Nobody I'd ever met.

"I love Sundays too," I told her.

"Even after a game like tonight?"

My head dropped back as Allie climbed carefully off my lap and moved to the side of the couch. It was hard to think straight when she looked the way that she looked, so I closed my eyes.

It took me a minute to answer. "Yeah, even after a game like tonight." I turned my head toward her and found her watching me curiously. How did I put into words that even after the losses, the ones that hurt mentally as much as they did physically, I'd never want to do anything else?

Her eyes dipped to the bruise on my side, but she didn't touch me. "Does that surprise you?" I asked.

Leaning forward to plant a hot, fast kiss on my lips, Allie smiled against my mouth. I found myself smiling back.

"No," she answered.

Then she was off the couch and wrapping her ruined dress around her shoulders while I chuckled under my breath. It was eerie how she seemed to be reading my mind tonight.

"Thanks," she said quietly.

"You're welcome?"

Allie laughed, looking down the length of me, my body still sprawled on the couch. I wasn't sure I could move.

"See you next week?"

Maybe she'd be my downfall. Maybe this would blow up in our faces. Maybe there'd be a day that I regretted that I ever had this stupid idea.

But it wasn't tonight.

"Next week," I told her.

And she was gone.

WASHINGTON WOLVES

S omehow, without conscious action, my days turned from unknown and overwhelming to expected and routine.

Paige liked to randomly quiz me on what the team might be doing on any given day. Even if I wasn't required to, I enjoyed spending weekdays just observing the inner workings of the Washington Wolves.

It was a well-oiled machine, no wheel or cog unimportant.

Raymond, a custodian who'd worked there for twenty years, talked to me about the stadium improvements that helped bump up season ticket sales in the early 2000s. Marie, an accountant who'd started a couple of years ago, told me that one of the things she admired about my dad was his ability to remember everyone's name.

No matter their job description, no matter how long they'd been there. When he walked the halls, if he saw you, he smiled. He greeted you by name and asked if he didn't know it.

Employees who felt respected showed more respect to their jobs. That was what Ignacio, who loved spraying the lines on the field as part of his maintenance job, told me when we spoke on a Wednesday afternoon. The practice field empty except for the two of us because the team was in the film room reviewing their game plan for an away game in Cincinnati.

Apparently, my father gave Ignacio a referral to an immigration lawyer when his mom and sister wanted to come to the States. That nugget hit me like a metal club into the heart, because I was still trying to balance the man I remembered as distant and in a state of constant work as someone who'd refer a lawyer to a groundskeeper.

Tuesdays were my favorite day to be at the facility because even though it was the players' day "off," they were everywhere. Lifting weights and sharing music, laughing together and swearing at each other. They were huddled in film rooms, watching the same thirty-second stretch of film on a jarring loop, back and forth, back and forth, back and forth, seeing something in a defensive formation that would probably elude me forever.

They were there, pushing each other to be better when they could be doing anything else.

I'd learned that every pre-game night, the players stayed in hotel rooms, whether we were home or away.

Their practice days during the game week were seamless. One day was practicing first and second down as the game plan crafted by the coaches dictated. Well, coaches and the captains. Often, I saw Logan, Dayvon, Luke, and a few others huddled around clipboards, flipping printed pages and discussing routes with their coordinators.

Did my eyes stray to Luke more than others?

I'd neither confirm nor deny. Except he was the only ass I watched religiously as it flexed underneath his black athletic shorts.

What that man's ass could do was nothing short of freaking miraculous. I practically had bruises on my inner thighs to prove it from our night on the couch five days earlier.

If he ever noticed me watching practices from a distance, wandering the halls with one employee or another, he never so much as looked. Not once.

Stupid discipline.

Then I shook my head and turned to leave the fields where they were practicing their two-minute drills. As I walked away, I felt a quick snap of awareness, something hot that trickled down my spine, but I didn't turn to look. If he could show discipline in public, then damn it, so could I.

But I made sure to put just a teeny extra swing in my hips, just in case. Sunday night, we'd be at the same hotel in Cincinnati, so he could damn well watch what would be waiting for him.

———

Something else I learned about football, in the wake of this slowly unfolding relationship with Luke Pierson, was how much one sweaty man in a strange uniform could turn me on, even with half a stadium between us. Cognizant of cameras aimed in my direction from the front row of my suite, I made sure not to gawk and drool, lick my lips like he was a perfectly seared eight-ounce filet after a week-long juice cleanse.

But in my head, when that man leapt over, *over!*, a defender and ran ten yards into the end zone, I wanted nothing more than to rip my top off and scream like I was in the front row of a Justin Timberlake concert and he'd just pointed straight at me.

His arms lifted over his head, the grass stains on his white pants, the bulge in his biceps and sweat coating his face made me terribly, terribly hungry.

Someday, I wanted him just like that. So while I was cheering and high-fiving people next to me, smiling happily as though my investment was doing precisely what I needed it to, I was imagining all the ways we could utilize the king-size bed waiting in my room.

Or the tub.

It was big. And had jets.

I walked to the locker room on a veritable cloud, the kind of cloud that can only precede a really good orgasm and did my duty round before their clothes started coming off.

Luke was by his locker, surrounded by dancing teammates that were making him laugh, and I could only see the side of his strong profile.

Truly, it wasn't fair. His smile—with bright white teeth and small dimple to the left of his mouth— made him so handsome that it was painful to look at. His hair was wet and messy, the white undershirt soaked with sweat. When he lifted his arm to give someone a fist bump, the white tape wrapped around his wrist was stained green from the grass.

And I had to press my thighs together.

Whyyyyyy was that so motherbleeping hot? It was grass-stained tape! I was losing my mind.

But past it was the corded muscle of his forearm marked with black ink. I had a bright, searing memory of his hand braced on my stomach while he knelt between my legs, his hips moving with unerring accuracy, fast enough to make my skin shake, slow enough to make me incinerate with blind pleasure.

My throat tightened in anticipation, and it felt like I was swallowing a chunk of concrete through sheer will, but the need for oxygen was so great with how much my brain was spinning.

Want.

Want.

Want.

It was my own personal victory chant, and I'd repeat it until the moment he knocked on my door. Then it would change.

Mine.

Mine.

Mine.

"Girl, you've got that look," Dayvon said, coming up to me and slinging a heavy arm around my shoulders, which was becoming his post-game tradition.

"Wh-what look?" I choked, tearing my eyes away from sweaty Luke Pierson and his black magic pheromones.

"That fire." He nodded as though I'd done something right. "It's how we look before a big game, and we know we are about to throw shit down, and nobody will stop us."

I laughed, and it came out a tinge hysterical, but he was so amped on the win, he didn't seem to notice.

"It's a good look on you, Sutton." He walked away, pointing a finger at me while he did. "Don't lose that fire. We take our cues from you, boss lady."

It was enough to make me blink.

I *was* the boss. Even if a lot of it was in name only. I didn't create their game plans; I didn't run practices or call plays. But this locker room wasn't the place for me to practice my sex eyes on Luke.

While I firmly believed there was nothing wrong with what we were doing because we were both consenting adults, I absolutely did not want it to affect the team. Affect how they viewed me, especially when I was so new within this stitched together family.

With a deep, sweaty-man-smell-filled breath, I smiled at Coach Klein and lifted my chin. Then with no fanfare, I left the locker room alone to find my driver.

———

The text came first as I turned to view my reflection over my shoulder.

My sleep tank was white, and I wore nothing under it. My shorts were black, as unadorned as the tank, and barely covered much more than underwear would. My hair was wild around my shoulders. Face bare.

LP: Room number?

My lips twisted into a smirk.

. . .

Me: So demanding. Can't you ask nicely?

LP: ... please

Me: 1625

The dots bounced on the screen but then disappeared, and I wondered whether he noticed I was on a different floor than the rest of the team.

That was no accident because I'm no idiot.

Plus, I'd already slept with Luke, so the likelihood of anything noiseless happening within the walls of either hotel room was slim to none. I ran a hand over my stomach and found it already shaking. My fingers were a little numb, and I shook them out.

"He's just a man," I whispered to my reflection. "He's just a regular man."

Even as the lie passed my lips, I forced myself to believe it. Because even the way I'd undressed, taken off my makeup, and undone my hair with just my fingers was a testament to how untrue that was.

It felt like Luke preferred the most stripped-down version of Alexandra Sutton. Not only him but me too. He didn't get the version of me that the rest of the world did. He got reality, not fantasy. And the fact that he did seem to prefer that made me want him even more.

The knock on my door came just a short minute after I'd sent my room number.

A *knock on the door* made my cheeks flush, for crying out loud.

I licked my lips and straightened, then tossed my hair like I was channeling Kate Upton.

His hands were clasped behind his back when I pulled the door open, using it to cover my body.

The sweat was gone. The grass-stained tape and damp under-shirt were gone. In its place was clean, shower-wet hair. A face that needed a shave, but thank the Lord hadn't gotten one, because it made the angle of his jaw look dangerously sharp as if I might cut my tongue if I licked at it with too much pressure.

I think I wanted to test that theory.

Covering his broad chest was a button shirt so blue that it made his normally brown eyes glow almost golden bronze. And those eyes held all the heat that I'd missed during the days wandering the facility, and the hours I'd lay in bed thinking about how he'd made my body feel the week before. My fingers curled into the surface of the door as we stared at each other.

Then he dipped his chin and walked through the opening with a strong, loose-limbed stride that ate up the ground from the impossible to ignore length of his legs.

With just the tip of my finger, I pushed the door shut and then flipped the deadbolt.

He watched with a lifted brow. "You think I'm going to try to escape?"

Moving slowly in his direction, I peeled the tank top off.

"Nope." I dropped the shirt on the floor next to me.

If I thought his eyes were heated before, I'd been so, so wrong. "I was going to do that."

I shook my head. "My turn tonight."

"You think so?" he asked gruffly when the tips of my fingers traced the edge of my sleep shorts, which had nothing under them, and started inching them down my hips.

Luke started unbuttoning his shirt, and I shook my head, instantly stilling the motion of my hands. He froze, narrowing his eyes.

"My turn tonight," I repeated. "I got a room on a different floor on purpose, Mr. Pierson, and I intend to make the most of that. So keep your hands by your side, and I'll let you know when you can do any touching."

"What?" he said in a low, warning voice.

"With anything other than your mouth," I clarified.

He held his hands out in a conciliatory gesture even as his gaze scorched my skin. It made my breasts feel heavy and tender even though he'd yet to touch them, and goose bumps pebbled over my arms as I slid off the last piece of clothing covering me.

"Holy shit, Allie," he breathed. "You're killing me."

"Oh, just wait," I said with dark promise.

I stood in front of him, and I could see the thick column of his throat move in a long swallow. The tips of my chest brushed against his shirt, and I leaned up on tiptoe so I could speak against the corner of his mouth.

"Before I'm done with you," I paused and licked my lips, glancing his in the process, "you'll beg."

Luke turned his head, his breath coming fast and furious. As if his violent reaction to my little test of how far I could push him was being held in check by a single, whisper-thin strand of thread.

That was all that separated me from civilized, disciplined Luke, the one who kept his eyes off me in public, the one who never sent me a single loaded glance when we were outside the safe, agreed upon parameters of Sunday nights, and the *other* Luke.

The other Luke was the one who tore clothes from my body with nothing more than the strength in his fingers. The one who bent my body in curves and angles with his unleashed strength, driven by instinct and something primal that was probably only ever channeled on the field.

But with me, it was darker, more elemental because no eyes were on us. No one to enforce rules or limits or levels of what was acceptable.

It was just us and what we wanted.

The thing that made him snap was when I arched my back and nipped at his chin with the edges of my teeth.

I practically purred when he licked at my tongue and dove his hands into my hair with scalp-tingling strength, tugging at the hair as his teeth tugged at my lips.

My fingers tore at his shirt, scratched down the skin of his chest as he angled my head for a deeper kiss and palmed my bottom roughly.

His shirt joined mine on the floor, his pants next, then my body was tossed on the bed just a breath later. His words against my skin were part command and part entreaty.

"More," he said.

"Yes."

His eyes heated again briefly when he saw two condoms on the nightstand instead of one like the other night.

With demanding hands, he turned me on my side but stayed on his knees on the bed. My back arched, and I braced my hands on the headboard while his free hand traced the line and bumps of my spine, down the length of my bent leg.

Once he was covered, he lifted my top leg and then stopped.

My eyes flew open, darting to him.

"What are you waiting for?" I tried to turn, tried to open my legs around his slim hips, the taper of muscle like the bottom of a V.

"For you to beg," he said with a cocky smile.

I groaned out a laugh, which made his smile soften into something more real than he'd ever given me before.

In my head, I heard the snap of a puzzle piece clicking into place as his hips slid forward, slow, slow, slow.

It wasn't until hours later, when I drifted off to sleep, sore and alone in my big hotel bed, that I could name it.

Happiness.

And that was more terrifying than any level of pleasure he could possibly bring me because of how much we both stood to lose.

CHAPTER 21
LUKE

WASHINGTON WOLVES

I should have known that something would go wrong. That I'd start to slip.

It started on Tuesday morning when I drank my smoothie at the kitchen counter and found myself staring at the sliders leading into Allie's home. Behind the glass, I saw no movement, no sign she was awake and starting her day.

Instead of thinking about which films I would study that day, or how badly I needed to work on my quads, which felt tight after Sunday's game, I was wondering what her bedroom looked like, and how she looked in it.

While I was doing that, I missed a call from Randall about a new endorsement deal from a shoe company who'd loved my *SI* cover. By the time I called him back, he was in another meeting.

Distraction.

It was understandable, I told myself, that someone like Allie would distract me. At least, that was what I kept repeating to myself on Wednesday when I caught a glimpse of her out of the corner of my eye as I barked out a play while we practiced first down sequences against the practice squad.

But I called the wrong play, so when I heaved the ball to my tight end, the ball sailed ten yards past him, bouncing ineffectually on the ground. He gave me a curious look, but when I stayed quiet, he knew that the fault was mine.

"Keep your focus, Piers," Coach yelled from the sidelines.

My eyes burned hot from the effort to stay zeroed in on anything but her, even when I walked to the drink table and I could have taken a quick glance. It was the thinnest version of control I was able to master when it came to her, something I'd honed over my career.

Discipline.

That was what I needed. To counteract the distraction of Allie, I needed to keep a tight-fisted grip on the discipline that I was known for.

Demand.

Thursday night, I lifted weights in my basement and made demands of my body that I normally wouldn't during a game week. I pushed my muscles to the point of shaking and wondered if I'd lost my mind for doing just one more set of reps.

Since we were nearing the midpoint of the season, my aches and pains were taking longer to disappear, and I was moving slower on Mondays and Tuesdays, praying that I could make it through another week without anything more serious than that and some bruises on my body from unrelenting linemen.

And then, desire.

Friday was when I should have heard the blaring sirens in my head, warning me at car piercing levels that Allie was becoming a problem. Because after I bid my mom farewell and thanked her for making dinner for Faith, and after I read four books to my daughter who so desperately needed some of my attention, I found myself sitting on the couch, staring at my phone.

I could text her. See what she was doing.

Friday was close enough to Sunday, right? Sunday night was a night game anyway—our first of the season—which meant high pressure, more people watching, and a late night before needing to be back at work Monday morning.

But the desire to see Allie, to try to capture what we'd only had moments of the past two weeks was growing larger than any concern I might have about what this distraction was doing to me.

It was only a distraction, but I was unable to harness it by discipline, it became impossible to demand from my head, and I was completely driven by desire. Desire I'd never, ever experienced. I'd had good sex before. I'd had great sex before.

But there was something with her, something indefinable, something that had dug its fist root-deep inside me and was growing beyond my control.

Which was why I clenched my teeth, put my phone down, and forced myself to go to bed at a good time on Friday night.

Alone.

Saturday was a little bit better. The game walkthrough was seamless, even if Jack commented on how tense I was, and the team arrived at our usual hotel with little fanfare. Some guys went out, usually the younger ones, but the veterans knew to keep our heads down, get good sleep, and wake refreshed.

I barely noticed the room around me when I woke on Sunday because they all started to look the same after a while. Nondescript lamps and artwork that failed to stand out beyond a few splashes of colors. Sterile sheets folded into tight edges and pillows that were always too soft. Showers that could never accommodate my height, and sinks that were too short for me.

But all those warning signs, one for each day of the week, that I stubbornly ignored, that I refused to properly name, were nothing compared to the disaster of what happened on the field.

Reporters after the game would speculate that maybe there was miscommunication between my receivers and me, which was partially true. Jack ran a ten-yard post route when he was supposed to go fifteen on a fade, resulting in an interception that was only saved from becoming a pick-six when I tackled the jackass myself.

My center blocked left when he was supposed to block right, and I was knocked back so hard that I saw stars for a minute, breath coming slow back into my lungs.

Bottom line, we sucked.

We were off rhythm.

Distracted.

It became such an ugly word in my head, a whisper through the week that grew louder in the deafening quiet of the locker room afterward. Ugly because it was my own damn fault.

Being disappointed in your teammates for not grabbing a perfectly thrown ball wasn't an easy feeling to swallow, but what was worse was walking into the post-game press conference knowing that I couldn't pass this off onto anyone else's shoulders. Not that I ever would.

Making excuses was for the weak and unprepared. And that wasn't me. Which was why I stood behind the podium and pointed at a reporter in the front row.

"What happened out there, Luke?" she said, glancing up from her notepad.

I lifted my chin. "We lost because we didn't play well, and our opponents did. Simple as that."

"Luke," someone from the other side of the room called, and I nodded. "We're not used to seeing so much miscommunication on offense. Are the rookies still having a hard time learning the play-book? We know yours is extensive."

I gritted my teeth, his insinuation clear. Blame the new guys for not doing their homework because it makes for a better headline. Jack was no rookie. He was one of the best receivers in the NFL two years running, and there was no way in hell I'd be throwing him under the bus.

"It's not on the rookies," I told him. "If there's a miscommunication, it's on me as the quarterback. I'm the one who takes the game plan and puts it into action out on the field, and if they heard something other than what I intended, then we'll come back next week and practice harder to make sure we're all on the right page as a team."

Hands lifted, people yelled my name, and I sighed, squinting into the bright lights aimed at me, pointing somewhere in the middle. "Last one, guys. I'm pretty beat, as you can imagine."

There was a ripple of laughter, as intended, when someone spoke up. I heard his voice and my back tensed.

"How's the new owner doing, Luke? She, uhh, still proving to be a bit of distraction for ya?"

Reporters murmured uncomfortably, and I pinned him with a hard look. Ava from PR started up onto the stage, and I held up a hand.

"We're here to talk about the game," I answered tightly, trying desperately to soften my face into something less homicidal. "If you have a question about that, I'd be happy to answer."

He smiled. It was greasy and slick like oil spreading over his face. "I saw a magazine cover at the grocery store yesterday, said she was pregnant with a player's baby already, but there's no way to tell whose."

"Asshole," someone muttered in the front row.

I kept my eyes pinned on him like I could inflict bodily harm. "Unless you have a question, I suggest you refrain from reporting on crappy tabloid covers," I said firmly.

He shrugged. "Can't say I blame you for taking the spotlight off her, though that seems to be her greatest contribution to the team."

Gloves. Off.

I straightened to my full height as a hush fell over the room. Reporters got fired for so much less than that, and if me giving an answer would make his stupid, sexist sound bite go viral, then so be it.

"I'd like to see you handle that situation with an ounce of the integrity that Al-" I tripped over *Allie* even though that was what she asked us all to call her, "Miss Sutton has. She was thrown into a huge role unexpectedly, one that is vital to any successful team in this league, and she's proven herself day in and day out to be committed and intelligent, and there is not one person in the entire

Wolves organization who would say otherwise. In just a few short months, she's earned our respect, and she's earned that title, talking to a janitor about his job and how it could be better just as she'd talk to Jack or me or the CEO. If you're insinuating that a woman who happens to be young and happens to be attractive can't do a damn good job, then you're living in the wrong century."

I walked off to some whistles and claps. Ava smiled in the dark area next to the stage, her eyebrows raised in surprise.

My nerves jangled uncomfortably at what I'd just allowed myself to say. To the press. To the people who would love nothing more than to twist and tangle my words into more.

But everything was true.

As I drove home, the headlights of my car cutting bright slices of light through the dark streets, I knew with painful clarity that if Faith was thrust into the same situation as Allie, I'd be so fucking proud of her if she handled herself the way Allie had.

But it didn't mean we should keep doing what we were doing.

When I pulled my car into the garage and waited for the door to close, I remembered something that Allie had said to me.

Don't make me look stupid.

And that was what would happen if anyone found out. If anyone knew.

They'd judge her at the precise moment that they slapped me on the back in congratulations.

It felt like a lifetime ago that we'd stood in my backyard and I'd comforted and calmed her with no fucking clue how much she'd end up meaning to me.

I wasn't even sure I could put a name to it right now. It had taken me long enough to admit I was simply attracted to her. Anything more than that felt akin to scaling Mt. Everest with no preparation.

I couldn't go there right now. It wouldn't help anything. Not her. Not me. Over and over in my head, I repeated that as I walked into my dark house.

There was a note for me on the counter from my mom, who usually had Faith sleepover at their house on night games.

Proud of you, son. No matter what.

I rolled my head around on my neck, a few satisfying pops punching through the silence of the kitchen. Would she be proud of me if she knew what I was doing with Allie?

She wouldn't care if I was sleeping with someone, but she'd care about what could happen as a result of sleeping with this particular person.

"This has to stop," I said out loud, testing the words on my tongue, feeling the unbearable weight of them as they hit the air. Immediately I wanted to take them back, let them be unheard in the universe, sweep them away because the thought of it had the same effect on my lungs as being sacked by a three-hundred-pound lineman.

I braced my hands on the counter and hung my head, taking a few steadying moments. Firming up what I was about to do, I knew I respected Allie enough to tell her that we couldn't do this anymore. That I couldn't do this to *her* anymore.

Why was my heart racing like that?

Why couldn't I take in a full breath?

My lungs were banded tight as if someone had wrapped a rubber band one too many times and they couldn't expand to their regular capacity.

I pinched my eyes shut and saw her in the hotel room last week, naked, standing in front of me and making demands that no woman would have ever made of me because she viewed me as an equal.

Then I was moving, down the steps, toward the slider, knowing with unerring certainty that she was downstairs waiting for me. My skin felt cold with panic, hot with anticipation of seeing her, everything tilted and unsteady, rocking around me like I was afloat and unanchored.

The lights were on over her patio, but she wasn't there as I looked over the hedge, and the breath whooshed uncomfortably from my mouth.

Just as I was going to push through the ever-widening gap in the hedge, I heard her voice behind me.

"Hey," she said softly.

I turned slowly, and when I saw her sitting at the edge of my pool—a happy product of an abnormally warm October day—bare legs dangling into the water, hair pulled up off her face, something strange happened.

The cold panic thawed into something warm and smooth. The world around me settled instantly, the horizon straight and flat and right where it should be.

Allie stood slowly, and that was when I saw what was covering her body.

My jersey.

Nothing under it by the looks of it.

Even with the lights from her backyard, her face was hardly visible in the shadows once she was facing away from the pool.

But her eyes on me held me fast in place, the anchor that I couldn't find just a few moments earlier.

"Hey," I said back, woefully inadequate for what was churning violently inside me.

I can't do this was one massive, side-knocking wave of thought.

I have to touch you again was another.

I refuse to be what might ruin you was the last.

Allie lessened the gap between us, unafraid of closing the distance, showing just how much more courageous she was than me with each step over the soft grass.

"I'm sorry about the game," she said, eyes lit and wicked in her face. No, not wicked. That wasn't the right word anymore. It didn't feel right to label this as something wrong even if it was dangerous for both of us.

Those eyes were almost invasive in how much intimacy I saw there. Not wicked at all.

When did this happen?

Was I so lost in the searing pleasure that I missed the frightening shift underneath it?

I once learned about the tectonic plates, deep under the ocean's surface. Just one fraction of an inch could trigger earthquakes, tsunamis, and unimaginable destruction and chaos.

That was what Allie felt like.

An unimaginable, life-altering change I hadn't seen coming.

Slowly, I lifted my hand and slid my fingers along her jaw, savoring the silk of her skin over the bone. I was so much stronger, it would take me nothing to break her if that's what I wanted.

When my other hand came up and traced the line of her nose, spread my fingers along her cheek so I could feel the fan of her eyelashes along my fingertips when she blinked, her delicate brows bent slightly in confusion.

"Are you okay?"

"You are perfect," I told her, the thing I'd kept swallowed down from our first night together, suddenly needing her to hear the words.

She smiled, but it was a confused smile. "Luke," she said even as she nuzzled into the warmth of my hand.

I couldn't bear it. Couldn't bear saying the words. My hands slid down her shoulders, and I gathered her to me, tight, tight, nowhere nearly tight enough, even as she wrapped her arms around my back.

Blindly, I sought out her mouth, and she let out a breathy, relieved gasp when our lips met, over and over.

Sweet and slow, we kissed, her hands clutching my back, up into my hair, and my fingers digging into the material of my jersey.

Just one more time, I promised myself. Just one more night.

My kisses turned harder, pulling a whimper from her mouth when my hands gripped underneath the jersey, and I found nothing but smooth, endless skin.

"You waiting for me like this is every fantasy come to life, Allie," I whispered into her ear, pulling on the lobe with my teeth. That made her arch up on tiptoe, gasping loudly. I spoke into her neck next after I licked the length of it. "It feels like it could never be better than this, but it always is, isn't it?"

"Yes," she moaned. "Luke, please."

I pulled back and touched my forehead to hers. "Tell me," I said fiercely, needing something in return, even though she couldn't possibly know, couldn't possibly understand what her words would mean to me later.

"Let's go inside," she said, her arms wrapped tight around my neck.

"Tell me," I said again, working my hand slowly up her waist, under the jersey until my hand was filled with soft, warm flesh, her heartbeat wild under my palm. "Tell me and I'll take you to my bed. I'll do anything. Anything you want."

Allie sobbed out a breath, her body winding tighter and tighter against mine, against my seeking fingers between her legs as I contemplated taking her right there on the grass.

"I-I, oh holy shit." She dropped her head back. "I didn't know, Luke. I didn't know it could feel like this. This good, this ... this, oh please stop if you expect me to be able to think."

I chuckled against her skin and slowed my hand. "I can accept that for now."

She lifted her head, blinking slowly, as I pulled my hands out from underneath the jersey, wound my fingers between hers and led her into my house.

As we ascended the stairs, I felt her questioning look but ignored it. My room was dark when we walked in, and I shut the door behind us. More than anything, I wanted this one memory of Allie in my bed, between my sheets, just one night where maybe she could fall asleep next to me.

"What about Faith?" she asked.

Extracting my fingers from hers, I tucked her silk-soft hair behind one ear, then dragged the edge of my thumb along the arch of her cheekbone. "She's at my parents'."

"Luke," she said, shaking her head slowly as she glanced around my room. "Are you sure?"

In answer, I kissed her softly, only breaking away to pull the jersey off her body. She took my cue, slowly undressing me until I was only in my boxer briefs. Every brush of her fingers, every place she kissed as she uncovered the skin made my hands shake with the need to do the same.

She stood at the edge of my bed and held out her hand, but I stood for a moment and simply stared. Then I spanned her hips with both hands, turning us so that I could stretch fully out on the bed. Allie smiled and pushed me back lightly.

There was only one source of light in the room, but it cut straight across the bed like a blade, and when Allie crawled over me, the moonlight illuminated every inch of her. All I'd had of her was stolen moments like this in the dark, and she deserved so much more than that.

She leaned over me, and we kissed again, the mood so muted and soft as if time had slowed to something elastic and malleable. My hands on her back, hers gripping my face as she moved in small circles over me as if I was already inside her.

"Allie, Allie," I whispered.

She straightened, bracing her hands on my chest, and suddenly, it felt wrong. She felt too far away, and I rolled us.

On a sharp inhale, she pulled her leg up, tucking her knee tight against my side. I gripped her thigh tightly and held her eyes as I pushed forward into her.

Her chin jerked up, and I could tell she was holding her sounds. But I wanted them. I wanted to take them into me like I was in her.

Together we moved, soft and slow, so slow, that when sweat started to pool on my back, and her hips started to rise against mine restlessly, I knew the time for slow was done.

Faster and faster, more and harder.

It wasn't enough. It felt like nothing could ever be enough.

I wrapped myself around her as tightly as I could, just short of hurting her, and she gasped into my ear as we came together.

I slumped to the side, so I didn't crush her, and Allie brushed the hair out of her face with visibly shaking hands. I finished for her, tucking a blond tangle behind her ear again.

Her mouth opened to speak, but I leaned forward and silenced her with a kiss. No tongue. No teeth. Just my lips against hers.

Then I slid an arm under her shoulders and tucked her into my side, reaching blindly with my hand so I could drag the sheet over our bodies.

"Sleep," I whispered against her forehead.

No longer did I want to question why I was doing the things I was doing. It felt right to speak the word to her with all the subtext beneath it. It felt right for her to curl into my arms and let her boneless body soften even further.

After a moment of loaded silence, her questions almost a tangible presence between us, I felt her relax. Her arm slid across my stomach, and she laid her head on my chest, her breath finally evening out after a few minutes.

Sleep came much later for me as I watched the light slowly move from the bed, leaving us in darkness.

A fitting analogy for what I knew I had to do.

CHAPTER 22
ALLIE

WASHINGTON
WOLVES

The first indication that I was waking up under not-normal circumstances was that everything smelled like a man. Manly man.

Like the kind of man smell that made you close your eyes, dig your nose in the nearest fabric, and inhale like a crack addict who just got a rolled dollar bill shoved up under your nose.

So naturally, that was what I did.

Since I woke to an unfamiliar pillow clutched in my arms, I curled into it and took the most blissful, long, sex-induced inhale of my life.

Luke.

It smelled like Luke.

And since I was currently alone in his California King Bed, I knew that it was just from being in his bed, in his room, in his home.

From the brightness of the sky, I knew he'd already be at the facilities, probably getting a massage or his bones cracked into place, which ... ooh, I stretched and winced.

I could use a little of that too.

A blissed-out smile spread across my face because holy hell, that night had been one for the record books.

I knew it made me a very, very bad owner to say, but if losing a game did that to a man, then I'd be awfully tempted to tell them to lose more often.

Turning on my back, I ran a hand over my forehead to clear my face of my tangled, bird's nest hair and tried to do the same to my tangled, bird's nest thoughts.

Some things I knew for sure.

One- Something was different last night. When I saw the post-game press conference from the comfort of my living room, I saw in his eyes the moment he realized what he'd said about me. Nothing was inappropriate, nothing that could be twisted into a story that was ugly or sordid, but I was watching him through the lens of our little ... agreement.

Two- That agreement was shot to shit into a million teeny, tiny pieces now. The second Luke brought me up those stairs, we clicked into a new category. What? No freaking idea. But that brought me to bullet point numero tres.

Three- I wanted more than Sunday nights. And I was pretty sure Luke did too. He held me like I was precious. Made of glass. Something to be cherished and taken care of. But screwed me senseless while also being cherished. In public, to reporters, he spoke of me with respect. With a protectiveness that had made my eyes water.

"What is happening here?" I asked the empty room.

It didn't answer.

I turned over again, studying his private space. The ceilings, much like my own, were peaked and white, with open beams stretching across the length and ending at a massive wall of windows. The windows faced the lake, as did mine, and were thankfully covered by white lined curtains.

The bed was on a simple iron frame and clad in a light gray bedspread. An empty fireplace broke up the far wall, and on either side of the warm-toned brick were open shelves lined with books, some old trophies, a few framed photos of Faith, and an older couple who must be his parents.

Next to the fireplace was a brown leather club chair with a short, fat floor lamp just behind it, perfect for reading.

On either side of the bed were dark mahogany end tables, mine empty and slightly dusty, his holding a water bottle, a phone charging cord, and a few loose coins. Doorways on the other wall led to a bathroom and maybe his closet. It was clean and simple but not boring.

I mean, I could spruce it up pretty quickly if he was interested in that sort of thing.

As soon as the thought grew wings, I smacked my forehead.

Turns out, it was completely unnecessary as a distraction technique because from outside the shut and hopefully locked door, I heard Faith giggle, then a woman respond.

My mouth fell open. My cheeks burned hot. My heart threatened to crack its way out of my chest.

His mom and daughter were riiiiight outside the room. And I was five minutes away from doing the walk of shame in front of them because I had no clue what time it was, and I was supposed to meet with Joy this morning.

Freaking awesome.

I sat up and blew out a quick breath. My choices were limited. When I'd walked over last night, I left my phone sitting in my own bedroom because I thought I'd be gone for thirty minutes max, so texting Luke to see how long they might be home was out of the question. I could don the jersey I wore over here, shimmy down the edge of the deck and pray no one saw me, or I could snag some clothes from his closet, lift my chin, and accept the situation for what it was.

Shitty. Embarrassing. Absolutely, completely, soul-crushingly mortifying.

Beyond that, I had to take a second and drop my head in my hands and breathe through the sharp flutters of panic.

I'd never met his mom before.

And I was about to walk out of his bedroom, which shouted a whole host of truths that even Faith would catch on to.

I whimpered a bit because the last thing I wanted to do was get her twisted up in the middle of this before Luke was ready.

Which was why people normally, like, woke the other person up and kindly told them to vacate back to their own house before their impressionable six-and-a-half-year-old daughter saw them.

Lifting my head, I took a deep breath and stared at the door.

I flung the covers from me and peeked around the edge of the closet, just to make sure it didn't like, secretly connect to the kitchen or anything.

Whew.

Without spending too much time digging through his walk-in closet, I found a pair of black athletic shorts that I rolled twice around my hips so that they didn't fall. Even though it was painfully obvious and horribly cliché, I slipped the jersey back over my head because I couldn't think of a better alternative in his closet when it came to braless apparel.

In the floor-length mirror, I did what I could by combing through my hair with my fingers, tugging it together into a quick braid that came over the front of my shoulder.

Not the worst I'd looked, I thought wryly. Just not how I ever imagined meeting his mother.

With that, I whimpered again and marched to my fate.

When I quietly opened his bedroom door and peeked out, his mom did an almost comical double take as she was flipping pancakes on a large electric griddle.

Her hair was short and peppered with gray, nothing about her like Luke because of how short and petite she was.

Except for her eyes. She had the exact same eyes as he did.

Faith was mid-chew when she noticed her grandma staring at something. When she saw me, she gasped, flying off the stool with pancake bulging in her cheek.

Her cast-clad arm wrapped around my waist.

"Miss Allie! Hi! What are you doing here? Did you just come to say hi?"

Her face was sticky with syrup, and I smoothed a hand down

her neatly braided hair, trying not to laugh hysterically at the fact that yup, I'd definitely come over to say hi. I'd said hi three times last night.

Luke's mom recovered remarkably well, much better than I did, as I was still trying to force words out of my useless mouth.

"Faith, get your tushy back here and finish those pancakes. We leave for school in fifteen minutes."

When she did as she was asked, I steadied my breathing, and extended my hand to Luke's mom, as though I wasn't currently without underwear and wearing her son's gym shorts.

"I'm Allie Sutton. It's a pleasure to meet you."

She took it firmly, eyes twinkling, lips curved slyly. "Roxanne Pierson. I've heard so many good things about you." Her eyes darted to Faith, who was happily munching her pancakes. "From my son and my granddaughter."

My cheeks may have matched the red on the jersey, but Roxanne didn't seem to mind.

"Oh," I stammered, "that's ... nice."

Even if it was wildly untrue. I could just about imagine some of the stuff Luke might have said about me just a few short weeks ago.

"I told her you looked like Barbie," Faith said.

Roxanne and I laughed. Unlike mine, I doubted her laugh was to cover up the rapidly growing mania crawling over my skin because I was the one stuck in a kitchen that wasn't mine, with a mother and a daughter of the man I was casually, maybe not casually sleeping with.

But that wasn't Faith's fault, and God love her, she thought I looked like Barbie.

"Well, I don't know about that," I told Faith with a smile. "But you're sweet to say so."

"Pancake?" Roxanne asked with an expert flip of her wrist. Another golden-brown circle appeared on the steaming hot griddle. The sweet smell of batter filled my nose, a strange and unexpected replacement from the smell of Luke from when I woke.

Outside of a restaurant, when was the last time someone made me breakfast?

Paige poured me some Fruit Loops last week, but no matter what she might say, that didn't count.

When I was Faith's age, I had a housekeeper who would cook for me, who'd pour a large cup of orange juice for my dad before he straightened his tie, said hello to me, and wished me a good day at school before he went to work.

I blinked out of the memory and into the much warmer one in front of me. "Oh, no thank you. I'll, umm, I'll just eat at home. I have a meeting that I need to get ready for."

Roxanne opened her mouth to say something when Faith turned and pinned me with a disconcertingly direct look for a six, almost seven-year-old. "Do you work as much as my daddy does?"

My eyebrows popped up in surprise. Roxanne did the same.

"No," I answered after a beat. "Your daddy works a lot more hours than I do. To be good at what he does takes a lot more time than my job does."

It was a careful answer, but truthful all the same.

Faith didn't react as I expected her to. She bent her eyebrows in and twirled the tines of her fork in a spot of syrup on her white plate. As soon as she stopped, the syrup slowly filled right back in. "Do you know how long Daddy will play football?"

When I imagined how this walk of shame would play out, it wasn't this.

Roxanne sent her granddaughter a soft smile but didn't brush her question aside. Nor did she rush to answer it and avert the spotlight from me. I couldn't blame her since I'd gotten myself into this situation.

The situation being Faith, right smack dab in the middle of whatever Luke and I were doing. The thought of brushing her off and telling her to talk to her dad made my stomach curl unpleasantly. Her sweet, big brown eyes did weird things to my chest, so I rolled my teeth between my lips for a second while I thought about what to say.

"I don't know, Faith. I've never talked to your dad about that." Or a whole hell of a lot, really, which made this conversation even more bizarre. Again, I wondered why he'd brought me to his bed, to his room. Why he'd left me sleeping alone when he could have woken me early and asked me to slip out before Faith, before his mother, woke up.

Most of all, I wondered why he'd reached for me again and again as the moon switched places with the sun.

Maybe I was reading too much into it. Maybe he thought I'd sleep well past when they'd be out the door for school.

So many maybes that only one man could answer if he so chose.

"Could you," the little girl asked tentatively, licking her lips before giving her grandma a quick glance, "could you maybe fire him so he's always home with me?"

Oof. I made a sound as I slowly sat next to her on one of the empty barstools. Roxanne gave me a small, encouraging smile. Wasn't this a grandma question to answer? I was nowhere near qualified to tell this adorable little thing why I couldn't fire her dad.

Honestly, I probably wasn't even qualified to have any conversation with her because I'd hack my hair off with a rusty blade before I gave her the wrong impression about what I was in Luke's life.

I knew the kind of damage that might do to a kid like her.

So instead of rubbing her back like my hand itched to do, I curled my fingers around each other and set them carefully in my lap.

"You must miss him a lot, huh?" I asked.

She nodded.

Deep breath, Allie, and holy crap, don't screw this up.

"I can't fire your dad because you miss him, sweetheart." Her face fell, and I lifted a hand, softly laying it on her bird-like little shoulder. "But you know what's amazing?"

She looked up at me. "What?"

"Men like your dad only work that hard for a couple of reasons. And one of them is because they love something so much that it's worth all those hours, and all the stuff he has to do to be good at his job. I've heard him talk about you, sweetie, and he loves you so much more than anything else in this world. If he didn't, he wouldn't be doing all this to make sure you have the most amazing life possible. That's why he works so hard. For you." I let out a slow breath, surprised at the lump stuck in my throat, wide like a boulder and as immovable as one. "My dad worked a lot too," I found myself saying, my voice thick and syrupy. "And it was really hard for me to understand at the time why he couldn't be with me instead. And I missed him terribly when he wasn't around."

Roxanne let out a tiny sniff, but I didn't look away from Faith, who was watching me, *me*, as if I had all the answers in the world.

"Now I see just what all his work has done for my life." Where were these words coming from? They couldn't be coming from me because that voice was all warbly and full of tears. "Without all the work he did, I couldn't have traveled the world or seen so many beautiful places." I squeezed her shoulder and tugged at the edge of her braid as I felt a tear spill over down my cheek. "I wouldn't know people like you, and your dad, if mine hadn't worked so hard. And I wish I could thank him for that. For the opportunity I have because of everything he did."

Faith's lip wobbled, and the icy sweep of panic I felt whipped away any lump in my throat. Please, please don't let her cry.

"I'm sorry I made you sad, Miss Allie," she whispered.

"Oh, sweetie, I'm not sad." I gathered her in a hug when she flung herself at me. I could hardly look at Roxanne for fear of what I'd see.

Then her little hand came up and pressed against my cheek. "Look, you're crying."

Well, if I wasn't before, I certainly was after that. My vision blurred dangerously, and I used my free hand to swipe at my face. "Oh, that, it's okay. Just ... I think I've got pancake smoke in my eyes."

I started to stand because this had gone waaaay too deep, way too fast.

When you start with me naked in Luke's bed and end with three women crying in the kitchen, it's time to get the hell out of dodge.

Roxanne cleared her throat, giving me a surreptitious pat on the shoulder. Oh hell no, if she hugged me, I'd lose my shit, fall into her arms, and unload twenty years of repressed grief or something. That one tear that fell was more than I could even process right now.

"Faith, honey, we need to get you to school."

Faith nodded, giving me a smile as I walked toward the slider. "Bye, Miss Allie."

The walk from his deck, down the stairs, and over to mine was short. Yet it felt like a mile.

What the *hell* had just happened?

And why was my first instinct to pick up my phone and call him, make sure it was okay, that I'd done okay with Faith.

I just ... wanted to hear his voice.

Oh, this was bad. This was such a very, very inconvenient time to feel stupid, fluttery, inconvenient, falling in love type of feelings.

In. Con. Ven. Ient.

Then I snorted as I let myself into the lower level of my house. The moment he turned to me last night and saw me waiting for him, I should have known I was falling for him.

Because at that moment, Luke Pierson looked at me in a way no one ever had before.

Before he ever laid a hand on me, kissed me, told me I was perfect, I saw the overwhelming relief, the staggering need on his face to find me there.

And I felt truly beautiful.

Even before that, I should have known. But that didn't matter because when I started feeling it was irrelevant. It didn't change the fact that Luke and I had a list of complications a hundred yards long, literally, that was standing between us. If that was even something he'd want to explore.

What I would do with these pesky, fizzy feelings, I didn't have to decide just yet. They would keep just fine for another day. Or another week, if we kept to the same schedule. I climbed the stairs with a dopey smile on my face because, after my meeting with Joy, I would be able to crawl into my own bed and relive every ache-inducing second of last night. Maybe after a hot bath and a couple of Advil, that is.

Paige was standing behind the couch, phone in hand, when she saw me. "Holy shit, Allie, if you're going to go next door for a sleepover, take your *phone with you.*"

I lifted my eyebrows at the sharp tone of her voice, so I tried to laugh it off. "Aren't really pockets in this outfit, if you know what I mean."

Paige's face went sheet white, and I narrowed my eyes. "What?"

She swallowed nervously, then jerked her chin at the TV. "You have a problem. Ava has been calling you nonstop for the last hour."

The sound was muted, but in a dark, grainy shot behind the reporter's head was a picture of me, tongue shoved in Luke's mouth, and his hand up underneath the jersey I'd been wearing last night.

My entire body started shaking as I read the headline along the top.

Wolves' QB tries out new position with sexy team owner.

That was pretty much when I passed out; Paige's voice the last thing I heard as my vision turned black.

CHAPTER 23
LUKE

WASHINGTON WOLVES

My masseuse, a square-shaped guy named Ivan, who was in his fifties with fists the size of boulders, told me that he'd had to work extra on my shoulders than usual.

No shit.

Waking up with a warm, soft body curled around mine, knowing that I'd need to talk to her tonight and explain why we couldn't do this anymore, was definitely giving me a few knots over my already weighed-down shoulder blades. I left the treatment room feeling loose and warm after almost two hours of Ivan's expertise. It was the only reason I didn't feel more banged up than I did at this point in the season.

The hallway was empty, but heavy footsteps jogging in my direction had me turning.

Jack's face was red and sweaty. "Pierson, holy balls, dude, I've been looking everywhere for you."

I hooked my thumb over my shoulder at the room I'd just exited. "I had a session with Ivan."

His normally carefree face looked grim. "Ava isn't far behind me, but I didn't think you'd want to hear it from her."

I squared my shoulders, sliding into the leader role that came naturally. "What happened?"

"You got your phone on you?" he asked warily.

I shook my head. "It's in my locker. Jack, what *happened?*"

His cheeks puffed out as he expelled a slow hiss of air, and he handed me his phone.

My heart chugged a heavy, awkward beat as my eyes struggled to comprehend what I was seeing in front of me.

I mean, I knew what I was seeing.

I'd been there.

My thumb scrolled, and I sank against the wall. The article blurred, my tongue turned into sand, and I couldn't figure out how I was still standing because my heart was frozen solid in my chest, prickling my veins with ice all the way to my fingertips.

"What the hell?" I whispered.

Oh God, Allie. My stomach turned over dangerously.

"Dude, I never saw this coming," Jack said quietly.

My eyes pinched shut. *Tell me about it*, was what I wanted to say. I should have known. I should have listened to my gut. The moment I realized that it couldn't continue, I knew it was because of shit like this.

The selfish, weak moment I'd allowed myself, touching her before we were inside because I couldn't not touch her, allowing myself just one more night with her, turned out to be me loading the weapon that I'd never want to be aimed at us. At me. At her.

"Pierson," Ava's voice barked from down the hallway. The sharp click-clack of her heels on the linoleum sounded like bullets being fired. "A word, please."

Jack gave me a grim smile, which I wanted to return, but my face was numb. Dread had me moving sluggishly even as my mind raced with feverish intensity, a revolving door that I couldn't jump out of.

Me.

Allie.

What I knew I should have done.

Doing what I wanted instead.

Taking her to my bed.

Waking with her head on my chest, her hand over my heart.

Not wanting to leave her there because I didn't want to leave.

Faith.

How I'd explain this to her because unless I hid her away for a couple of weeks, she'd hear it from some idiot kid at school.

Doing the exact thing I promised myself I'd protect her from since she was a baby—putting her in the middle of a media storm.

My stomach twisted and churned, empty except for a growing pile of disappointment that was sitting like rocks.

I'd failed.

Failed.

Failed.

Funny how just a few hours earlier, I only imagined failure as not winning more games. Not winning another Lombardi trophy. Now, I just wanted to get home to make sure I didn't have a flock of vultures with cameras and microphones camped out in my driveway, shouting questions at my home.

Ava perched her hands on her hips and watched me carefully as I walked into the empty conference room.

"Care to explain how this happened?" she asked as soon as she cleared the doorway.

Instead of answering, I stared at the nondescript table, trying to decide if I would injure my arm if I were to pick it up and hurl it across the room.

Not worth the risk, so I sat on it instead, hanging my hands between my open legs and staring at her for a beat.

"Not really," I told her.

Ava growled under her breath. "Of all the stubborn men on this team, you are without a doubt the biggest pain in my ass. You and Logan. I'd have a better conversation with tree stumps than you two."

I lifted my eyebrows but didn't respond. She wasn't wrong. I had about as much use for PR as I did the media, so I'd never gone out of my way to make her job easier. I didn't know what Logan's problem was, nor did I particularly care.

I was just trying not to break furniture. Or have a heart attack.

My molars crunched together, imagining all the people seeing Allie and me like that. The headline had been something ridiculous, clearly a gossip site.

"What do you want me to say, Ava?" I spoke slowly, holding her eyes, daring her to get pissy with me right now. "We're consenting adults, and some asshole out on a boat got lucky with his timing."

She narrowed her eyes. "So it was a one-time thing?"

Just the fact that she dared ask me about it, that I'd put myself in a position where she was required to in order to do her job had me walking a razor-thin edge of keeping my temper in check. My voice was quiet and dangerous when I answered. "That's none of your business."

"It is my job, though, Pierson," she explained patiently. "You want to screw each other five ways every day, I don't give a shit, but the moment it ends up on every gossip site, every entertainment channel, then I am allowed to ask you questions about it. There is a picture of you groping the new owner, and she is in your yard, wearing your jersey and not much else." With each word, her volume increased, her stance got taller, and I was breathing like a bull ready to charge. "So help me, Pierson, you will make this right somehow. Do you understand me?"

Like a dog trapped into a corner, I felt the hair stand along my back. A visible warning to whoever might approach, but if Ava saw it, she ignored it.

I leaned forward and pinned her with a level look. "I will make this right with the people who are directly involved, and I don't need you to tell me how to do that."

Ava threw her hands up in the air. "Pierson, I am not asking you for much here. Part of your job is dealing with the media, which you have known since you were in college and you had to deal with them. They don't go away simply because you will it to happen. This story will not go away quietly unless you address it head-on and tell them what happened and why they need to move on. You're smart enough to know that, aren't you?"

With a clean, almost audible snap, I felt the muzzle drop.

"And do what?" I yelled. "Go stand in front of a podium and tell them that every Sunday night, I was screwing the new boss because that was the arrangement we made? Do you think that would help *anything?*"

She wasn't amused. "Well, not if you phrase it like that. But how you phrase it is my job. All you have to do is read from the paper and walk off the stage. There will be no questions from the media, which they'll know beforehand."

I laughed under my breath. There was no way I was doing that.

Clearly struggling with her own temper, Ava took a minute and paced the front of the room. The silence had my shoulders sagging. What a giant clusterfuck.

And I could have avoided all of it if I'd paid attention to my instinct. I'd be on my way into a team meeting like usual. Allie would be off doing whatever she normally did on a Monday afternoon.

What did she do on Monday afternoons? I'd never asked her. With shame, I had to own up to the ugly truth of how I'd treated her.

That I couldn't be bothered to ask her something as simple as how she spent her time during the week because I was afraid of knowing too much beyond how her body fit against mine.

That knowledge was dangerous enough, anything beyond that felt like I was tempting fate. Getting in too deep with Allie, trying to imagine how her presence in my life would rock it to its core, was the single most terrifying thing I could've imagined.

Before this.

Now I'd exposed her to the entire world.

Ava spoke, and until I heard her words, I was relieved at the interruption to my thoughts.

"We can say it in a respectful way, okay? Because it's not just about you. She's the owner. We are in a tenuous time right now, Pierson, where workplace indiscretions are being shoved under a microscope of consent and power and manipulation." She smoothed a hand down her hair while I chewed on what she'd said. It tasted bitter as only the truth can.

She was calmer when she spoke again. "You and Allie began a romantic relationship at the beginning of the season, you were neighbors before any of this started, before you had any idea who she was. Leave it at that. Let them infer the rest." She stopped and tipped her head forward. "It could work. If nothing else, the press will eat up a romance between you two."

"Absolutely not."

Her head snapped up. "Are you serious?"

Ava wasn't around when the media feeding frenzy of Cassandra's death was circling around me, their sharp gray fins clear everywhere I looked. She had no idea how absolutely, one hundred percent serious I was about not tossing them bloody chunks of the story just to slake their appetite.

"There's no way to romanticize this," I said in a low voice. "I won't stand up there and say that Allie is my girlfriend because she's not."

"He's right," a quiet voice came from the doorway.

My head snapped around, as did Ava's.

Allie stood inside the entrance to the room, her hair pulled up into a messy bun, her face covered with mirrored sunglasses, her clothes simple and dark.

As if she'd just come from a funeral.

I stood. "Allie ..."

She pulled off her sunglasses, and I felt like I'd been sacked.

Her eyes were rimmed red, her face pale and drawn.

Because of me. I wanted to go to her even though I knew that I shouldn't. And definitely not in front of Ava. For a long, horrible, frozen moment, we just stared at each other.

I'm so sorry, I tried to tell her with my eyes, not willing to give anything away while we had an audience. There were enough people watching us as it was.

Allie blinked, then turned and closed the door behind her.

"Now what?" she asked, her voice scratchy and raw.

At the sound of her voice, I dropped my head into my hands.

Now what indeed?

CHAPTER 24
ALLIE

WASHINGTON WOLVES

I wanted to be mad at him.

I wanted to look at him across that empty conference room and feel angry, self-righteous fire in my veins simply from the sight of him. But I didn't.

What I felt was soul-shriveling embarrassment because now I was being dissected, my old pictures being thrown up on new stories as some sort of proof that the way I'd lived before should have given a hint that this would happen.

The shot of me on the rocks in Aruba was a particular favorite this morning on the entertainment sites, maybe because my arched back and skimpy red bikini made me look more like the kind of person who slept with someone who worked for her. Like it reinforced whatever narrative they'd chosen for the juicy tidbit Luke and I had just handed them.

There was no regret for what I'd done months ago, years ago, because I looked damn good in that bathing suit, but it was that in a matter of weeks, I'd turned into a punchline. Fodder for some late-night TV anchor who wanted a quippy top ten list.

Luke wouldn't be a punchline. *Who could blame him?* was something I read on Twitter before Paige ripped my phone out of my hands

And in his eyes, I could see the devastation. He'd rip down every word, every picture, every comment with his bare hands, if he could.

But it was impossible. This was something he had no control over.

What people said. About him, or me, or us together. What it looked like to the outside world had absolutely no bearing on what it looked like between us.

And even that was subjective because not once had Luke given me verbal clues as to what was going on in his head. Now all I knew was that he was sorry. That he wanted it to be gone, but he had no way to make that happen.

I knew that because that was what I saw on his face when he looked at me with apology screaming from the depths of his dark eyes. I had to close my own eyes against it because as much I wanted to be mad at him over this, my heart was shredded to ribbons in my chest over how I felt that very morning in his bed.

Ava gave me a sympathetic look, but her tone was all business.

"You're in agreement, Allie?"

With my back still against the door, I nodded. My fingers knit together tightly at the pulse of silence that came with my decision. Even if it hurt to hear Luke say that I wasn't his girlfriend, it was the truth. Something I couldn't argue with. To stand in front of the media and try to spin something sweet and innocent would feel like plucking glass shards from my skin.

I wasn't capable of it at the moment. Just convincing Paige to smuggle me into the facility, past a waiting horde of news vans, took enough of my energy. But sitting at home wasn't helping. Amazing how hiding under your covers and crying didn't *actually* make your problems go away.

"Okay," Ava said in a crisp voice. "We'll issue a press release from the front office, saying that you and Luke had private lives outside of the Washington Wolves, and they'll remain private, considering that you're both consenting adults and there's nothing in Luke's contract that prohibits a relationship between the two of you."

It was a scrubbed-clean version of the truth.

The bare facts boiled down to a sanitized version that would provide little for the media to work with.

I hated it.

Neither Luke or I spoke, and Ava glanced at us briefly before directing her attention back to her phone.

"We'll talk to the team at the meeting that starts in"—she looked at the clock on the wall—"twenty minutes. Let them know that outside of these walls, they're strictly on a 'no comment' basis, and if anyone utters a word to the media other than that, they'll get a stiletto up their piss hole."

Her attempt at a joke had me smiling slightly, but Luke only dropped his head down so that I couldn't see his face at all.

The smile fell when I imagined facing the team again. Just like that, it was as if someone lit a match behind my eyes, igniting the short, thin fuse on my emotional leash. What would they think of me?

I cleared my throat, just to make sure I would not cry if I spoke. "Do ... do you need me at that meeting?"

Even though vomiting seemed like an appropriate response to the thought of attending, I'd do it. I'd face them and look in their eyes, accept whatever judgment they'd have for me. Risk being able to put a tangible moment to the loss of respect that I might see aimed back at me.

But Ava shook her head. "No, unless it was something you'd normally attend, I think it's better if you don't. But after we issue this press release, I think it's best if we return to business as usual. On game day, you do whatever you'd normally do." She paused and held my eyes when my breathing increased audibly. "If you're comfortable with it."

I chewed on my bottom lip and risked a glance at Luke. He'd lifted his head and was watching me carefully. A muscle in the side of his jaw popped when he clenched his jaw.

I wish you could've kissed me out in the sun.

The thought came from nowhere, and then it was my turn to drop my head so I could shackle my emotions down with iron chains. When I'd willed the tears back with clenched fists, I looked up again.

"I'll see how I feel on Sunday." It was all I was willing to promise at that point.

She nodded. "Fair enough. Who knows, maybe this will have all blown over by then. Another Kardashian baby might enter the world, and believe me, that'll distract them from just about anything."

"Ava," Luke said, still looking directly at me, "can I get a minute with Allie? I'll be at the meeting before it starts."

If she was surprised, she did an excellent job of hiding it. "Of course." She touched my arm as I moved out of her way. "Let me know if you need anything, okay? I'm an excellent drinking companion."

I gave her a weak smile. "Thanks, I will."

With the click of the door being closed, we were alone.

Luke straightened, wiping a hand over his mouth. "Allie, I'm so sorry about all this."

"It's not your fault," I answered.

He uttered a dry laugh. "Isn't it?"

Our eyes held until my vision blurred.

"Allie, please don't cry," he begged quietly. A single tear dashed down my cheek, and I brushed it away, but I knew by the way his arms popped when he clenched his hands together that he saw it. His brows furrowed over his tortured eyes, but he didn't look away. Like it was his penance, his punishment. I knew what he was remembering. I'd asked him to go inside. But he'd touched me first as though he couldn't not touch me.

But that didn't matter. Even if the only thing they'd seen was us walking into his house, it was damning enough to still make the headlines. Saying that to Luke would make little difference, though.

"I had plans," I heard myself saying.

He took a deep breath and let it out through pursed lips. "What do you mean?"

"I-I wanted to start a foundation." I didn't brush away the tears that fell now. It was pointless. My heart hurt so badly, standing a mere five or six feet away from him, telling him the most personal, secret thing since the day we'd met. Now, when it didn't matter and couldn't make it better, I was showing him the most tender side of my underbelly. The thing that could hurt me the most. "Helping young girls learn to be leaders, how to make an impact in the lives of people around them when they're not given the same opportunities as others. How not to waste the ones they are." My throat thickened, and I had to stop, just so that I didn't unleash some ugly, snot-filled sob. "Faith gave me the idea, actually."

"God, Allie," he said, leaning forward like he would stand.

"This was something I never knew I wanted," I told him, suddenly unsure if I was talking about the foundation, about him, or about us. "But that doesn't matter, you know? All that matters is that one day you wake up and you *do* want it. And now I feel like it was taken away from me," I said angrily. "By some asshole with a zoom lens. I didn't even get the chance to turn it into something amazing. Something special."

"You still *can*," he replied fiercely

I let out a watery laugh, my cheeks wet with tears. "Would you send your daughter to me now? If you didn't know me, know what happened, would you trust me to mentor her?"

His breathing picked up speed. He stood and paced in front of the table, his hands fisted by his side. "Fuck," he yelled, then he kicked out the chair next to the table. It clattered to the side. He glanced at me. "Sorry. I really want to punch the wall or something, but ..." He held up his hands, worth millions, and shrugged helplessly.

"It's okay," I replied because even though it wasn't okay, I really didn't want him to break any bones.

"I knew that night that we couldn't keep doing this," he muttered, pacing again.

I froze. "You what?"

His nostrils flared out as he stopped and stared at me, unseeing. "I left the press conference and knew we had to stop. I'd said too much, that asshole had baited me too easily, and if anyone found out, *shit*, then this is exactly what would happen."

That.

That was the piece I'd been missing in all this. The look in his eye when he turned and saw me sitting by his pool. He'd been preparing to end it.

I looked away and stared at the white wall until my eyes burned from the need to blink, but I would not let another tear fall until I was alone. That was why he brought me into his bed. Why he touched me that way, why he said the things he did because he knew it was the last time.

And I'd woken up, sniffing his pillows like a silly little girl.

Like a suit of armor unfolding, I shored up every side of my aching, tender, torn heart. Slowly, I nodded. With shaking fingers, I reached up and slid my sunglasses back down to cover my sandy, gritty eyes.

It never would have worked. Whatever visions had danced through my head that very morning would never have worked because he was too afraid of something going wrong on his watch. The idea that strangers could peer easily into his personal life was the worst thing Luke could imagine, especially when he couldn't control the outcome for the people surrounding him.

And briefly, I had been one of those people. For a second, it was as if someone reached into my chest and squeezed, wringing every ounce of pain from the realization that he still resided there for me. But he didn't need to know that. Not now.

I'd get over it.

I'd *make* myself get over it.

"You're right," I told him.

He blinked at my even tone. "I am?"

I swept my fingers under my eyes and pinched my cheeks. "Well, not about it being your fault." I looked down at the watch on my wrist. "I was part of this too, and I knew the consequences as well as you did. But I still chose to ignore them."

"Allie," he said slowly, clearly confused at the sudden shift in my mood.

I held up a hand. "No, I'm not mad at you, Luke. It is what it is."

His eyes narrowed. "That's fine, but …"

"Really, there's no need for self-flagellation. It was my choice to wait for you outside half naked." I forced a smile on my face, but it must have looked like a grimace because he made a matching facial expression. "The news will move on. They always do eventually." Luke opened his mouth, but I waved him off. "Don't you have a meeting to get to?"

Instead of leaving, of agreeing, or even looking relieved in the slightest, Luke stared at me as though I was a puzzle he couldn't figure out.

In my chest, my heart hammered wildly because I was hanging on by the most fragile of threads. Staring him full in the face even though he couldn't see my eyes, I knew he'd probably hold me if I went to him, making each frayed edge that much closer to coming undone.

Eventually, he nodded. "Yeah."

"Good luck. Don't let them give you too much shit about it."

"Are you sure you're okay?" he asked, clearly not buying my little act, which was unfortunate because I was pretty sure I just delivered a performance that should make the Academy sit up and take notice.

"I'm okay," I told him.

With one last searching look at the mirrored lenses, he left, and I let out a shaky exhale. Then I sank down onto the floor, tossed my glasses to the floor, and wrapped my arms around my knees, letting the tears fall.

Because it felt like he was pulling my heart behind him with every step, and I'd never get it back.

When Joy found me on the floor fifteen minutes later, she helped me stand, dried my face off with a white handkerchief, and walked me back to where Paige was waiting anxiously.

She took my face in her hands before I left. "Honey, you're a Sutton. And that's no wimpy breed. You take today and cry, but tomorrow, tomorrow you straighten that spine and keep doing your job."

"Okay," I promised her.

Joy gave me a tight hug before Paige folded me into the car.

Tomorrow.

Tomorrow I'd straighten my spine and keep doing my job.

WASHINGTON
WOLVES

"You sure you don't want me to come out there with you?" Paige asked in a quiet voice, her hand on my back. The tunnel out to the field looked eighteen miles long.

I set my shoulders and took a deep breath. "No, it's business as usual. I've survived the past five days, so I can survive one walk-through on that field."

Her face mirrored the apprehension currently warping my stomach into twist ties. You know, those bendy things that hold together bread bags? And if they're wound too much, you couldn't find the beginning of it, couldn't figure out what direction it needed to go in order to smooth everything out correctly.

That was how my entire body felt.

I'd gotten three massages this week, all at the house, because leaving that place was highly overrated. Grocery delivery kept us alive, as did massive amounts of wine, ice cream, and Chinese.

Not in that order.

Though the wine had preceded every major decision Paige and I had made since The Incident, as we'd taken to calling it.

Wine helped us decide that I should pay an exorbitant amount of money to have my stylist come chop my hair above my shoulders from the comfort (and privacy) of my own bathroom. Something fresh and new.

Wine helped us decide that inheriting a football team from your father was stupid, even if I didn't really think it was stupid at all.

Wine helped us decide that Luke was definitely probably most likely hopefully just afraid of how awesome it was between us, so he was choosing the safe route for him and his daughter by maintaining his distance. Not once had I caught a glimpse of him at home. Faith either.

Not a single glimpse.

It almost made it worse. As if he hadn't existed at all.

By Friday, I'd had to tell wine we were breaking up for a few days because I needed to not be hungover for the game on Sunday. First game since The Incident, at home, against our biggest division rival, and the team was currently ahead of us by one game in the division standings.

Even without The Incident, it would be a tense game. Joy told me that they were known for a lot of things, in addition to winning games this year. Trash talk. Some questionable plays. Fans so violently passionate for their team that they showed up looking like warriors from a bygone era, all mildly terrifying if you didn't know what to expect.

I'd stayed out of the office all week, and I'd woken up Sunday morning knowing that I needed to be at the game. Business as usual. I'd walk the field during warm-ups because that was what I'd normally do. I'd greet the team, some of whom had reached out via text or email to let me know they had my back, and I'd watch from the safety of my luxury suite.

Paige, who'd been by my side all week, doing whatever I needed her to do, did not want me to go out there. Joy thought it would be good for me. Good for the team.

She'd thrown that last gem in there, probably knowing it would smack the hell out of my cowardice and force me back into the land of the living.

Business as usual.

I could do this. Because it was a home game, I just had one security guard walk with me, a menacing looking man with eyes that never stopped scanning and a neck the size of my entire body. I think his name was Rico, but I also wasn't positive he could speak, so I didn't ask.

With one last concerned look at the field, where we could hear the thump of music, the laughter of the players, and fans shuffling around vying for autographs, Paige squeezed my hand. "Well, I won't be far if you need me to rough anyone up."

Rico cleared his throat, and I tried not to laugh. I gave my friend a brief hug. "It's fine. I don't feel unsafe, I just feel ..." I searched for the right word. "Exposed. And I hate that."

Her eyes were sad. "That'll fade eventually. Just, just go out there, don't look at anyone other than your players, do your thing, and we'll go order a fantastic Bloody Mary in your suite, okay?"

I nodded. "Okay."

As I walked down the tunnel, I smoothed a hand down the front of my white Wolves tank top. I'd covered it with a tailored black blazer and kept my hair pinned back from my face. Instead of heels, which were a giant pain in the ass on the field, I went with plain white Keds.

Business as usual.

No one would be dissecting my outfit. No one would care that I was out there. I repeated it over and over like a prayer.

Business as usual.

The retractable roof was open, allowing the sun to stream in along with a slow, cool October breeze. I kept my chin up and my eyes straight forward as I exited the tunnel, and like he was waiting for me, Dayvon slid in front of me, dancing through his warm-up.

I couldn't help but smile when he extended his elbow to me and kept singing with whatever pop song was playing. I didn't recognize it, but that wasn't surprising.

"Thank you," I told him under my breath, folding my hand around his massive arm.

"Girl, no thanks necessary." He glanced at me out the corner of his eye. "You're probably the reason he was in such a damn good mood those few weeks. Boy needed to relax a bit."

It felt wrong to laugh but also so, so good. So sweetly relieving, along with the sun, the fresh air, knowing that the hardest part—walking out here at all—was over.

He walked with me as the guys stood from their stretches, one by one smiling at me, giving me high fives, a couple of hugs, every single one greeting me with respect, with purpose, and letting me know I had their support.

Jack winked at me before he took off running to catch a ball thrown by, yep, Luke. When I glanced his direction, his head was down, listening to whatever his QB coach was telling him. Now that was one thing I hadn't considered. Eyes would definitely be watching us for that.

As much as I didn't want to, I allowed my eyes to scan the sidelines, where all the cameras lined up and all the reporters would stand during the game. Half of those cameras were already trained directly on me.

My heart thudded uncomfortably, which made me tighten my hand on Dayvon's arm.

From behind me, Jack jogged up, tossing the ball to someone on the field staff before he nudged me with his shoulder.

"Miss Sutton," he said with a wide grin. "How you doin' today?"

I shrugged, feeling completely overwhelmed with the wide swing of my emotions. How was it possible to feel so much in such a short span of time?

"Oh," I told him airily, "just peachy."

We smiled at each other as someone whistled sharply to gain our attention from the other side of the field. Jack's smile fell instantly, and Dayvon turned me so that I was behind him when I heard one of the opposing players yell out.

"Y'all got any openings for a guy like me?"

I looked around Dayvon's shoulder and saw the guy stretching his thick arms over his head. He had his eyes pinned on me and a wicked smile on his face.

"Why don't you worry about your own damn team," Dayvon told him firmly.

Whoever he was, the number twenty-two in faded black on his T-shirt, ignored Dayvon and kept his eyes in my direction, sliding them down my body. "You sure, baby? You're the boss, right? You could bring me over for some fun."

Rico grabbed my arm and pulled me from Dayvon just as Jack started marching forward.

"What'd you say, Marks?"

He stuck his tongue out and waggled it. "You heard me just fine, rookie. So did she."

"You wanna repeat that, asshole?" he yelled, his arms spread wide. "Come on, you get in my face and say that again."

My skin felt tight and cold, my fingers clammy and useless as I was walked back to the tunnel.

Dayvon used both hands to hold Jack back, speaking to him low enough that I couldn't hear him over the blood roaring in my ears. Luke strode over, pinning me with one brief, loaded look before he glanced at Rico with a nod.

Then he stepped next to Jack, telling him to calm down. The other player was pulled back by his own teammates, which was probably wise since half of the Wolves lineup was making their way over to Jack, who was still breathing like a bull.

My heart hurt. It was the only way I could describe it. I felt beat up. Tired. Exhausted to the marrow of my bones.

Paige rushed toward me. "Oh my gosh, Allie, what did that asshole say?"

"Nothing worth repeating." I rubbed my hands up and down my arms, suddenly cold. "Can we just go up? I think I need that Bloody Mary."

_____

Luke

If someone didn't muzzle Marks, someone would end up bleeding on the field. And it wouldn't be anyone from the Wolves.

With two minutes left in the game, we'd heard just about everything come out of his giant, idiotic, never-silent mouth, and by some miracle, every member of our team had kept their hands off his throat.

The chippy atmosphere on the field made me feel jittery, unable to hold still.

I barked plays louder than usual, the words snarling out of my mouth like my jaws could barely hold on to them.

In front of me, Gomez was snapping the ball faster and harder, blade-straight into my waiting hands. My throws were instant, slicing the air so that their defensive line didn't have a chance in hell of touching me. My O-line was blocking like they were made of cement, nothing was coming through them.

Tackles were rougher.

Catches snatched from the air with furious accuracy.

If there was anything, *anything*, good about all the trash talk coming from him, unchecked by his teammates or coaches, it was that he had us playing with an angry, almost violent precision. The only thing keeping us from throwing down, fifty guys against one, was the fact that we were winning. That we were kicking their ass.

But did that shut him up?

Not a chance in hell.

"I wanna break that dude's arms," Jack growled next to me in the huddle. This came right after he jogged backward after Jack ran a ten-yard route for first down, taunting him in a singsong voice after he took Jack to the turf.

Me fucking too. That was what I wanted to say. But no one needed to be incited right now.

"Come on," I barked. "First down, second down, first down. We aren't giving those assholes a chance to stop us on third, okay? We shut him up by winning."

Everyone nodded, clenching and unclenching fists, punching their pads just to release some of the spitting, fiery testosterone that had us practically shaking.

And I'd never wanted to win a game so badly.

It was taking every ounce of my mental and physical discipline not to march up to him, rip his helmet off, and bash his teeth in with it, which was harder than I'd expected. My nerves were on their last white-knuckled grip on the edge of a wet cliff.

All week, I'd shut out the noise. The moment I walked from the conference room, the moment I saw her determination to make it less than it was, I'd slapped my blinders on with steady hands, met my teammates' eyes, and told them that now was the time to prove we were a team. If they had something to say about it, they could do it now or keep their mouths shut.

I'd been met with silence.

Each day was survived with a single-minded intensity that I hadn't felt in a long time. I practiced each day with an inflexible, iron-wrapped stubbornness, working my muscles until I was soaked with sweat and well past the point of exhaustion. I watched film late after I'd tucked in Faith, which served as a perfect distraction to what had happened, to how I felt like that biggest asshole on the planet.

And now this clown was poking at the bruise, and if he kept it up, I'd rip his finger off and shove it down his throat.

"Oooooh, I see her up there, Pierson. You got that shit all nice and warmed up for me?" Marks called out.

I clenched my jaw and refused to look at him. Even though in my head, I was imagining how many ways I could break a man's arm.

"Loudmouth son of a bitch," Gomez muttered under his breath, popping his knuckles.

I smacked the side of his helmet. "Let's go."

We lined up, the home crowd quieted, my receivers split left and right, but Marks didn't follow Jack as he normally would as the corner. Over the top my O-line, his D-line, he weaved back and forth as I called my play, like a snake uncoiling out of a basket. They were lining up to blitz, to rush straight at me with everything they had. His eyes, blue and cold and fixed on me, never blinked. Not once.

My fingers flexed.

"Easy ninety-four," I yelled, pointing at Marks so that Ryan, my left tackle, saw him and would protect my blind side. "Easy ninety-four. Hut!"

Snap.

Ball in hand.

Crowd roared.

I jogged back a few steps, pulled my arm back, and hefted it twenty yards where my tight end Rateliff would be running his fade route.

From the corner of my eye, as the ball sailed perfectly in a tight spiral through the air, I saw Marks lower his helmet, spin around Ryan, and launch at me. I tried to drop back, but the top of his helmet hit the front of mine, leveling me in an instant.

"Hell yeah," he roared in my face, spit hitting my skin. Before he got up, he gripped the front of my facemask and yanked my head closer. I shoved at him, but he was holding too tightly. "She like to be on top too, Pierson? I bet she does."

I was just about to punch him in the kidneys when he was yanked off by Gomez, who pushed Marks a bit harder than he should have. Gomez reached a hand out to help me up. Marks danced in front of me while I struggled to control the furious drumbeat of my heart screaming at me to hurt, hurt, hurt.

"You like being down there?" he taunted, unconcerned with the flag just thrown on his completely illegal hit or the official running over to calm him down. "I bet she liked being down there too. I'll make that bitch choke on it when I get a hold of her."

My entire body froze, and my vision sliced to one spot in the entire arena, nothing else. No one else. No coaches or teammates, no reporters, no cameras, no fans, nothing but me and him and the roar that came out of my mouth.

I launched at him, both hands on the base of his helmet, which I ripped off as I took him down to the field.

He punched my side as my teammates and his descended on us like a swarm of angry bees.

There were no whistles, no flags, no penalties in my head.

Just pure, hot rage. A beast unleashed, I wanted nothing more than to take every word he'd thrown into the air and shove them back where no one could see them, no one could hear them, just in case they made it up to where she sat, hiding from the eyes that had been on her all week.

My arm cocked back, my balled-up fist cracked against his nose once, twice, a sickening, gratifying snap of bone and rush of blood against my hand, and we rolled once, he caught the side of my helmet with his fist just before someone ripped us apart.

"Hey, get your shit together, Pierson," Coach screamed in my face, both hands fisted in my jersey while referees tried to untangle the mess of shoving and yelling and swearing in the mass of uniforms around us. "You just broke his nose, you idiot."

My chest was heaving, my fist throbbing, and as my blood red vision cleared, I heard the referee say that both Marks and I were ejected from the game. The crowd didn't boo, though. Up on the giant screens, they showed a replay of his mouth moving, then me ripping his helmet off, followed by a live shot of him with a balled-up, blood-soaked towel against his nose.

The fans roared.

With a grim smile, I accepted the back slaps of my teammates as I walked down the tunnel and off the field so that my backup could kneel on the last series, finalizing the win.

I'd pay for it. Financially, for sure, when the league fined me. When I had to explain to Faith why Daddy got into a fight with another player. But as I showered, ignored reporters, listened to

Coach give his post-game speech, I couldn't bring myself to have the slightest pang of misgiving over what I'd done.

At that moment, after *hours* of hearing him talk about her, talk about us, turn it into something ugly, and her into some sort of empty vessel, I had to reckon with the truth that defending Allie's honor was more important than whatever consequences were headed my way. Maybe she hadn't seen it. Maybe she'd only catch a highlight and think that I was reacting to a shady late hit.

But as my car turned the corner to home, hours after I broke Marks's nose, I saw the moving van in front of Allie's house.

She'd seen. She'd definitely seen.

And now she was running away.

CHAPTER 26
ALLIE

"Here's what I can't figure out," Paige said around a mouthful of ice cream.

I twisted my spoon in the bottom of my white bowl, eyes staring out at the sound, which was easy because my father's house in Edmonds had been built with panoramic views of water and trees and white-capped mountain peaks. "What's that?" I asked.

"Why did he stay here?" She glanced around. "This house is massive. It was just him, right? He never remarried?"

Snuggling into the deep couch cushions, I sighed. "Nope. Just him."

It wasn't a truth that made me feel guilty anymore.

This big house, the one I'd been brought home from the hospital to, was indeed massive. Over five thousand square feet of beautifully decorated, perfectly impersonal space that I could now use as my own hideout. I'd like to think that my father would be okay with it, no matter what drove me there in the middle of the night.

It wasn't until we woke late that morning, stumbling down the hallway until we found a coffee machine buried in a cupboard, that Paige had been treated to the multi-million-dollar views from my childhood home.

What the property lacked in acreage, it made up for in endless stretches of sapphire blue water, diamond dots over the surface from the sun reflecting off it. The tall spears of trees were the only thing that interrupted the view between us and the mountains in the distance.

It was impossibly beautiful.

And I could hardly pay attention to it.

Like a twitch I couldn't stop, an itch under my skin that never went away, I slid my phone over and tapped on the YouTube app. As it had been since yesterday, the clip of the on-field fight was right on top. I kept the sound off because if Paige had any idea how many times I'd watched it in the past twenty-seven hours, she'd stab the screen out with her ice cream spoon.

Every action played out in my head before a single image moved on the screen. I'd watched it so many times, to affirm my decision, remind myself what was at stake, and maybe, sort of, because it gave me a sick sense of satisfaction to see Marks bleed his way off the field courtesy of Luke.

The players lined up.

Marks swayed in place, almost like he was dancing, straight across from Luke. Others were in motion, but once the ball was snapped, those were the only two I watched. Marks held where he was until the ball was in the air, then he lowered his head like a bull and charged.

One spin around the tackle, Luke tried to duck out of his path, and boom. They were down.

That was when my stomach curled around uncomfortably because he was clearly mouthing off as he held Luke down on the field. Even when they were separated, Luke standing up, Marks never got out of his face.

The whistles were blowing, a bright yellow flag fluttered to the ground, and everything stilled. Or just Luke. The way he held his body reminded me of how the air took on a strange, electric sort of pause before a tornado, with yellow clouds and an unnatural sort of prickle in the air.

A warning. It was a warning.

Even though I wanted to look away, I didn't.

He launched at Marks, ripping his helmet off as they tumbled to the ground. His fist smashed into Marks's face once, twice, before they rolled and were separated. They got lost in the shuffle, in the messy shoving and pushing and yelling that erupted on the field from both sides.

"I like the lake house better," Paige said quietly, interrupting my hundredth viewing. As though I was a guilty child caught with her hand in the cookie jar, I locked my phone screen and turned it over.

"Me too," I agreed. Looking around, I didn't see any mark of my father. Not in any of it. The master bedroom, large and slightly stale, with a view fit for a king, still sat empty. I'd chosen a guest room down the hall, as had Paige.

"Why couldn't we stay there again?"

I cut her a dry look. "Seriously?"

Paige batted her eyelashes. I hated how long they were. "Seriously. If you have to go this far to avoid him ..." She tapped a finger against her chin. "I mean, it's not like you saw him at all last week. Me thinks you're running scared."

My fingers fairly itched to pull up the replay again. See Luke's grimly satisfied smile as he walked off the field. I wanted to kiss that smile off his face, taste it with my tongue, see if it transferred that same bloodthirsty satisfaction into my body as I imagined it would.

"That guy, Marks," I explained. "It's like his sole purpose was to put on display exactly how much of a distraction I truly am. I gave him every piece of ammunition." I shook my head. "Or Luke and I did. I know it's not just my fault."

"Damn right, it's not," Paige mumbled around her spoon.

"I just need to let them finish the season without getting in the way."

"You weren't in the way before," she insisted.

I lifted an eyebrow.

"Whatever. I still think the fight was a good thing."

"How do you figure?" I held up a hand. "Look how easily that guy got under Luke's skin. He's known for being level-headed. The one who keeps the guys in check on the field when things get out of hand. He can't start breaking noses when someone spouts off about his Sunday night booty call with me," I said just a touch too bitterly.

Paige whistled under her breath. "Yeah, okay, we can take that route if you'd like."

When she cracked her knuckles, I rolled my eyes.

Paige faced me from her corner of the massive L-shaped couch. "If Luke is known for being level-headed, then obviously you're under his skin too. He wouldn't start fights on the field for a"—she made a disgusted face—"Sunday night booty call."

If I'd watched that video a hundred times in the last day, then I'd relived our conversation in the conference room a thousand. If I could dissect each inch of his handsome face, decipher what each bend of his brow meant, why his broad, strong shoulders seemed so weighted down, maybe I could ...

No.

I didn't need to dissect anything.

Luke was a leader even if I was the boss. And he'd failed me. Or at least in his mind, he'd failed me. No matter what was written on his face, in his shoulders, the grim set of his mouth, or what fights he got into, it had to be rooted in that failure.

"Okay, fine," I conceded. "Maybe he looked at me as more than a booty call. But it doesn't matter."

Paige clapped her hands together. "You're right. It doesn't."

I narrowed my eyes at her cheery response.

She shrugged. "What? You've given zero indication that you want more than that from him, so why would it? You'll stay here until the season ends, gain much-needed space from all that chaos, and then next season, you two can smile when you pass each other in the hall, and it'll be professional and friendly and polite. You'll co-exist." She lifted an imperious, perfectly arched auburn eyebrow. "Right?"

I must have looked as grumpy as I felt. "I hate you," I muttered.

Paige laughed.

There was a large pillow wedged under my elbow, and I yanked it out so I could wrap my arms around it. In lieu of a dog or a man to cuddle with, it would have to do.

"I mean," Paige continued, "the reason it's neither here nor there why he started that fight is because you don't want to pursue a relationship with him, *right*?"

"You're seriously going to make me say it?"

"Yes," she cried. "Come on. I've never seen you like this over a guy. It's about damn time."

"For what? Have another man in my life willing to set me aside because I'm too much of a complication?" A tear slid hot down my cheek, and Paige's face fell instantly. "My dad shipped me away to boarding school because he had no idea what to do with me when it was just the two of us."

She scooted across the couch so she was closer to me. "Honey, I'm sorry, I didn't mean to bring up a sore subject."

I sniffed and rubbed at the aching spot behind my breastbone. "It's okay. I don't think I even made the connection until just now." I looked around. "I think it's being in this house."

"That makes sense." Her hand rubbed my knee.

"I know my father loved me, but he just didn't know how to make a life for me that didn't completely interrupt his in the process." I pinched the bridge of my nose to stem more rising tears, then spoke quietly. "I want someone who's willing to fight for me."

"Just not ... like ... literally fight because, Allie girl, Luke definitely already did that."

I smiled. "No, I'm not talking literally, but I am glad he did that, too."

"I didn't think that's what you meant."

"I want," I whispered, staring up at the ceiling, "I want someone who doesn't sit back and look at how the landscape of their life will change by adding me into it and weigh whether I'm worth the change. I want them to pull me into it with both hands and make it something new without a second thought."

Paige laid her head on my shoulder. "You deserve that. A hundred times over."

I stopped fighting the tears because more than anything, I wanted to be saying this to Luke. I wanted him to hear the words scrawled over my bruised heart, the piece of me that missed him most of all.

"I want someone who loves me so much that they can't stand the idea of us hiding in the shadows. I want them to love me so much that all the ugly and harsh that can come with the light doesn't bother them because we'd be facing it together." I exhaled a small sob. "I don't want to beg for that."

"Do you feel like you were with him?"

One more tear slid down the side of my face unchecked until it disappeared into my hairline. "No. It felt ... good. It felt right."

I missed him. With Luke, it wasn't so much that I felt like a different person. I'd just felt like a stronger, more powerful version of who I already was. Now, I was just willing to admit my own worth, know that I was worth more than one night a week.

He was too, for that matter. He just wasn't at a place where he wanted the risk. And I wouldn't be anyone's safety net, conveniently placed and safe to fall into.

I wanted to be the wild, the free fall, the leap off a cliff into something exhilarating.

Eventually, I'd be able to be in the same room as him and not see how he was that for me even if it was for a brief time.

"So you're like, in love with him, huh?" Paige asked quietly.

I chewed the inside of my cheek. I didn't want to cry anymore. Falling in love was supposed to be good, wasn't it? Not something that made you cry, but I guess that was what happened when you tumbled on the same day that someone set a bomb off in your personal life.

But was I in love with Luke Pierson?

Yeah.

It was pretty much the only reason all this would make me so miserable because sitting on a strange couch in the house I grew up in, I wasn't thinking about the embarrassment anymore. I wasn't thinking about who'd seen what, or if the fans lost respect for me. I was thinking about him.

"Does it matter?" I asked Paige. Or the universe. Or whoever might be listening.

She didn't answer. No one did. It sure would have been nice if a booming voice told me what to do. But there was no one. Just me, trying to figure out what the hell came next.

"What are you gonna do?"

"Besides go sleep for two days?"

"Yup."

My head leaned against hers, and as she had all week, she propped me up. Kept me sane. "I'll do my job. Let him do his. Eventually, it won't hurt so much."

I almost believed it.

CHAPTER 27
LUKE

WASHINGTON WOLVES

When you've built your entire career on your ability to pick up on the slightest change in the environment around you, something slightly annoying happened. You couldn't shut it off.

Even when I wasn't on the field with the clock running, I noticed the people around me. How they were standing. Whether they were carrying their weight differently after a particularly brutal game. After Jack injured his knee his rookie season, I found myself watching the way he walked for two solid months. It drove me crazy, but long ago, I'd accepted it as a part of me. Part of what made me good at my job.

It was also why I didn't think myself insane for studying Allie the way I did for the next three weeks.

In my head, I told myself it was because I barely saw her. The house next to mine was empty and quiet, no lights in windows or terrible music coming from her little bright blue speaker that always accompanied her outside. The first week after my fight with Marks, I saw her twice, brief glimpses down hallways and through open doorways.

We won on the road that first week, cementing our division

lead by two games. She didn't join the team for the first time all season.

The second week, I noticed that her hair was shorter. The cheekbones on her face were a bit more pronounced as though maybe she hadn't been eating enough. If she saw me, if she noticed me, she gave me absolutely no indication of it.

Not in the hitch of her breath, a pause in whatever conversation she was having, no flick of her eyes in my direction.

The third week, we won at home by one point. The cameras panned to her suite, and I saw her high-fiving fans in the row in front of hers. It was the only time I saw her on game day. She'd taken a hiatus from doing her pre-game walk on the field, and none of us could blame her. I'd have stopped too.

They moved the cameras away before I could see her face fully, gauge if she looked well. If she looked happy.

Not once in three weeks did I see her eyes unless her face was in profile.

It did weird things to my head when I found myself wondering things like were they still the same color or had I imagined it?

I saw the slight upturn in her straight, perfect nose. I saw the stubborn angle of her delicate jaw. The curve of her smile, to varying degrees, depending on who she was speaking to. Those were things I saw. But not her eyes. And I hated that I couldn't use them to know what she was thinking. How she was feeling.

"Are you sure you don't know where she's living, Daddy?" Faith asked me on week three. Standing at the hedge, which was taller than her, she looked so sad that I almost lied, almost told her that Allie would be back soon, just to see her smile about it.

"I think she's living in the house she grew up in, turbo."

Faith sighed and spun back around to me. It was Tuesday, our day off during game week. I'd already lifted for the day, so I would spend the rest of the afternoon with her before watching film once she was tucked into bed.

"It was *so fun* to have her here that one morning," she said between twirls. I'd heard this twenty-two times in the past three weeks. "She's nice. And doesn't treat me like a baby."

Not being treated like a baby was a big deal to a six-year-old. My initial panic at being told that Allie had walked out of my room during their morning pancakes had been short-lived because apparently, she handled it like a champ.

Besides, I couldn't really be mad. In my sex-clouded brain, I'd completely forgotten to double-check with my mom that they wouldn't be stopping by the house before school that day.

"And," Faith continued like she was trying to convince me of something, "Grandma really liked her."

I'd also heard that a few times, from the direction of the woman who gave birth to me. My dad, as usual, had stayed stoically silent, content to let Mom voice their joint opinion. Maybe if I'd been married for forty-two years, I would do the same thing.

Better head on her shoulders than most of the men I know, were the precise words my mom had used, *including my idiot son who can't figure out what's right in front of him.*

That was what she didn't understand. What none of them could understand even if I'd been capable of explaining it to them. My life was controlled chaos, at all times.

I had a daughter who fell off playgrounds and in the next instant, had a broken arm, even though I was ten feet away from her, watching her every move.

I had a football team that looked to me to lead them, to see things they didn't see on the field, and predict outcomes like we had a chess set in front of us, carefully carved pieces that could be moved at will.

A coach who threatened me within an inch of my life if I ever started another fight on the field again.

My job would've consumed my life if it wasn't for Faith, who made me pay attention to some of the things I'd normally miss. The tiny purple flowers that were growing along the east side of our house that someone else had planted. The fairies planted them, according to her. She got what was left of me after meetings and weights and notes and game plans and hours of film, and it still didn't feel like I was giving her enough.

How could I possibly set any more pieces aside for another person?

I had to grit my teeth as I stared at the pool. Where she'd waited for me. For the first time in my life, I'd experienced that strange dichotomy that I'd heard talked about.

Two sides of the same coin.

Peace and fire.

Heat and calm.

She'd given me both, which seemed impossible.

I rubbed at my forehead when I felt my thoughts drifting away from Faith. This was why I couldn't even contemplate it. How could I possibly *try* to make a regular relationship work? Keeping her in a neat, small box of time hadn't felt like it was working. Even after only a few weeks of that, she'd pushed the edges open until I felt powerless against what I wanted from her, what I wanted out of my time with her. Powerless against wanting more time with her.

My phone buzzed next to me, and I saw a text on my lock screen.

Dayvon: Open up. I'm at the front door with leftovers

I shook my head. "Faith, run around the front and grab Mr. Dayvon. He's here with food."

She squealed and took off, a flurry of pink ruffles and long brown hair. When he came around the side of the house, she was up on his back, chattering happily in his ear. Something made him let out a booming laugh, and I found myself smiling.

"What'd you bring me?"

With the hand not bracing my daughter's slight form, he held up a large paper bag. "Tamales. Monique said you looked scrawny last week."

When he was closer, he tossed the bag, and I caught it. Dayvon used his massive paws to heft Faith up on his cement beam shoulders, where she screamed happily and grabbed him around the face to hold on.

I opened the bag and inhaled gratefully. They'd be my dinner. Probably tomorrow night too. While I rolled the seams of the bag over into tight edges and set it on the lawn, I watched Dayvon make my daughter laugh. He had four boys of his own, the youngest only a couple of years older than Faith.

He and Monique got married right out of college, a ceremony I'd attended as one of his rookie year teammates since we'd entered the draft at the same time. He'd gone in the first round, and I was a couple of rounds later, needing to grow into my talent a bit more.

The ring on his finger glinted brightly in the sun, and I found myself staring at it.

"Does she get stressed during the season?" I heard myself ask him.

Without any further clarification of who I was asking about, Dayvon shook his head. "Nah. We dated all through college too, man. By the time I hit the pros, she knew what she was getting into." With a roar, he dipped forward so he could deposit Faith safely on the grass. "Why don't you go draw Miss Monique a pretty picture, baby girl? She'd love that."

"Okay!" Faith ran off into the house.

Sitting heavily in the chair next to me, Dayvon tipped his head back and sighed contentedly. "Man, I need a place on the water like this."

"Yeah," I drawled, "just watch out for assholes on boats with cameras."

He scratched the side of his face and chuckled. "No shit." Then he cut me a sideways look. "Haven't seen much of her lately."

Quite stubbornly, I refused to look at her house. "Same here. I think she moved into Robert's house for a bit."

"Scare her off, did ya?"

I rolled my eyes. "I don't have time for a woman. You know that."

Dayvon tipped his head back, hooting loudly. His whole chest shook from the force of his laughter. When I crossed my arms over my middle and said nothing, he laughed even harder. He used the edge of his thumb to wipe at the skin underneath his eyes.

"Oh, man," he yelled. "That's some funny shit."

"I'm not trying to be funny."

"No, I don't think you are." He stared at the lake, shaking his head. "You think she's stupid, is that it?"

"What?" I sat up. "I never said that. No," I insisted. "Of course, I don't think she's stupid."

"So then don't blame shit that has nothing to do with why you're sitting here alone and why she's off in that house when she probably wants to be here." He clucked his tongue like a chicken.

So I told him that was exactly what he sounded like.

"You *need* a mother hen, son," he said. "If Monique was here, she'd smack you so hard."

I stayed stubbornly silent.

"Tell me this," he said. "And I won't ask details because God knows I like Allie too much to know that shit about her, but when you were with her, how'd you feel?" When I gave him a skeptical look, he held up his hands. "What? I've been married for twelve years. I know how to talk about feelings, man. Not my problem if you don't. Just, don't answer if you don't want to. But without all the extra noise, just you and her, what was it like?"

Effortless.

Impossible to describe.

Instinctive.

Nothing we'd done made me second-guess myself, not until the moment everything went wrong at the press conference.

"Doesn't your ma ask you about stuff like this?" he asked.

I shook my head. "We weren't the family who shared our emotions. It was more like ..." I thought for a minute about my childhood, college, when Cassandra died, and my parents moved out here to help with Faith, so I wasn't paying strangers to help raise her. "We showed our love by showing up. We didn't need to put the words on it like pretty labels. You just be there."

Dayvon nodded slowly. "I feel you."

In my seat, I shifted slightly. "What does that have to do with anything?"

"Emotional intelligence of a rock, man," he muttered up at the sky. "I think it wouldn't matter if you woke up with little hearts floating around your big ole head, you still wouldn't admit what you feel."

"That's not true." I scoffed. "It just feels ... impossible, I guess. Everyone would be watching us."

"So what?"

Dayvon leaned forward. "Let's play a game real quick. Don't think too hard, just say the first thing that comes to your head. Was your life better with her in it?"

Yes.

My mouth stayed zipped shut.

"Do you miss her?"

Hell yes.

"How many times have you seen her in the past few weeks?"

Twelve.

A tease, just a taste, when I wanted to gorge endlessly. In the silence, I could feel my heart thudding uncomfortably, which was probably exactly what the asshole wanted.

He must have seen something on my face because he chuckled under his breath.

"Do you trust her? Did she put constraints on your time? Complain about what you do? My guess is that I know the answer to every single one of those questions." He sighed when I finally looked over at him. "Man, doing what we do? Do you know how hard it is to find a woman who's got the strength to put up with the work and the commitment? I don't care what anyone says, what they have to do is harder. So much harder. Monique is the strongest person I've ever met in my entire life, but don't you dare tell my ma that if you ever meet her."

I laughed.

He wasn't done, though. "You want to know why I've never once been tempted to cheat on my wife when most guys wouldn't think twice? Because I don't want to. There ain't nothing out there that's better than what I've got at home. No one who could ever compare. Maybe your family defines love as showing up, but I think it's that I know there's nothing better. No one better than her for me. I could see a thousand women. I don't care what they look like, or what they promise me, there's nothing better out there for me than Monique. And I trust that like I trust nothing else in this world."

I hung my head down, my arms dangling between my legs while I struggled to breathe.

"So I don't know why you're fighting against it so hard because the way I see it, you've been a grumpy pain in the ass the past few weeks for a reason. You're working yourself too hard because you can't get her out of your head, right?"

I pushed my tongue into the side of my cheek.

"It can't be that easy, can it?" I asked, voice rough and rusty and coming from somewhere deep in my chest. A part of my body I didn't normally speak from. It grew into something bigger, wider, too much to be contained within my skin.

Could I imagine someone better for me than Allie?

Hell no.

I'd never been tempted by anyone until her. I'd never come close to accepting the slightest risk of upsetting my life until her. And she hadn't upset it at all.

She'd fit into it.

Into me.

"Holy shit," I breathed uncomfortably. My ribs pinched until I had to suck in a deep, cleansing breath through my nose. Everything rearranged inside me to make room. But my brain, always logical, always reacting to what was presented in front of me, rattled and churned to life slowly as I realized the utterly, stupidly transparent truth of what I refused to admit. "It's that easy, isn't it?"

He leaned back, stretching his long legs in front of him, his hands folded over his stomach. The picture of smug satisfaction. "Yup."

I glanced at him. "What do you get out of this little sermon?"

"My wife bet me I wouldn't be able to get you to admit it. I get the satisfaction of being right, my friend."

Faith came running out of the house and thrust a paper filled with pink and purple stickers and scribbles in every color of the rainbow. "Do you think she'll like it?"

"Aww, yeah, I do. I bet she'll put it right on the front of our fridge, baby."

I patted my lap, and Faith hopped up, snuggling into my side. "That's really pretty, turbo. Good job."

"What are you gonna do about it?" Dayvon asked.

I breathed in the soft scent of Faith's hair. "Not sure yet."

He grinned. "Make it big. Women like that."

"About what?" Faith asked, smacking a kiss on my cheek.

Over her head, Dayvon and I shared a look. "Well, I don't have a plan yet, but do you think I should figure out a way that we could see Allie more? I know you miss her."

"Yes," she screeched into my ear, and I winced. "Can she come over again? Please, please, please?"

"We'll see," I told her, unwilling to promise anything more.

Because first, I had to see if she'd even hear me out.

That was what I knew I had to do and just pray she didn't kill me for it.

WASHINGTON
WOLVES

"Explain to me why we're here so early again?" I asked Paige, who hustled us into my suite well over an hour before kickoff.

I mean, yes, I understood the significance of playing on Monday night. Ratings were higher, games were usually more important, and it was our first one all year. Because of everything that had happened, and it being a division game in the latter half of the season, there was a lot riding on it.

"I, umm, just really wanted to get comfy." She wouldn't look me in the eye. Against one wall, there was a massive floor-to-ceiling entertainment center with large flat screen TV mounted against the wall and surrounded by built-in bookcases. "If you were a remote, where would you be hiding?"

From the mahogany coffee table, I handed her the remote she needed. "Were you day drinking again?"

"It was touch and go there for a couple of hours," she muttered. "But no."

"What is going on?"

Outside the box and the relative privacy of the glass doors leading out to our two rows of cushioned seats, I could hear muffled music. The players were stretching, and I tried not to stare down at them, so small on the bright green grass. I tried not to pick out where Luke was tossing the ball to someone else in tight pants and a T-shirt.

Paige didn't answer, fumbling with the remotes and squinting at the TV when the guide appeared. "Finally, good grief."

"Paige," I huffed, crossing my arms over my black long-sleeve t-shirt. Joy had picked out the fitted V-neck style from the pro shop, something new we'd gotten in last week because she said it looked good on me. Written down one sleeve was *Washington* and along the other was *Wolves*. Over my heart was the red, black, and white logo of the howling beast. Briefly, I laid my hand over it, the silly little drawing that had become so ridiculously dear to me in such a short time.

"There," she breathed when she found the Monday Night Football countdown that was currently being filmed on the very field we looked down on.

"Seriously?" I asked her. "We're *at the game*, so why do we need to watch this?"

For the first time since we got in the car, she cut me an apprehensive look. "I just ... really want to watch Jon Gruden's interview. I love his Monday night interviews."

"Since *when*?"

"Since now."

I shook my head and picked up the catering menu but tossed it down again because nothing sounded good. For the first time all season, we'd be the only ones in the box. Usually, I invited different family members of the players or gave passes to employees to use for friends and family, but Paige really wanted us to relax tonight and not feel like we had to entertain.

I sank onto the couch and propped my sneaker-clad feet on the coffee table while the announcers gave updates from around the league.

"It's important for the Wolves to win tonight," one said, giving a nod back to the field behind them. "They've got a two-game lead in their division, but they end out the season with one of the toughest stretches all year. Two back-to-back away games against two of the best scoring defenses in the league. They've stayed healthy, which is huge, but they've also been plagued with distraction on and off the field."

Paige looked at me, and I crossed my arms over my stomach, determined not to show how uncomfortable this made me. This was the stuff that Luke hated. The rhetoric. The narrative that you couldn't control. People who didn't know you dissecting your life, your livelihood, colored with their own bias.

Gruden nodded. "Indeed, they have. One thing we know about Luke Pierson, besides his huge arm and ability to manage the game, is that he's not prone to those kinds of distractions. He normally avoids guys like me, so when he called and asked if he could sit down with me, I was more than a bit surprised."

I sat up slowly, my lips falling open.

The other two at the curved table laughed. "Us too," the third announcer said. "We thought you were kidding."

Gruden held up his hands, an affable smile wide on his face. "I'd never lie about the elusive Luke Pierson asking for a one on one." He looked straight at the camera. "So here you go. My most surprising and revealing interview of the season."

My heart catapulted up into my throat as I sat forward fully, my knees bouncing in place. The camera cut to a dark room, only two chairs facing each other with lights behind each.

Gruden sat in one. Luke in the other.

I had to cover my mouth with a shaky hand at how good he looked. His hair had been recently cut close to the scalp. It would be soft against my hand. He was wearing a simple white dress shirt with a light blue plaid pattern that made his skin look golden and healthy. His shoulders stretched the seams when he shifted in his seat.

"Thanks for having me," he told Jon.

"I was a bit surprised, man. You don't usually call me to have a chat."

Luke gave a look that was half grimace, half smile. "Yeah, sorry about that. I haven't always had the best of luck with the media."

"How so?"

He took a deep breath, visibly prepping himself before he spoke. In the set of his jaw, I could see how uncomfortable he was. My hands wanted to crash through the glass to get to him even though I was just seeing an image of him, a replay of something that had probably been shot the day before. Maybe even earlier.

"I've always struggled with the feeling that when I spoke to the media, I was defending myself. Defending how we played, how we didn't play, defending the things that happened off the field that might have affected our game." He swallowed and looked down. "When my daughter's mother died, it only magnified that feeling because I had no desire to explain any of that. It was private to me, and it was difficult to see my silence taken as tacit agreement to a made-up story about what my life had been like with her."

"And by that, you mean that your relationship was more serious than it was in reality."

"Yeah." Luke stared past Gruden's shoulder for a minute. "Cassandra, Faith's mother, wasn't someone who I knew all that well. Not really. And I regret that, especially for my daughter. I wish I could tell her more about what her mother was like, but I can't. And when I was suddenly stuck in the trenches of being a single father, I wasn't ready to open myself up to that conversation, and it really affected how I started dealing with the media."

Gruden leaned back, folding his arms and shaking his head. I couldn't believe what I was seeing. "Man, and here I thought we'd talk pass rush and how you read a blitz so well."

Luke laughed, and my heart somersaulted, sluggish and lovesick. "We can do that, too."

"But that's not why you wanted to sit down with me?"

Another heavy exhale that I felt in the tip of my fingers, a rush of blood with hot anticipation. "No. It's not."

"You want to talk about Alexandra Sutton." Not a question. No surprise in his eyes.

"I think I'm having a panic attack," I whispered. Paige rubbed my back. Beyond the glass, I realized I heard an echo of Gruden's words. My eyes darted out, and with a dawning sense of horror, I realized that they were projecting the interview up on the main screens of the field. During warm-ups. For everyone to see. "Holy shiiiiiiiiit," I breathed. Both hands covered my mouth now, and I fought the urge to go lock myself in the bathroom.

Luke's smile was soft. Soft! It was sweet. And he looked like he might vomit.

OMG, join the club.

"I do," Luke said. He licked his lips. "I'm not someone who believes that regret is this big evil to be avoided. It's how we learn. If we won every single game, we'd never be forced to sit back and rethink our strategy, to replay our choices, see where we could have been better, been faster. Regretting the ability to get to know Cassandra is something I can't change, but I can change the regret I have over not speaking to the media a couple of weeks ago when Allie's and my privacy was clearly invaded. It doesn't matter that there are no legal ramifications for the person who took our picture during a private moment because I regret not protecting someone who I very much respect and care for."

"So that's why we're here? You want to apologize to her?"

"Yes and no," Luke replied. "I've already apologized to Allie for the pictures even though I'm not the one who took them or sold them to the media. And I've apologized to my teammates for the distraction it caused as a consequence."

"The fight with Marks," Gruden said.

Luke shook his head, grinning a little. A dimple popped next to his lips, and I fought the urge to swoon. I didn't know I could want to swoon through panic, but there I was. Heart-eyes all around, I was helpless against them.

"The fight with Marks was ill-advised," he said carefully. "But that is *not* something I regret."

Gruden lifted his eyebrows. "No? That was a hefty fine you were given."

Luke leaned forward. "Not for one second would I take that back. I'd pay twice that much and still do it again."

"Why?"

"Because no one will ever speak about her the way Marks did and get away with it. Not in front of me," he said with terrifying, incredible certainty.

My heart. Poof. It was gone somewhere in a glittery cloud of pink. Paige sighed, and I felt my lips twitch into a helpless smile. From outside the glass, I heard applause. Cheering.

Gruden grinned. "Because she's your boss?"

Luke rubbed the back of his neck, one side of his mouth hooked up in a smile so sexy, so heartbreaking, that I felt my breath catch before he said a single word. "Because I fell in love with her."

I gasped. "Did he? Did he just ..."

Paige sniffled. "He totally did. Oh, my word, Allie."

"You love her," Gruden clarified. "Does she know that?"

His shit-eating grin was one of a sports reporter who knew he just got the scoop of the season. One that would be replayed a million times. And that was just by me. I stood slowly, my ears ringing, my heart racing, my blood screaming to go find him.

For me. He did this for me.

Luke shook his head. "She doesn't."

Gruden tilted his head. "Why do it this way? You don't strike me as the guy who puts this on display."

Luke laughed. "I'm not. But I'm doing this for her. She's given the whole team space for the past few weeks so we could focus on winning, and I wanted her to know, in front of however many people are watching this, that win or lose, she's what I want. If she'll have me."

"This isn't live, though," Gruden said. "How will you get your answer?"

He lifted his hands and shrugged. "I guess if you guys are kind of enough to show this while I'm still down on the field warming up tomorrow night, then she'll be able to find me pretty easily."

I was standing before my heart chugged out another single beat, and I couldn't feel my hands as I flung the door of the box open. The fans that were dotted around the stands roared when I appeared. My eyes raced over the field until I saw him, standing at midfield, holding a bouquet of bright pink tulips in one hand, a jersey in the other, and wearing a hopeful smile on his face.

Down the cement steps I flew, people cheering and clapping, darting out of my path as I made my way down to the field. When I reached the barrier, two smiling security guards greeted me. People patted me on the back as I waited for them to open the gate down to the field, and I swiped happy tears from my face. When my foot touched the field, Luke started jogging my way, dropping the flowers and the jersey as we got closer.

I couldn't run fast enough.

My body yearned to fly, to erase the space between us, to be wrapped in his arms in front of the world with the bright lights overhead. Even players from the opposing team hooted and hollered as we ran toward each other. But nothing, nothing matched the sheer explosion of sound in the arena when I launched myself into his waiting arms.

They banded around me like iron, and he exhaled heavily into my hair while I wrapped my legs around his waist and my arms around his neck. I was so safe, so surrounded. Loved. It was too big for my ribs, too pure to be real.

But it *was* real.

"I love you, too," I whispered in his ear.

He leaned back to see my face, and for one moment, we smiled at each other. His mouth took mine in a searching, sweet kiss, and everything was gone except us. All I could see and feel and smell and taste was Luke.

The whole world could've been watching, and it wouldn't have mattered.

WASHINGTON WOLVES

Luke

Fifteen months later

"I really, really wish I didn't have to go," I said against Allie's smiling lips.

Her laughter was throaty and quiet, so I touched my mouth to the side of her neck to feel the vibrations of that sound underneath her skin.

"You don't have a choice," she answered.

Outside of our bedroom door, I could hear Faith banging around in the kitchen, making me some sort of good luck cookies that I would probably pass off to some of the younger guys who could still get away with eating sugary shit like that before a big game.

This, of course, being the biggest game.

How fortunate that Seattle had been chosen a couple of years ago as the host for the Super Bowl this year. Made our commute awfully convenient.

But I didn't want to go to a hotel even if it was how we did things. I wanted to stay in my home, with my fiancée and my daughter. I wanted to wake up with Allie tucked into my side as I always did. I wanted to get up and help Faith make her pancakes, as that was the only thing Allie wouldn't immediately puke up these days.

And at seven weeks pregnant, she puked a lot. According to her, Rico carried a puke bag in his pocket now when he did the pre-game walkthrough on the field. Thank goodness she hadn't had to use it yet, because then the media would definitely hear the good news before we were ready for them to.

I wrapped my arms around Allie and growled unhappily, which made her laugh again.

"You know, for a guy about to play in the Super Bowl, you should be a lot more focused on the game than you currently are." Her words were light and teasing, and she rubbed her nose against mine as she said them.

I ran my hand up her back and kissed her again. "I'll be focused tomorrow. Actually, as soon as I walk out the door, I'll forget you exist."

She pinched my side, and I twisted away laughing.

"Liar."

Humming, I leaned in and pulled her lower lip between my teeth. Allie sighed contentedly and met my kiss, snaking her tongue into my mouth and gripping my hair tightly.

Something crashed outside the door, and she broke away on a laugh. "I should probably go see what she's doing."

"You're going to help her bake?" My eyebrows lifted skeptically. "I think I'll leave now before it gets too messy."

Allie snuggled in closer and pressed her forehead to the side of my throat. "Probably for the best. You know what happens when I get involved in her little experiments."

I chuckled, but mess or no mess, even if I wouldn't eat what Faith was baking, the moments that my two favorite girls stood in the kitchen and spilled flour and sugar and cinnamon and whatever the hell else unhealthy creations they loved to share were some of my favorite moments in the world.

Allie and I might not be married yet—we'd scheduled that event for two weeks after the Super Bowl, just in case we made it that far—but the moment we made our relationship oh-so-very public, she'd stepped into Faith's life like she'd been born to mother her.

Actually, that on-field display was what put us on *Sports Illustrated* for the second time that season. Every photographer in the place caught it from a different angle, but the best one made the cover, which was currently framed in my office downstairs.

Allie in my arms, us smiling at each other, just before she kissed me. It might have broken the internet for a few days—our story and my very public declaration—but it died down quickly enough.

We got engaged quietly six months later, which was when she moved in, and at the beginning of the following season, we set our wedding date. It would be a quiet affair, close friends and family, a handful of teammates and front office staff, on Orcas Island, overlooking the water.

"I know this is a bad owner thing for me to say," Allie whispered, "but I'll be really happy not to have to share you for a few months. Just the three of us, living life, sounds pretty perfect right now."

This. This was why I didn't want to leave.

I wanted to win. I wanted that so bad it made my body shake. We'd missed the Super Bowl the year before after a grueling, last-minute loss in the AFC Championship, and everything about this past season felt like vindication.

For me, certainly. But Allie too. She'd defied the odds as well, and as much as I wanted to be standing in a fall of red and black confetti twenty-four hours later for myself, for my teammates, I wanted it for her too.

She'd be able to hold the trophy and do it while wearing my ring on her finger, with our child inside her.

The thought had my inner caveman growling again, my arms banding around her slender form even more tightly.

"Do you think we'll win?" she asked as if she read my thoughts.

I breathed in slowly. Before a game like this, I was strict in my avoidance of all the talking heads. No *SportsCenter*. No *Pardon the Interruption*. No *Mike and Mike in the Morning*. I didn't want to know what they had to say.

If we won, it would be because we were more prepared. Because we would play better. The preparation was something I was confident in.

And our play would be decided tomorrow evening. There was nothing I could do about that until the moment the ball was kicked into the air.

But I knew what I felt in my gut. I'd felt it all week. That churning, bubbling sense of anticipation that came before a big win. When everything clicked seamlessly into place.

"Yeah, I think we will," I told her. If anyone else had asked me, I'd never say that out loud. "I can feel it, Allie. It feels like our time."

She smiled. Her hand came up to cup the side of my face, and I turned so I could kiss her palm. "I'm so proud of you. Have I told you that today?"

"Not yet." I kissed her. "You're slackin', Sutton."

Her blue-green eyes got serious when I pulled back. They searched my face intently, the way they did when it felt like she was able to read my mind. She was the only one who could.

"I don't care if you never played another snap or won another game, there's no one on this earth who I'm more proud of. As good as you are out there, it's nothing compared to the man you are right here."

Allie moved against me, not to incite or entice, but to wrap herself around me so fully, so completely that I felt her everywhere. What had I ever done before her love?

It was impossible to try to remember what each day was like before I had her in it. Thank God I didn't have to.

"I love you," I said against the silky smooth skin of her forehead, then I kissed her there.

"I love you too," she whispered back. Another crash in the kitchen had Allie exhaling a laugh, carefully extricating herself from my arms. "I better go help her."

"I should go anyway." My hand pulled her back for one more searching, deep kiss.

Allie smirked as she stood off the bed, and I gave a quick caress against her still flat belly. "You better pretend you're going to eat those cookies, Pierson." She gave me a warning look and left the room.

I heard Faith laugh as soon as Allie joined her, and I smiled instantly at the sound.

Maybe I'd hold the trophy one more time, and maybe I wouldn't.

But for the rest of my life, I'd already won.

The End

ACKNOWLEDGMENTS

Full disclosure time, this book was HARD for me to write at the beginning of the process. And also the middle of the process. Somewhere around the end, it started getting easier, and it's completely thanks to the people who allowed me to talk (read 'rage obsessively') about why being a writer was stupid, and writing books was dumb, and I was never going to do this to myself again.

My husband (aside from his terrible title suggestions) was definitely one of those people. He herded the boys out of the house more than once because these two fictional people, and the new fictional world I was entering into, were almost causing me to have a mental breakdown. If that's not love, I don't know what is.

Fiona Cole championed Luke and Allie from the beginning, and never made me feel crazy for how much I was doubting myself and doubting the story. You have the patience of a saint, my friend, and I'm a better writer because of your ability to see what my story is missing, what my characters need, and what I couldn't figure out. #dreamteam.

Kandi Steiner and Kathryn Andrews, my football loving girls, and Amy Daws, who made time in their crazy schedules to read for me, pet my hair when I needed it, kicked my ass when I needed that too. Your feedback and friendship are invaluable to me!

It should also be said that Amy is the one who came up with the title of the book, so she gets an extra gold star for that too.

In keeping with the theme of 'how many times can Karla doubt herself during this process', I also need to thank Brittainy Cherry, for a particularly timely pep talk, and asking me the exact questions that I needed to be asked to figure out why I couldn't figure out Luke. You are a freaking GEM in this community, BCherry.

Caitlin Terpstra for always being so fast as a beta reader!

Najla Qamber for being incredibly patient with me, and so amazingly talented, as I changed about a thousand things on the cover for Bombshell. You are the BEST.

Jenny Sims with Editing4Indies for the proofreading, Enticing Journey for help with my promo, along with Book Ends Tours.

All the bloggers and readers who've joined me in this crazy journey over the past 3+ years, you are, quite literally, the reason I'm able to keep doing it. THANK YOU.

I should also note, that while I am an AVID football watcher, and I certainly did my research on what Allie might go through as a new owner, I took a bit of creative license in order to create the world of the Washington Wolves, so any errors are mine alone.

Last, and never, ever least, my Lord and Savior, Jesus Christ.

OTHER BOOKS BY KARLA SORENSEN
(AVAILABLE TO READ WITH YOUR KU SUBSCRIPTION)

Wilder Family Series

One and Only

The Wolves: a Football Dynasty (second gen)

The Lie

The Plan

The Crush

The Ward Sisters

Focused

Faked

Floored

Forbidden

The Washington Wolves

The Bombshell Effect

The Ex Effect

The Marriage Effect

The Bachelors of the Ridge

Dylan

Garrett

Cole

Michael

Tristan

Three Little Words

Love at First Sight

ABOUT THE AUTHOR

Karla Sorensen has been an avid reader her entire life, preferring stories with a happily-ever-after over just about any other kind. And considering she has an entire line item in her budget for books, she realized it might just be cheaper to write her own stories. She still keeps her toes in the world of health care marketing, where she made her living pre-babies. Now she stays home, writing and mommy-ing full time (this translates to almost every day being a 'pajama day' at the Sorensen household…don't judge). She lives in West Michigan with her husband, two exceptionally adorable sons, and big, shaggy rescue dog.

Find Karla online:
karlasorensen.com
karla@karlasorensen.com
Facebook
Facebook Reader Group

Printed in Great Britain
by Amazon